Inheritance

Inheritance

Mystery Suspense Thriller

Philip L. Levin

To Larna –
I'm honored to be
invited to Turner County 2013 –

Philip Levin
July 14 2013

iUniverse, Inc.
New York Bloomington Shanghai

Inheritance
Mystery Suspense Thriller

iUniverse books may be ordered through booksellers or by contacting:

iUniverse
1663 Liberty Drive
Bloomington, IN 47403
www.iuniverse.com
1-800-Authors (1-800-288-4677)

2nd Edition

ISBN: 978-0-595-49883-3 (pbk)
ISBN: 978-0-595-61291-8 (ebk)

Printed in the United States of America

Dedication

My mother, Beatrice Levin, published over two dozens books and thousands of articles. She taught creative writing at high school and college levels. My father, Franklyn K. Levin, edited *Geophysics* magazine and published extensively in scientific journals. Now in their eighties, they continue productive lives.

Characters

Bellows, Sally	Cocktail Waitress
Bevis, Marvin	Construction Company Owner
Birchman, Scott	Car Dealer
Byrd, Sam	Police Sergeant
Carter, Carl and Debbie	Clinic Counselors
Cohen, Nathan	Soldier
Dove, Anna Marie (Dovie)	Dancer and Artist
Dupree, Barbara	Real Estate Developer
Garcia, Lupretto (Lupè)	Laborer
Garcia, Maria	Lupretto's Wife (Recently Missing)
Gonzalez, Juanita	Maria's Mother, Martha's Sister (Deceased)
Gonzalez, Martha	Rebecca Smyth's Cook
Hopsteader, David	Lupè's Defense Attorney
Harper, Harry	Barbara Dupree's Attorney
Jack	Homeless Fellow
Jones, Sidney (Turtle)	Dovie's Boyfriend
Kriten, Peter	Finance Editor
Matthews, Bryan	Meredith Tracy's Attorney
McDonald, Bruce	Ex-Public Works Department Manager
Merino, Luke	Sports Writer
Morales, Jesus	Investigative Reporter
Randolph, Robert (Bob)	City Editor
Scouras, Fred	Art Dealer
Silverman, Sophie	Patricia's Elderly Neighbor
Smyth, Rebecca (Becky)	Model
Sweeney, Mel	Police Detective

Tracy, Herbert	Patricia's Grandfather (Deceased)
Tracy, Meredith	Patricia's Mother
Tracy, Patricia (Tricia)	Columnist
Tracy, Richard	Patricia's Father (Deceased)
Trevino, Alma	Patricia's Attorney
Tucker, William (Bill)	Sailor

Note: Although the locations are based on real Corpus Christi landmarks, all characters and events in this novel are entirely fictional. Any similarity to real people or events is entirely coincidental.

Preface

Sunday, the day preceding the novel's commencement, Detective Mel Sweeney interviews Lupè Garcia regarding his wife's disappearance. That transcript appears as Chapter Two.

Inheritance

Mystery Suspense Thriller

Philip L. Levin

Tracy's Tidbits
by Patricia Tracy

Corpus Christi Caller Times
Monday, September 12, 1994

Law and Disorder

We live in a society of law and disorder. Our laws set up standards, and our citizens disobey them. The degree of disobedience sets the mores of society. The law says drive fifty-five miles an hour. Those who go that slowly obstruct traffic. Most drivers pop along at sixty. Tooling down the highway at a hundred endangers the citizenry. Noise limits hardly matter when you turn your radio up for your favorite song. They make more sense when that dressed out Cadillac next to you bounces your car with the rhythm from his huge bass speakers. How much harm is there in an occasional puff of marijuana? Devastation comes when disrespect of illegal substances leads to cocaine or heroin. When a man hits his wife we look the other way. Does society have to wait for murder before intervening?

Maria Garcia suffered for years, a helpless victim of her husband's belligerent drunkenness and documented violent abuse. Several times she filed charges of battery against her husband, Lupè, yet our legal system allowed him to walk away unpunished. Two weeks ago Maria disappeared. She and Lupè spent the last known evening of her life drinking at The Lonesome Coyote, a local bar, where witnesses watched Lupè become loopy. Now, the best excuse Loopy Lupè can give is that maybe Maria suddenly decided to go visit relatives in the Valley.

Without a body, police can do nothing. Where might the body be, if it were to be somewhere? Noting a freshly capped abandoned well in the backyard of the Garcia property, Detective Mel Sweeney petitioned to dig up the well as a possible location of the missing Mrs. Garcia. Judge Parker, previously mentioned in my columns in reference to light sentences for criminals, turned down his request.

Our lawmakers legislate morality. Society decides when actions exceed acceptable limits. We count on our judges' judgments to dijudicate these limits. Without enforcement of society's morality, daredevils drive dangerously, pushers propagate poppies, and murderers meander menacingly. Please, Judge Parker, enforce the law. Help us secure a safe society.

1

The telephone ring startled Tricia, resulting in her making a jagged eyeliner mark across her lid. She wiped it clean as she hurried into her bedroom to grab the receiver.

"Tricia Tracy here." She brought the phone back to the bathroom to finish applying her make-up.

"Hi Tricia, it's Dovie. I've got a mystery for you to solve!"

Tricia smiled, picturing Anna Marie Dove in her black leotard, prancing around her little cluttered home. "A mystery, huh? You have my full attention. Tell me more."

"It's something I have to show you. How about over lunch? Can you join Turtle and me for some freshly picked vegetables?"

Tricia picked up her date book to check her day's schedule. Other than the mayor's reception tonight, she was free. She had planned to head into the newspaper building before lunch, but could easily put her work off until the afternoon.

"Lunch sounds good, Dovie. Are you going to give me a hint about the mystery?"

"Okay, but only a tease. It's something Turtle discovered while cleaning a car he bought last night."

"That could be a fuzzball. You can do better than that!"

"It has to do with a lot of money."

"A mystery about a lot of money? I can hardly wait! I'll see you in half an hour."

She slipped a yellow sundress over her trim twenty-four year old body, followed by yellow half-heels onto her nylon encompassed feet. Climbing into her yellow Ferrari, she careened along Shoreline Drive before turning up Naples road to Dovie's home.

Acorns from the tall oaks shading the fifty-year old clapboard home crunched under Tricia's feet as she balanced her way up the cracked sidewalk. The door opened to reveal a diminutive bundle of energy.

Dovie barely topped five feet, with black hair swept back, small eyes, and a sensuous mouth. At thirty-four, her constant dancing kept her lithe and muscular. Tricia met her in a friendly hug.

Making their way past antique dressers and breakfronts overcrowded with worldwide knickknacks, they settled onto a pair of mismatched overstuffed chairs. Dovie poured two cups of herbal tea from a silver serving set.

"How have you been?" Tricia asked.

"Just fine. And you?"

"Good. Now that we've got the niceties out of the way, tell me about this mystery."

Dovie laughed. "I'm surprised you could hold your curiosity for even those thirty seconds! Anyway, it's Turtle's discovery. Let's see if I can get him to tell you about it." Dovie turned to the hallway door and shouted, "Turtle! Come in here and say hello to Tricia."

From deep in the house Tricia heard a rumble of thunder. "Who?"

Dovie went into the bedroom. Tricia could hear her voice drifting back.

"We invited Tricia over for lunch. She wants you to tell her about that intriguing note you found. Come join us for tea."

Dovie returned to her chair. "Turtle's doing much better, Tricia. We journeyed out on two car purchase trips last week. He even went to the store for me and brought back a pint of whipping cream. I was very proud of him."

Turtle emerged, a ponderous reticence wearing shorts and a huge T-shirt. African-American features of broad nose and thick lips accented his noncommittal expression. Dovie sometimes referred to Sidney Jones as her teddy bear. Tricia thought the label was half right; he looked like a bear, sure enough.

Tricia waved. "Hello, Turtle. Good to see you again."

He stood solemnly. "'Yo, Tricia," he boomed. "S'all right?"

"Sure. Same old stuff, really; tanning at the beach, writing for the paper, partying with the socialites, and dating old Mel. How about you? Anything new?"

He shrugged.

"Now, Turtle," Dovie said. "Tell Tricia how you're doing. Let's hear about your car business."

Turtle's slow gaze moved for a moment onto Dovie before falling down to his feet. "You tell 'er."

Dovie sighed and, with a plaintive look, turned to Tricia. "He's really doing much better. He'll warm up after lunch. I'll be right back with the food."

"Can I help?" Tricia asked.

"Sure." Dovie pointed to a half dozen newspapers neatly stacked underneath the table. "Your papers are ready, Turtle. Why don't you enjoy them while Tricia and I bring lunch to the table?"

In the kitchen, Dovie directed Tricia to the utensils and asked her to pull down three brightly colored plates. Dovie poured the ratatouille into a bowl and put it on a tray with the bread and salad. Returning to Turtle with feast in hand, Dovie served portions to all.

"So," Tricia asked, as she ate. "What is this mystery you promised? You said Turtle found something valuable? I've been imagining all sorts of things, like maybe a diamond brooch or an ancient manuscript?"

"You're so silly, Tricia," Dovie said, and giggled. "Turtle loves to buy and sell cars, don't you Sweetheart?"

Dovie turned to Turtle, waiting to hear the affirmative grunt. Mounds of newspapers spread around him like sand dunes at Padre Island beach. His half gray hair stood short; half inch soldiers standing sentinel, guarding the quiet man's thoughts. Tricia knew little of the causes of Turtle's reticence. "War experiences," Dovie had said. Tricia hadn't appreciated any improvement in his social skills in the year she'd known him.

"Turtle finds car deals in these papers that we get from all over the area. If he can get a good deal, I'll drive him out, and he'll bring it back, clean it up, and drop it off at a local car lot where he sells it on commission. All sorts of things fall out of people's pockets and get lost in the seat cushions. One time my man found a solid gold money clip with five fifty dollar bills."

"What did Turtle find this time?" Tricia asked eagerly.

Dovie smiled with delight. "I hope it tickles your fancy as much as it did ours."

Turtle handed Tricia a document detailing a failed water perking inspection. In the upper margin of the report, someone had jotted in neat blocked script, "Bruce says it's going to cost $50,000 to get this changed."

"Fifty thousand dollars! Sounds like a substantial bribe to me!"

"I thought it would intrigue you, Tricia. Seems like a big scandal a super reporter like you could expose."

Tricia felt a slight burn on her cheeks. "Thanks for the compliment. I'm a feature columnist, though, not an investigative reporter. I'll show this to Bob Randolph today. Maybe after he's seen what a good job I did with today's column about that Garcia fellow he'll want me to investigate this scandal too. Whose car was it?"

"Barbara Dupree." Turtle's deep voice pronounced each syllable slowly and precisely, as if each sound received close inspection, tender packing, and gentle delivery.

"I've never heard of her."

"Me either," Dovie said. "Turtle said she lives in a huge ugly home in one of those new developments out near the river. He bought her one year old Lexus for a bargain. He said it's in great shape."

"A Lexus, huh?" Tricia's asked. "What color?"

"Blue," Turtle said. "Want?"

"Thanks anyway. I'm happy with my Ferrari."

"And now that we've finished eating," Dovie announced, "it's time to dance. Come on, Tricia. I've got some new steps I want to show you. Turtle will play his flute for us, won't you, dear?"

"It's a little too hot for me to dance, but I'd enjoy watching you."

Tricia and Turtle followed Dovie to the backyard, a riot of green vines and overhung trees, surrounded by an eight foot privacy fence. Metal and ceramic icons formed a mishmash of decorations. Sundials and birdbaths decorated narrow pebbled paths. Tricia relaxed on a clover patch in the shade.

Turtle settled on a bench beneath the gargantuan oak tree. Fitting the sections of his flute together, he floated a happy Irish melody. Dovie pranced and twirled in time to the music, pointed toe ballet poses accenting stylish jumps and spins, dancing until her entire outfit became dark with sweat. She stopped abruptly, panting and flushed.

Tricia asked, "Dovie, are you okay?"

Before answering, she took a long draught from her water bottle. "Just great, Tricia, just great. Tomorrow afternoon I'll try to drag Turtle out to Cole Park for a performance. You should stop by and watch."

"Maybe I can make it. Right now I better get to work."

Passing back through the house and out the front door, Tricia climbed into her car, and sped downtown to her newspaper office.

2

Interview: Lupretto Garcia
Date: Sun. Sept. 11
Location: Police Station

Sweeney: Lupè, I've turned on my recorder. Do you
                give permission for this interview to be
                recorded?

Garcia: Only 'cause Hopscotch says you can. You
                sure, Hopscotch?

Hopsteader: Mr. Garcia, as we just discussed, record-
                ing is common for these types of inter-
                views. It prevents misrepresentation of
                your words. Naturally, Mel, you'll send a
                transcript to my office promptly.

Garcia: Okay, cop man. You gonna tape.

Sweeney: For the record, today's date is Sunday,
                September eleventh. Present for this
                interview are Lupretto Garcia, known as
                Lupè, David Hopsteader, his attorney,
                Samuel Byrd, police sergeant, and me, Mel
                Sweeney, detective. Lupè, this isn't our
                first interview. I talked to you Tuesday.

Garcia: Yeah, you and your friend here came bus-
                tin' in my door.

Sweeney: As I recall, Lupè, you invited us in. In
                the five days that have passed, have you
                had any further thoughts about what might
                have happened to your wife?

Garcia: I don't know nothin'. My old lady split, that's all. She run off like the *puta*[1] she is. She no good, cop man. Maybe she find a skinny cop like you to screw?

Sweeney: You told me last week that she was sup-posed to be visiting relatives for Labor Day weekend. Yet she disappeared a week before. Didn't you wonder where she went?

Garcia: Like I said, cop man. I figured she decided to leave sooner. She got a right to go visit her family, *¿verdad?*[2]

Sweeney: I worked on a case last month — a spouse murder. All their friends said they were the happiest couple around. You and Maria weren't like that, now were you?

Garcia: We got along *bastante*[3]. We fight. We make up. I don't know why she go. I don't know where she go.

Sweeney: You like to drink, don't you, Lupè?

Garcia: What-cha mean, cop man?

Sweeney: According to my records, you've been arrested multiple times for drunkenness. You've had your driver's license revoked for DWI.

Garcia: I like my *cerveza*. So what?

Sweeney: And when you get drunk, you get violent. Isn't that right, Lupè?

Garcia: No, man. I ain't violent.

---

1   Tramp

Sweeney: Let's see now. According to this record, you have eight arrests for assault, sometimes with battery. You've been treated four times at the hospital for injuries, including twice for multiple stab wounds. Even spent six months in the pen for manslaughter, huh? That's big time, Garcia.

Garcia: It was self defense. I'm a nice guy.

Hopsteader: I believe the conviction was involuntary homicide, Mel.

Sweeney: Let's talk about your relationship with Maria, shall we? When you got drunk, you liked to beat up on her, didn't you?

Garcia: No, man. I don't hit that *puta* hard.

Sweeney: Three times Maria charged you with battery. Once the judge issued a court order to keep you away.

Garcia: She like to joke. She dropped those charges, didn't she, cop man?

Sweeney: I have here seven hospital records from when she went for injuries that you caused her.

Hopsteader: There is no evidence that my client ever caused injury to his wife.

Sweeney: Well how do you explain the injuries, then?

Garcia: She fall a lot.

Sweeney: From what I gather from the neighbors, you're pretty abusive, Lupè. You didn't let her work, didn't like her going out with friends, beat her to keep her under control. Do you think she liked being hit?

Garcia: *Cuando mujera es una puta, si!*[2] I never
                 hit her hard. *Porqué* you don't go look for
                 Maria instead of hassling me?

Sweeney: I am trying to find her, Lupè. You told me
                 the last time you remember seeing her was
                 Friday night, August 26th. Tell me what
                 you remember.

Garcia: Like most Fridays, I get *mi dinero*. Me
                 and Maria go to the Lonesome Coyote. Maria
                 drives us home.

Sweeney: You said she wasn't home when you woke up
                 Saturday morning?

Garcia: That's right. *Desvanecerse.*[3] Gone.

Sweeney: She packed her suitcase and left, is that
                 right?

Garcia: I ain't saying she packed anything.

Sweeney: Last week you said she packed up a suit-
                 case and left. Now you're claiming that
                 she didn't?

Garcia: *Tonto*[4]. I told you I thought she'd packed
                 for the visit to McAllen. Now I ain't sure.
                 I'm tellin' you she left, cop man. Either
                 she packed or she didn't. What difference
                 does it make? She own *nada* worth taking any-
                 way. She left and I ain't seen her since.

Sweeney: Nothing, huh? Do you recognize these,
                 Lupè?

Garcia: You settin' me up? I'm no thief.

---

2   Yes, when a woman's a whore.

3   Disappeared

4   Stupid

Sweeney:	You don't recognize this necklace? Or this broach? Or this ring? Any of these, Lupè?
Garcia:	No. *¿Que paso?*
Sweeney:	You sure?
Hopsteader:	Are you badgering Mr. Garcia for a reason, Mel? He said he doesn't recognize those pieces of jewelry. Are they supposed to be relevant?
Sweeney:	We found these wrapped in a scarf in a drawer of Maria's dresser, David.
Garcia:	You're lying, *vaca tonto.*[5] Maria ain't never had that kind of stuff. Hey, Hopscotch, can they go through Maria's stuff like that?
Hopsteader:	Good question, Lupè. May I see your search warrant, Mel?
Byrd:	Here.
Garcia:	If that's Maria's stuff, can I have it? Sell it?
Hopsteader:	Are you keeping these as evidence, Mel?
Sweeney:	For now. Unless we find that they belong to someone else, then, yes, Lupè, we'll return these pieces to you. It sure does seem strange that Maria would run off and leave all this behind, don't you think?
Garcia:	*No se nada*[6]. Why you care about these details? Go do your job. Go find Maria.
Sweeney:	Sometimes the littlest details can make a difference. Last year I worked on a cat

---

5   Stupid cow

6   I know nothing about that

burglary case that came down to paint residue left on the window sill. Turned out
the robber was a painter. Are you a handy-
man, Lupè? You like to make repairs around
the house?

Garcia: *Eres loco*[7]. I work hard for Bevis all day,
cop man. When I get home I don't work.

Sweeney: No? We found concrete residue in your
wheelbarrow that appears to be fresh. What
did you do with that concrete?

Garcia: That ain't even my wheelbarrow. I borrowed
it from work last year. We do concrete work
on the job. That's old dust, cop man.

Sweeney: It looks like you recently put concrete
in that old well in your back yard, Lupè.
There's splattered concrete all around the
opening. Why'd you do that?

Garcia: I don't know what you're talkin' about,
cop man. You think Maria's in that well?
Go dig her up.

Sweeney: I'd like to, Lupè, but the only way to do
that is to bring in heavy equipment, like
a steam shovel. The houses in your neighborhood are too closely packed to get one
in without tearing down a house. So far
Judge Parker won't let me do that.

Hopsteader: Lupè still has his home because we have a
judicial branch that prevents you destroy-
ing our citizens' homes on wild goose
chases, Mel.

Sweeney: Speaking of having your home, tell me about
your dog.

---

7   You're crazy

Garcia: What about my dog?

Sweeney: Sherlock Holmes, the grand master detective of all time, thought it unusual when the dog didn't bark in the night. Does your dog bark a lot?

Garcia: He's supposed to bark, *tonto*. He's a dog.

Sweeney: The neighbors tell me he usually only barks when you're fighting with Maria or if strangers come around. He barked that night.

Garcia: Maybe Maria ran off with some stranger, ¿*Si*?

Sweeney: Lupè, not remembering is not an alibi. You got drunk. When you're drunk you beat up on Maria. No one has seen or heard from Maria since that night. I think you killed her. I don't think you meant to kill her, and that would be manslaughter rather than murder. But when you found she was dead, you must have hidden her body. I think you put it down the well and then capped it. That's obstruction of justice. If you admit you put the body in the well we'll work out a plea bargain. What do you say, Lupè?

Hopsteader: Before my client answers, I'll need a private conference with him.

Garcia: You don't need *nada*. I never seen no body. Maria ran off. *Qué tonto eres*[8]!

Sweeney: Okay, Lupè, we'll do it the hard way. Sam, book him on suspicion of murder.

---

8   You are so stupid!

Hopsteader: Mel, this is such a waste of time. You have
                 no evidence. Mere suspicions aren't enough
                 to convince Judge Parker to deny Garcia
                 his basic rights.

Sweeney: Why don't we let the judge make that deci-
                 sion, David?

End of recording.
MS/sb

3

At the city newsfloor Tricia weaved her way through the dozens of reporters' cubbyholes, each separated by half size corkboard walls. As she walked she hummed to the background of voices, phones, and printers.

"Hey Tidbit." Luke Merino, the sports writer, called to her as she walked past. He had been leaning back in his chair, and when he dropped the feet to the floor, an avalanche of papers from his desk joined the piles on the floor. Tricia watched him snatch a trophy of a club extended golfer as it tumbled through the air.

"Now that's an interesting style of decorating, Luke," Tricia said. "When the trash pile reaches your desktop do you raise your desk or just move to a new cubicle?"

Luke balanced the trophy on two mugs half full of old coffee. He kicked the papers out of his way and laughed. "Gotta keep the spiders active or their webs get too thick. Where you been? Randolph's been out here looking for you twice."

Tricia glanced across the room to the side office marked "Robert Randolph, City Editor." Through the open door she saw him peering at his computer monitor, a phone in one hand, a half eaten sandwich in the other.

"He must have loved today's *Tidbits*. Maybe he's got a great assignment for me?"

Luke guffawed. "Yeah, and maybe the Astros will win the World Series. Give it a rest, Tidbit. Uncle Bob knows you're not cut out to be an investigative reporter."

Tricia picked up the trophy and read the label out-loud. "Fifth place, Del Mar Open, 1990. Best you ever got was fifth place, Luke? You know what makes that so sad? I'm on my way up, on my way to being a world class reporter. You, on the other hand, peaked four years ago as a fifth rate golfer. You'll never be anything but a sports bum, a has-been who never was."

Luke laughed. "You? A world class reporter? Say, Tidbits, since you're so bright, how 'bout we take a break and go to my place and you can teach me a thing or two."

"Why are you such a boor?"

"Comes with the territory. Oh, by the way, your boyfriend called. He said he'd call you back. I advised him against it. I told him you'd left the country."

15

Tricia pointed her nose to the ceiling. "Don't call me Tidbits."

Turning her back on him, she stepped over to her clean cubicle. Tacked to the wall a calendar sat between two 8 x 10 photographs, one of Mel, the other of her father. In the middle of Tricia's computer screen a bright yellow post-it-note said "CALL ME PRONTO! RANDOLPH."

As she sat down she noticed a letter in her in-box. Recognizing her mother's handwriting, Tricia felt her jaw tense. She remembered the screaming fight she had with her the night after her father died. Although only fourteen, Tricia had moved out to the boathouse that night, never again stepping foot in her mother's home.

She dropped the letter into the trashcan unread. She drummed her fingers on the desktop a few times. She looked at the letter sitting on top of the trash pile. It stared up at her. She picked it up out of the can and ripped it open.

Dear Patricia,

I have sent your attorney's request for copies of those documents to Bryan Matthews. Let me remind you that Mr. Matthews' firm has reliably served as the attorneys of record for both the Tracy and the Randolph families for over sixty years. As you clearly are in need of legal services, I urge you to consider quality over flair.

Sincerely,

Meredith, your mother.

Tricia wondered what documents Alma Trevino, her attorney, wanted? Why had Alma sent the letter to Meredith instead of talking to Tricia about it? She made a mental note to ask Alma if she saw her at the Mayor's reception tonight.

Tricia played back her single phone message, finding it came from Bob Randolph.

"Your article about Garcia attracted a lot of attention, Tracy." His light Texas drawl stretched out each syllable. "Call me."

Tricia pressed in the extension of Randolph's desk.

"Randolph," he announced.

"It's me, Mr. Randolph. You called?"

"Tracy? You at your desk?" She confirmed her position for him.

"Wait for me. I'll be right there."

Tricia stood up to look over the cork divider in the direction of the editor's office. Just as she'd seen for fourteen months, the smiling fat man strolled leisurely among the nooks of the work spaces, stopping to offer advice or encouragement. Ruffs of peppered hair bounced merrily encircling his balding pate. She sat down just before he reached her.

"Good afternoon, Tracy. Enjoy a late luncheon?"

"Never know where the inspiration for the next column will come from, Mr. Randolph." Tricia smiled sweetly up at him.

"Your inspirations seem to come from strange places sometimes. This morning's *Tidbits* for example. The Caller Times doesn't need our feature columnist writing about criminal topics. Where did all this about the well and its possible hiding place for the body come from? Your boyfriend?"

"Yes sir, Mr. Randolph. Mel told me all about the case over dinner last night. It's a fascinating crime, really. Mel wants to have the house condemned so he can get a steam shovel in there to dig up the well, but Judge Parker won't let him."

"I happen to know these people, the Garcias. I can't see Lupè killing his wife and stuffing her body down the well. Did Sweeney okay you putting this in print? It seems to me the evidence is pretty flimsy."

Tricia felt her cheeks flush. "Um, well, not in so many words. The point of the story, though, is that Judge John Parker is being a twerp. My original title for the column read 'Judge John Jilts Justice.'"

The editor reached across his belly to scratch a sweat spot forming under his right armpit. "Judge John Jilts Justice? Hah. That's a good one. I understand your wanting to write about criminal activity, Tracy. When I started out as a cub reporter, I haunted the police station. All of our boys in blue knew me well. Made contacts, that's what I did. A good newspaperman's gotta make good contacts. It's what drives this business. Do you have good contacts, Tracy?"

"I think so, Mr. Randolph."

"You bet you do! You have great contacts. Those contacts are with Corpus' high society. You know what our readers like about your column? The Tracy name, 'cause everyone knows it's written by you, Patricia Tracy, of the famous Tracy family. This paper needs you to write about our city's high society ... the sparkling socialites. People like reading about famous names."

"That's a great phrase, 'sparkling socialites.' I'm going to use that in my column tonight."

"You're one of them, those sparkling socialites. They love to see their names in print and the public loves to read articles about the rich and famous. Let the investigative reporters like Morales write about the Smiths and Garcias. You know what I always tell my reporters, Tracy?"

"Names, sir. You always say names."

"Well, yes. That's true. But I also say, follow the money. You know who's representing Garcia in this case? Ever heard of David Hopsteader?"

"Sure," Tricia answered. "I've met him a few times socially. David Hopsteader is one of the most prominent criminal defense lawyers in the city. He's one of the principals of the group Barker, Gardener, and Hopsteader."

Bob nodded, his double chins bouncing lightly. "Yep, that's Hopsteader. He called the publisher to suggest that this morning's *Tidbits* constituted libel against his client. Now, how do you suppose a two-bit laborer like Garcia is paying for a high class attorney like Hopsteader?"

Tricia shrugged. "Pro bono?"

"My advice, Tracy, is stick to the society stuff. Lay off the Garcias and concentrate on the Hopsteaders and his ilk."

"Yes sir," Tricia said, displaying a slight pout. "Tonight I'll be at the mayor's reelection reception. Tomorrow's *Tracy's Tidbits* will feature Mayor Arthur Andrews' loud tie. Everyone will love hearing about that!"

"Good. That's just what your readers want to read, cutesy stories with a message. Set it at the Mayor's reception, throw in some famous names, add the moral, and get it to the paper no later than Ten PM. Okay?"

Bob patted her condescendingly on the top of her head, and turned away.

"Wait, Mr. Randolph. I just remembered I got hold of something else that could be worth investigating." Tricia opened her purse and brought out the perking report. Bob's left eyebrow rose on reading the item.

"Where'd you get this, Tracy?"

"A friend of mine found it in a car he bought from Barbara Dupree. Ever hear of her?"

Bob nodded. "This could be very interesting. Let's get some expert opinions." He picked up Tricia's phone, dialing an interoffice extension.

"Kriten? Randolph here. Got a minute? Good. See if Morales is available and meet me in the conference room. Thanks."

Tricia followed Bob to the glass walled conference chamber across the room. He stopped en route to make a handful of copies of the report.

As soon as Bob opened the door, Tricia's nose wrinkled in disgust at the reek of stale coffee, cigarette smoke, and body odors. He pressed the intercom button and ordered four coffees.

Bob sat on two of the plastic chairs, one huge buttock per chair. With a sweep of his hand, he cleared off enough trash to make part of the table useable. Tricia bushwhacked a trail through old coffee cups, newspaper scraps, and crumpled food wrappers to a chair opposite him.

A teenage boy entered with a handful of steaming coffee cups pinched in one hand and multicolored additive packages in the other. He dumped the packages and set the cups gently on the table beside them.

"Thank you, Stevens," Bob said. "Now go get some stirrers. You think we're going to use our fingers?"

"Er … no sir. Yes sir. Sorry Mr. Randolph. It won't happen again."

As the embarrassed young man hurried out the door, the editor called out, "And be sure you get someone to clean up this room when we're done."

Through the glass wall, Tricia saw Peter and Jesus coming across the room toward them. Jesus was talking adamantly, looking at Peter, who merely shook his head and shrugged. Peter held the door to allow the younger man to enter first.

Five feet eight inch Jesus Morales radiated energy. Swarthy good looks enhanced the burning intensity of his mahogany eyes. On his black pocketed tee shirt he proudly wore a button awarded him by his comrades at last year's Press Club banquet. Across a red background in large white letters it read "Poor K." The button had two meanings. As a twenty-seven year old, struggling on a reporter's salary to support a wife and four children, it stood for *poor kid*. Impoverished might be more precise. But the real motivation behind the label, which had become his nickname, was Jesus' incessant asking¿*porqué?* Why?

On entering the room he spotted Tricia. "Ah, *mia amiga*[1] Tricia. That was one *muy buen* column you wrote today. My compliments. It makes me wonder *porqué?* Why do the police suspect the well? I think there is more to tell on this story." He spoke with a fast paced Spanish accent.

Tricia blushed, acknowledging the compliment with a smile. She had a slight crush on this young fellow. Jesus came around the table to sit on Tricia's left.

Peter Kriten, the financial editor, walked in quietly, a stately fifty year old man with erect figure. Charcoal hair lay neatly combed above pale white skin, thin graying eyebrows, and Texas flag blue eyes. He carried a trim figure on his five foot ten frame, decorated by a neatly pressed pinstriped two-piece suit.

"Ah, Patricia, greetings," Peter said. He spoke with his upper lip stretched stiffly across his teeth, British style. "I have to disagree with Poor K. Your forte lies with your interactions among Corpus' upper class. I find your columns

---

1   My friend

about our local movers and shakers informative, and often hilarious. I advise you to stick to those topics." Peter placed himself at the table's end, between Jesus and Bob. Tricia glared at him.

"Coffee?" Bob offered. Tricia grimaced on the first sip of what must have been an ancient brew. Even with two creamers and two sweeteners stirred in with a pencil, the nasty taste punched through. Shuddering, she pushed the cup away. She noticed Bob finished his in two gulps. He then appropriated the cup unclaimed by Jesus. Peter smacked his lips and murmured, "Ah yes, three AM — a memorable vintage."

Bob handed out copies of the perking report.

"Where did this come from?" Peter asked.

"Barbara Dupree," Tricia said.

"Dupree? Oh my. That is interesting." Peter clasped his hands neatly on the table.

"What do you know about Dupree?" Bob asked.

Peter's crisp enunciation reminded Tricia of a BBC announcer. "Over the past eight years Mrs. Dupree has organized three property developments; Remington Grounds, Remington Heights, and Westchester Acres."

"Really!" Tricia exclaimed. "I'm surprised I haven't heard of her. She must come from money. I wonder why I've never met her at any of the functions?"

Peter snorted. "Oh she's got money now, but it's not old money like yours. With no education or social skills, she's used obnoxious persuasion, an abrasive voice, and semi-legal intimidation to gather that wealth."

"You make her sound so ugly, Peter," Tricia said. "Clearly this paper is proof that she's bribed someone. Mr. Randolph, let me investigate her and write a screaming expose!"

"*Con permission, Señorita,*[2]" Jesus said. "To me this woman deserves honor. She has accomplished much from little; organized the forces necessary in promoting her plans. This paper most likely reports one of the hundreds of obstacles that she overcame. Perhaps fifty thousand dollars for improvements. *Cuidado*[3]. Care before accusations."

Bob turned to Peter and asked, "Bribery or innocent expense?"

Peter flexed his fingers before answering. "Fifty thousand is a lot of money, and the wording here is suspicious. Still, Poor K could be right. Unfavorable perking reports are somewhat common. Like this one, each has a code number explaining why the property fails. This could be legitimate … but, I have my suspicions."

---

2   With your permission, Miss

3   Careful

"What have you heard?" Tricia asked, eager to hear new gossip.

Peter shot her a quick wink of intrigue. "Two months ago there was a big shake up at the Public Works Department. I've heard rumors from the banks where I sit on the Boards. No one's saying exactly what, but there apparently is a lot of money involved."

"A lot of money?" Bob asked. "You just said that fifty thousand is a lot of money."

Peter shook his head. "I'm hearing rumors of millions of dollars. I haven't heard all the details yet."

Bob stared at him. "You haven't heard the details yet? So why are you sitting here? You know what I always say to my reporters, Kriten? Follow the money. Go on, get to work! Follow that money."

Peter nodded, rising gracefully. "Of course, Robert. That's just what I had on my afternoon schedule; chasing rumors about the city public works department."

"Millions of dollars rumors are not your ordinary rumors. And, Kriten ..."

Peter paused at the door, "Yes, Robert?"

"Names. Get me names!"

"Right-o. Names it shall be." Peter waved good-bye to Jesus and Tricia, shutting the door gently behind him.

Bob turned to Jesus. "Morales, find out which property this report concerns. Determine whether the report was overturned, and, if so, why. And identify Bruce. This shouldn't take more than a couple of phone calls and maybe a trip to the courthouse."

"What about me?" Tricia asked.

"Why don't you handle the Barbara Dupree angle? Offer to interview her. She'll know who you are from the column, and probably jump at the chance to be in with the hotsie-totsies. Morales, you go with her and eavesdrop. Pose as her cameraman or something."

"Can I challenge her with ..." Tricia started to ask if she could show the perking report, but not wanting to give Bob the chance to say 'no,' finished with, "my credentials?"

"Of course, Tracy. Be proud of those credentials. After all, this is the best fangled newspaper on the Texas coast!" Sitting back on his haunches he laid his hands contentedly across his chest.

Tricia turned to Jesus. "What time's good for you?"

"*Siepre que quieres, Señorita*[4] You please name the time."

"Okay. Let's try for early tomorrow afternoon."

---

4   Whenever you want to, Miss.

Back at her desk, she pulled a Corpus Christi phone book out of a drawer and looked up Barbara Dupree's number. After four rings she waited until the end of the nasal voice on Barbara's answering machine.

"Mrs. Dupree, this is Patricia Tracy from the Caller Times. I write the feature column, *Tracy's Tidbits*. I'm interested in hearing about your new development and your future plans for that area of town. I was hoping to come out tomorrow afternoon and interview you. Could you please call me back at your convenience? If I'm not in, please leave a message on my voice mail or ask for my photographer, Jesus Morales. Looking forward to hearing from you. Thanks a lot."

Tricia called the paper's librarian, asking him to pull some references on Dupree.

She decided to venture a call to Mel's police station. Though he was usually out doing fieldwork, this time he answered his phone on the first ring.

"Mel Sweeney here."

Tricia looked at his picture smiling at her from the photograph. Clean shaven, his face bore thirty-two years of laugh lines below disheveled reddish brown hair. Green eyes twinkled above Irish turned up nose and boyish toothy smile. A blue paisley tie hung loosely knotted upon a loud green shirt.

"Hi Darling," Tricia greeted him happily.

"Tricia. Oh, hi." He sounded subdued.

"Did you see my column this morning, Mel? I wrote up that Lupè Garcia case you told me about last night. You sure provided some great information. Came out pretty good, don't you think?"

"Oh, yes, Tricia, it certainly caught my attention."

"What's the problem? Did I get something wrong? Didn't you tell me all that stuff?"

"Oh sure, Tricia. I told you that stuff. But it was supposed to be confidential."

"I'm so sorry, Mel. Did I mess things up? It seemed like such a good story."

"Well ... I suppose no harm was done with that. But why did you have to say those things about Judge Parker?"

"Why? What happened?"

Mel sighed. "At the bail hearing, Judge Parker proclaimed that he would not have the presumption of innocence distorted by a gossip mongering press. He set Garcia free. It reminds me of a case I had three months ago when a car thief paid his bail from the revenues he made from selling parts from stripped down cars. The judge regretted that one, though. The convict stepped outside the courthouse, hot-wired, and drove off in the judge's Mercedes."

"Gosh, Mel, The way you were talking I had the impression the case was airtight. At my end, Bob Randolph told me that David Hopsteader complained to the publisher."

"I guess I'll just have to work harder to find enough evidence to convince Parker. It reminds me of a case last year where the judge repeatedly dismissed the charges against this guy who wrote graffiti, until we caught the guy painting 'Judge Wilson is a queer' on the courthouse wall. After that Wilson put the guy away in the pokey for several months."

Tricia felt guilty. "Perhaps I can make it up to you over dinner before the mayor's reception. You'll pick me up at six?"

"Well, actually, Tricia, what with Garcia still on the lam I was thinking of passing on the reception in order to do more investigation."

Tricia's sense of guilt disappeared in a burst of exasperation.

"You're not going to stand me up again!"

"I'm sorry, Tricia. But duty calls. I've got to follow up some leads."

"Mel Sweeney, you're always standing me up! This is the second time this month you've broken a promise to attend a function with me."

"Darling … I love you. I want to be with you. Didn't I sit through that stupid play with you just last week? Right now, though, I'm real busy. I hate to stand you up, you know that. But this is my job — my life."

Tricia snapped a pencil in half, scooped up the pieces and threw them over the cubicle wall.

"Hey," Luke complained. "Just 'cause you're having a fight with your boyfriend doesn't mean you have to throw pencils at me."

She covered the mouthpiece and said, "Stop listening to my private conversations, Luke!"

She turned back to the phone. "Damn it, you have to make concessions! This is my job and my life too! Besides the fact that I love these high class social engagements, I have to attend them for the paper. I hate always going by myself. People are talking about me, staring at me, wondering why I'm always unescorted."

She stood up and looked over the wall of her cubicle. Luke had his ear against her wall. She knocked him on the head with the receiver, and when he looked up, she pointed to the other side of the newsroom. "Out, muddle head. This is a private conversation."

Luke shrugged and strolled out of his cubicle and down the hallway.

Back to the phone, Tricia pleaded, "Besides, aren't these parties sort of fun?"

"No. They're never fun. I find the conversations boring, and when I do tell my stories those snobs always make me feel like I'm some sort of boob.

You know I don't like your parties or those stuffed shirt crowds. But I do like you!"

Tricia realized she held the phone so tightly her fingers had turned white. "Thanks. I like you too. But we're just not meeting each other's needs here, are we? If we're going to be a couple I need you to want to be with me, to mingle with my friends and join me in the places I like to go."

Mel's voice sounded tense. "I've already told you I don't like that sort of thing. Pizza and beer, and then a movie, that's my idea of a good night out."

"How can I do my job at a movie? No one gossips at a movie."

"No gossip? Maybe it would be better if I didn't say some of the things to you. Police information about a pending case isn't supposed to be splashed in the paper like that."

Tricia felt her anger rising. "You told me all that stuff. Don't deny it. You didn't tell me not to print it."

Tricia could hear someone talking to Mel in the background. "Someone's here I've got to talk to, Tricia. I've got to go."

"I've got to go too! Good-bye Mel. If you're not going out with me tonight, don't make plans to go out with me again anytime soon!"

As she slammed down the receiver she heard him calling to her. She shrugged off a twinge of regret. Turning off her computer, Tricia headed out of the building, deciding to blow off steam with a car ride.

Tricia raced through Corpus Christi's palm-tree-lined streets and brightly painted houses topped with red clay roofs. Shooting up the bay bridge she slowed near the top to admire the promenade of huge boats; trawlers, military vessels, and tankers snaking out in river ribbon. Driving along the shore roads, catching reflections from sparkling sunbeams shimmering in Nueces Bay, serenity returned.

Once calmed, she raced for thrill rather than relief. Along small Texas farm roads, the Ferrari grabbed the seashell embossed highway at a hundred miles an hour, slowing to eighty for the curves. The air rushed through the convertible's open top, creating tumbleweed of Tricia's hair. Her eyes glowed behind her Oakley shades.

Tricia circled the outskirts of town, returning to her home in the secluded Lakewood Village Townhomes. Some days, when she had the time, Tricia would bring a romance novel out to the lake in the middle of the townhomes. She'd curl up under the weeping willow and read about dashing heroes or swashbuckling pirates. There would be no time for that today, as her long drive had brought her home late. She rushed inside to change.

4

Interview: Fred Scouras
Date: Monday, September 12
Location: Police Station

Sweeney: Hello Fred, good to see you again, my friend. For the record, today is Monday, September twelfth. Present for this interview are Fred Scouras, art dealer, Mel Sweeney, detective, and Sam Byrd, police sergeant.

Scouras: Always a pleasure, Mel. What can I do for you today? Come across some interesting art pieces you wish me to identify, as usual?

Sweeney: Yes, what do you think of these?

Scouras: Hmm. Gorgeous. This necklace has some exquisite emeralds and pear shaped diamonds. One certainly doesn't see this quality work very often.

Sweeney: Do you have any ideas how to trace these? I ran it through our computer and nothing like this has been reported stolen.

Scouras: You came to the right man, Mel. As it happens, tracing these will be simplicity itself. I know exactly where these two pieces came from, as I was the seller. This necklace I sold about two years ago to Mr. Robert Randolph. You know Mr. Randolph, of course? Works as the Caller Times editor. This broach is part of the Randolph family heirlooms. I believe I sold it to Robert's mother some thirty years ago. The ring I

don't recognize. Though it's pretty, it's
hardly unique like the other pieces.

Sweeney: Robert Randolph, huh? I wonder how they
ended up where we found them, huh Sam?
Have you sold him other pieces?

Scouras: Bob's a good client and long time friend
of mine. I've sold him several items of
various types, jewelry, wall hangings,
statues, even a rug or two. He's got sur-
prisingly good taste.

Sweeney: Wall hangings and rugs sound like he was
shopping for his personal use, huh Fred?

Scouras: Many times he specified something as a
gift, like he'd say, "Show me something
that would please a young woman of thirty
years."

Sweeney: I thought Bob was a bachelor. Very interesting. Okay, thanks Fred. I appreciate
your time.

Scouras: My pleasure. Are you going to be returning these pieces to Bob? I'd like to keep
track of them, for professional reasons.

Sweeney: For the moment they're evidence, but I do
plan to run them by Mr. Randolph and see
if he recognizes them. I'll let you know,
Fred.

End of Recording
MS/sb

5

At Mayor Arthur Andrews' reception, Tricia flitted from guest to guest, collecting gossip like a lepidopterist after his butterflies. Occasionally she'd pull out a pad and jot down a few notes.

"Hello, Tricia."

Tricia turned to the voice, finding Carl and Debbie Carter at her elbow. She smiled and leaned forward to catch Carl's kiss on her cheek, followed by Debbie's hug.

"Having a good time?" Debbie asked.

"Fabulous! Isn't the band great? Have you tried the canapés? The *foie gras* is scrumptious! What have you two been up to?"

Carl shook his head. "Busy! Suddenly there's a big supply of cocaine in town. We're seeing a surge of recurrent patients in the clinic."

Debbie nodded. "It's high quality and plentiful. Some of the addicts I had nursed off the stuff plunged right back in. There's such a plentiful supply of drug, it's going at half the usual price."

"That's a shame. I can't understand how people allow themselves to get involved with that terrible stuff. Everyone knows how addictive it is."

"Everyone knows how addictive cigarettes and coffee are, too, but that doesn't stop people from getting started," Carl observed.

"Cocaine is a hundred times worse," Debbie said. "It ruins people's lives. Once that monkey gets on your back, you'll give up everything to snort another line. Now there's a new variety, called crack. It's much more concentrated."

Tricia took a sip of her wine. "I think it's all a matter of will power. Look, I can drink this wine, or not, as I choose. It should be the same with cocaine, or, as Carl mentioned, cigarettes. Isn't that how you get people to stop their addictions, guys? Determination, yours and theirs. Where is all this coke coming from, anyway?"

"Some of it comes to town by land from Mexico, dodging the border control. Mostly it comes in from the port. Little pleasure boats bring in big shipments. The importers connect with distributors on the dock or by hanging out at a local bar. Look around this room, Tricia. I'd bet half the people here have used cocaine within the past few months. I could pick out a half dozen who've been to our clinic, not that I would identify them, of course."

"It's a tragic travesty of temperance, boisterous abusers of abashed bounty. Look at all these dressed-to-the-nines partiers; to think that some of them are high on cocaine right now!"

"Why don't you drop by the clinic sometime and we'll share some info with you."

"I'll do that. Could you send me some info to my home? My address is in the phone book."

Tricia bid them *adieu*. Finding a secluded corner, she wrote her article, transmitted it to the paper through a phone jack, and put away her computer.

Returning to the party, she spotted Alma Trevino near the far buffet table. The beauty of Alma's high Indian cheekbones, strong chin, and comely figure was offset by kinky black hair and an acne scared face. Tricia and Alma had been close friends since high school days when they teamed up as debate partners.

Tricia looked at the eye-patched man listening raptly to Alma, and stopped, stunned. His handsome features and mischievous smile made her catch her breath. Clearing her head with a shake, she waved as she approached.

"*Hola, mia amiga!*" Alma reached out and pulled Tricia to her for a big hug.

"*Hola* yourself, Alma. How goes the world of defending downtrodden victims of overpowering social forces?"

Alma's eyes danced with merriment. "I get my koodles making those fat-cat landlords squirm. Not everything I do involves suing someone, though."

She turned and indicated her companion. "Patricia Tracy, allow me to introduce William Tucker, a recent client of mine and escort of the evening. Bill, this is my good friend and high-class chronicler, known to her friends as 'Tricia'."

Bill bowed deeply at the waist, took hold of Tricia's outstretched hand and gently applied a kiss.

"Your beauty blinds me as I experienced only once before, on first sighting the glowing emerald shining from the forehead of the legendary Mekong Buddha in deep Cambodia. Forever more that fabled jewel's radiance will be faded in my memory in comparison to the loveliness of your countenance."

Tricia laughed. "What absolutely adorable bullshit, Bill. I accept your gallantry with a smile." Shivers rolled up her back as she gazed at his dashing good looks, from bronzed weathered skin to sensuous lips pursed in thought.

"Patricia Tracy. Now why would that name sound familiar?" His smile of greeting exposed even white teeth, with a gold cap glittering at the edge.

Tricia smiled back at him, dimples forming just beyond the corners of her mouth, giving her cheeks a rosy glow. "Perhaps you've read my column *Tracy's Tidbits* in the *Caller Times*? This morning's was about a suspected murderer."

"I must confess, I'm not a regular reader of the paper. Deliveries to the boat slips tend to be unreliable." Bill winked his hazel eye. Tricia looked at the left side, where a long sharp scar bisected his eyebrow and came out below the patch an inch onto his left cheek.

"I think I've heard your name in association with something else. Isn't there a Tracy building in town somewhere?" Bill leaned on his black polished walking stick, topped with a golden duck head sporting black onyx eyes.

Alma interjected, "Yes. The Tracy Building is on Sixth Street. There's Richard Tracy middle school, as well as a Randolph Tracy wing to the art museum and one on the First Baptist Church, just to get the list started. Wealthy Corpus Christi families lend their names to local artifacts. Perhaps you've seen their stone castle on Ocean Drive? It's quite a local eyesore … uh, I mean landmark."

Tricia and Bill laughed at Alma's joke. "How does it feel to live in a castle?" he asked.

"That's my Mom's place," Tricia said. "Despite Alma's name dropping, I'm not yet one of the richer members of the clan." In answer to his puzzled look she elaborated, "It's one of those legal entanglements known as trusts."

"That's right," Alma said. "Tricia's practically impoverished. Wait until you see the little clunker she's forced to drive. To bring bread to her table, she slaves away at these fabulous parties seeking important items for her newspaper column. Be careful what you say to her as it may end up in print."

"I love my job," Tricia said happily. "I meet interesting people, receive invitations to all the great parties, and my fancy clothes and travel expenses are tax deductible. What more could a girl ask for?"

Bill tossed his head, his auburn ponytail bouncing. Tricia estimated his diamond earring at a carat and a half.

"Ah, you like to travel? We share that interest. Travel and the search for adventure have always been my greatest passions. I just finished a four month sailing tour of the French Antilles. Have you been? No? Should you go I recommend climbing the volcano La Soufrière on Basse-Terre Island. A three hundred meter climb up the Chemin des Dames brings you through lush tropical flora. The view of the jungle foliage from the summit will forever be a welcome remembrance of unspoiled natural beauty — a source to contemplate to renew a peaceful spirit in my soul. On the way down the mountain you can view three of the world's most spectacular waterfalls. Do you speak French?"

Tricia nodded. *"Oui, monsieur, en peu."*

"Très bien. It's always best to know the native language. I would recommend the French Antilles over the Netherlands Antilles anytime. Curaças is extremely dry. There the jungle trees of Basse-Terre are replaced by cactus."

"Three hundred meters up a mountain is exhausting," Tricia said. "I did that once, climbing an extinct volcano in Hawaii."

"Ah, but you weren't acclimated. The climb will only take a couple of hours, and the cool breezes will ease your journey. It's nothing like the Masada in Israel. Have you climbed that? No? Hot and dry. No wonder the Romans had such a rough time in conquering it."

"If you two travel agents could interrupt your resumes," Alma said, "you'll note the party crowd is thinning. Bill's invited me out for a midnight sail on his boat, Tricia. Why don't you come along?"

Tricia looked at Bill who smiled and nodded.

"Sure, My Beauty. Come join us if you'd like. We'd planned to sail a few miles into the Gulf and return to anchor just off shore for the night. If you prefer not to spend the night, we can bring you back to the dock and drop you off before we head out again."

"I haven't spent a night out on a boat since my Dad died. If you're sure I wouldn't be in the way, I'd enjoy spending the night on the water."

"We'll have a fine time telling stories. The night temperature dips to a pleasant sixty-five. Do you have a sweater or other clothes with you?"

Tricia nodded. "In my car's trunk. But I haven't eaten supper yet. Should we go out first?"

"How about take out Chinese food?" Bill suggested.

"Great, I love it! We can call in an order from my car phone and pick it up on the way to the dock. Where is your boat, the 'T' head?"

"No, 'L'. Say, Alma's already been to my boat. Would it be all right with you, Alma, if I go with Tricia? I can show her where I'm berthed. We'll meet you there in half an hour."

"Sure. Just as long as you remember which woman you've got a date with tonight. Make mine governor's chicken."

As they walked Tricia noticed that Bill limped, using his cane lightly. Together the three of them stepped out of the country club's door onto the porch. Tricia signaled to the valet.

"Get my Ferrari please, Javier."

"Right away Miss Tracy," he called back, as he jogged away down the driveway.

"Tracy?" Out of the dark staggered a scowling Hispanic, his swarthy skin accentuated by the yellow glow of the incandescent coach lights. He flung a cigarette to the ground and stopped five feet from them.

"Tracy, the newspaper girl?" he asked. He stood still, a hulk of foul smelling menace staring into Tricia's face. Just a few inches taller than Tricia, his arms bulged with laborer's muscles, his belly with alcoholic fat.

Alma's "Who wants to know?" wasn't quite in time to stop Tricia's "Yes?" He brushed his shaggy brown hair back and spat onto Tricia.

"You ugly *puta*. Just because *eres blanco[1]* and rich don't give you the right to say I kill my wife."

Tricia realized the identity of this intruder. "Lupè Garcia?"

"No one calls Lupè a murderer and gets away with it. There ain't no proof I done nothin'. You better write an apology."

Alma took a step forward, which Tricia considered brave, considering how strongly Lupè stank of alcohol, sweat and grime. "I'm an attorney, Mr. Garcia. If you do not leave immediately we will have you arrested."

Without taking his dark eyes off of Tricia, Lupè turned his head slightly and spat on Alma.

"We're going inside to get some help," she announced, taking Tricia by the arm. Tricia shook her off, and Alma, clucking in disapproval, trotted back into the building.

Tricia stared at Lupè contemptuously. "I didn't write that you were a murderer, though the police know you killed Maria. Just because they didn't throw you in jail today doesn't mean you're going to get away with it, you drunken lout. Eventually Detective Sweeney will get enough proof, lock you up, and throw away the key."

Lupè cursed, spewing forth a long string of Spanish profanity. He whipped out a switchblade knife. Its straight silver blade glittered in the lamplights.

"They can't prove I killed Maria, you ugly *puta*, so maybe they'll prove I mark you!"

Lupè lunged for Tricia's face, the knife whistling through the air. She had no time to move, hardly enough to gasp. With a loud crack the weapon clattered across the pavement. Lupè yelped, holding his wrist tightly.

Bill stepped into the light, holding his walking stick in front of Lupè's face.

"Try it again and I'll break your other arm too, Lupè."

Lupè stepped back in surprise. Anger flashed in his eyes.

"Nate? What the hell are you doing with this ugly *puta*? And whatcha defending her for? I thought you was *mi amigo*."

"You know this fellow?" Tricia asked Bill. "Did he call you Nate?"

"*Vaya! Estas haciendo problemas.[2]*" Bill snarled at Lupè, a spicy foreignness to his Spanish accent.

---

1 You're white

2 Go away. You're causing problems.

From a stance of apparent submission, Lupè lunged at Bill, swinging a left hook toward his face. Bill ducked and smacked the back of Lupè's head with the brass duck head as he staggered past. Lupè crumpled to the ground with a groan. Sitting up, he felt the back of his head with his left hand. It came away bloody.

Alma stepped out of the door with a policeman as the valet pulled up with Tricia's Ferrari.

"Do you need some help?" the officer asked, surveying the scene.

"No," Bill said. "I think he's done."

The police officer nodded, and turned to glare down at Lupè. "What about you, Buster? You want a police escort out of here?"

"No," Lupè said, staggering to his feet. Glaring at Bill he muttered something in Spanish.

Bill replied, "*Cuidado, Señor. Tu hora esta viniendo.*[3]"

Lupè spat again, this time on the ground. His right hand hung loosely at his side. His left applied pressure to his scalp.

"You owe me for this Nate," he said. "*Acuerdo esta caro amarillo, también.*"[4] Turning, he stumbled off into the night.

"What happened?" Alma asked. "I'm guessing that was the Garcia you wrote about in your column this morning, huh?"

"Bill just saved my life," Tricia told her, "beating up Lupè Garcia in the process." She bent down at the curb and picked up Lupè's knife. Alma whistled with respect when Tricia held it up for her to see. She offered it to Bill, who placed it, folded, in his pocket.

"Come on, let's get out of here. I'll tell you all about it later tonight." Tricia handed Javier a twenty dollar bill and climbed into the Ferrari. Bill struggled through the other door, easing his stiff left leg through first. He pulled out a handkerchief and cleaned the duck's head as the stick rested between his legs. They shot off, leaving little memories of rubber at stops and turns.

---

3   Be careful, Sir. Your time will come soon.

4   I'll remember this yellow car, too.

6

Interview: Sally Bellows
Date: Monday September Twelve
Location: Lonesome Coyote Tavern

Sweeney: Miss Bellows, thank you for agreeing to let me tape this interview.

Bellows: It's only because you're insisting that I'm even talking to you, Detective Sweeney. I don't like the police and I don't like you. You're nothing but trouble. Do you remember me?

Sweeney: Vaguely. Wait, now I remember. I ticketed you in the emergency room for drunk driving about a year ago.

Bellows: Damn straight. I went to the E.R. 'cause I was in an accident and ended up getting a DWI ticket. You know how that affected my insurance rates? It wasn't even my fault, that accident.

Sweeney: I had no choice, Miss Bellows. You were driving intoxicated. Besides being illegal, driving under the influence is dangerous to you and to others. Last week we arrested a bank president who broke a kid's leg. He claimed no one could have stopped the way the kid shot out in front of him on his bike. Maybe the drinks he had weren't a factor, but maybe they were. I'm always very serious about drunk drivers, Miss Bellows.

               For the record, today is September twelve. Present for this interview are

33

Sally Bellows, cocktail waitress, Sam Byrd, police sergeant, and me, Mel Sweeney, police detective.

Bellows: Do I have to answer your questions, Detective?

Sweeney: Yes, the law says you have to answer my questions.

Bellows: What if I just say I don't remember anything? Then will you leave me alone? If I'm talking with you guys I'm not serving drinks. If I'm not serving drinks, then I'm not getting tips.

Sweeney: Please bring us two drinks, then. Mountain Dew for me, please. Sam? Make it two, please.

Bellows: Here. Don't break your budget. That'll be two bucks.

Sweeney: Thank you. You said you recognized Maria Garcia from the picture I just showed you.

Bellows: Yeah, I recognize her. She's been in here a few times.

Sweeney: Yesterday her husband Lupè told me that the last time he remembers seeing her was in this bar three Fridays ago. That'd be August 26th. Do you remember them here that night?

Bellows: I'm going to say I don't remember anything about that night, okay? Then will you leave me alone?

Sweeney: Lupè told me that he and Maria came here
                  pretty often. Tell me what they were like
                  when they were here.

Bellows: Okay, okay. Yeah, they came here often.
                  Just about every Friday night, in fact.
                  Lupè gets paid on Fridays, I think he
                  works construction or something. He and
                  Maria come in, they both drink a lot, and
                  then she drives him home. She handles her
                  liquor better. You ever ticket Maria for
                  drunk driving?

Sweeney: I investigate crimes, Miss Bellows. So,
                  when they drink, does Lupè get violent or
                  obnoxious?

Bellows: Sometimes, yeah. Depends on who's here.
                  Like any bar, we have our Friday night
                  regulars. There are a few that like to rile
                  Lupè up, and a few that he likes to hang
                  around with. Course, Maria could make any
                  fella pissed. The way she flirts, I mean.

Sweeney: A flirt? What does she do?

Bellows: None of your business. Always looking for
                  trouble, aren't you, Detective?

Sweeney: Well, I would like more information. Anyone
                  around here tonight who would know Lupè?
                  How about that guy over there?

Bellows: How about you leave my customers alone,
                  Detective? Hold on a minute, will ya? He
                  needs a refill. I'll be back.

Pause

Bellows: Okay. What were we talking about?

Sweeney: You were telling me about some of the peo-
              ple who are usually here on Friday nights
              when Lupè and Maria are drinking.

Bellows: Well there's this fat guy named Bob. Works
              at the newspaper I think. He's out here
              most Friday nights. There's a homeless guy
              named Jack. He doesn't drink, never has
              any money. He's here pretty often. I think
              he deals drugs, but I'm not sure. Shit, I
              shouldn't be telling you all this. See, I
              told you talking to you guys was going to
              be trouble. Now you're going to be has-
              sling poor little Jack, as if he doesn't
              have enough problems already.

Sweeney: You honestly don't remember anything spe-
              cial about the last night you saw Maria in
              here? You can't remember if she and Lupè
              talked to anyone special, or if he was
              particularly drunk, or even what time they
              left?

Bellows: Sorry, Detective. I just serve drinks. I'm
              not a babysitter.

Sweeney: Has Lupè been here since then? Have you
              seen him alone or with someone else the
              last Friday or two?

Bellows: Yeah, he was here last week. Talking with
              a new guy. A sailor I think. Lupè's a lot
              different without Maria around. More sul-
              len. Hold on, again, that guy wants some-
              thing. Is this going to take much longer?

Sweeney: No, I guess we're done. Here's your tip.

Bellows: Twenty bucks? Hey, maybe you aren't so bad,
              Detective. Now I'm sorta sorry I gave you
              such a hard time.

Sweeney: Don't mention it. Maybe we'll have more
                  luck returning later in the week. Some of
                  those people may be here then. Turn off
                  the recorder, Sam, and let's get out of
                  here.

End of Recording
MS/sb

7

Pulling her car phone out of a covered panel, Tricia punched in the automatic dialing of the Golden Dragon. "Make mine shrimp with lobster sauce," she told Bill, handing it to him.

Bill began speaking in tongues, or so it seemed to Tricia. She stopped the car and stared at him in astonishment as he babbled away. He hung up, saying "They said it'll take twenty minutes."

Tricia demanded, "What was that?"

"What? Oh, the order? I got beef with broccoli. I figured a shrimp dish and a chicken dish could use a beef with vegetable to round it out."

"No, silly. What language were you speaking?"

"Chinese, of course. Actually a Cantonese version that's common in Hong Kong. Most of these Chinese restaurants in America are run by immigrants from Hong Kong, though a good number of Vietnamese, Koreans, and other nationalities have set some up too."

As she resumed driving, Tricia asked, "How many languages do you speak, anyway?"

Bill shrugged and smiled. "Oh, a working vocabulary of twenty or so. Once, when I was a teenager, I went to school with a Greek friend. He taught me a dozen words in Greek, all expletives. One day I dropped by his home when his mother was giving a party. He brought me out to meet the guests, a smattering of prim old ladies sitting in a parlor, yakking away in Greek. He proudly announced that I knew some words in Greek. Naturally they insisted I speak. Can you imagine my embarrassment?"

"So what did you do?"

"I spoke the only non-curse Greek word I knew, '*Hola*,' to one and all. Also, I promised myself I'd learn a few key phrases in every language I encountered. It's great fun. I can ask 'Where's the toilet' in at least forty dialects."

Tricia laughed. "A useful phrase, I'm sure."

"With a mere four hundred words you can get by in almost any language. Here's a bit of trivia for you. What single word is the same in almost every language?"

Tricia considered for a moment. Even with her limited language skills she could eliminate most words. "Television?" she guessed.

Bill chuckled, a low pitched rumble like Gulf Coast surf rolling onto the beach. "A very good guess. Your cleverness matches your fine spirit, My Beauty. Actually, the word is Taxi."

A sudden squeal of tires interrupted their conversation as Tricia stomped on the brakes to avoid a dog on the road. He finished crossing in front of the vehicle before turning around and urinating on her tire. The two travelers laughed.

"That's gratitude for you," Tricia said. "I save his life and he pees on my car. Oh. By the way. Thanks for saving <u>my</u> life. I promise I won't pee on your boat."

"That Garcia fellow's a bad one, sure enough. I'd like to offer my services as bodyguard for the next few days in case he tries something again."

"Oh, he was just drunk. I don't think he'd be foolish enough to do that again. Besides, I think you broke his arm; and maybe gave him a concussion."

She glanced at Bill's face and found it very solemn.

"I recommend you take this man's threats more seriously, Tricia. He's mean and tough. Most men wouldn't have gotten up so quickly after such a head blow."

"I'm old enough to take care of myself, thank you just the same. Look, here's the Golden Dragon."

On the way to the 'L' head the heavy smells of the Chinese food filled the car. Tricia swung onto Shoreline Drive, bringing them the view of the bay at night. Out in the water boats blinked with green and red lights. Two drilling platforms decked in strings of white lights looked like distant Christmas trees.

At the dock they found Alma relaxing on board Bill's boat. Named *Adventure*, the thirty foot yacht had a full cabin, and rigging large enough for both sail and jib. Intricately carved woodwork and shiny polished brass fittings demonstrated the care the owner lavished on this, his home. After they each took a turn in the cabin to change clothes, Bill brought out cups, plates, and a couple of bottles of wine.

An hour later the *Adventure* had left the protection of the docks and headed into the Gulf. While the boat hopped through waves, a light breeze to port, they shared the Chinese food. After dinner Bill returned the boat to tranquil waters.

The silence of the sea delighted Tricia. Laid back on a cushion aft, she watched the trail of white foam swirl and close up behind. Bill, next to her, guided the rudder while Alma sat with her back against the cabin, facing them.

"Bill has offered to work as my bodyguard," Tricia informed Alma.

Alma snorted. "You, Tricia? No offense, Bill, but you might as well guard a *toro* in a bullfighting ring. This girl flirts with trouble so much that trouble thinks he's her fiancé."

"Nevertheless, my c.v. for bodyguarding duties is not without impressive references. I have indeed guarded the proverbial *toro* from the *toreadors*. You no doubt have heard of Gandhi?"

"Uh-oh," Alma said. "Sounds like one of Bill's long stories. We better load up with fresh drinks before he gets going." She poured another round of wine.

"Mahatma Gandhi from India?" Tricia asked dubiously. "Of course we've heard of him. You're not going to tell us you were his bodyguard?"

Bill shook his head, his good eye winking at her. "Certainly not, My Beauty. I refer to Rajiv Gandhi, Nehru's grandson. Rajiv was involved in a rather nasty reelection campaign in 1989. As his personal bodyguard, I accompanied him on his Soviet made helicopters and his private Boeing jet to various campaign spots.

"This story involves Rajiv's campaign stop in Calcutta. Have you been there? No? Well, let me tell you, it isn't a city for the fainthearted.

"The very name Calcutta conjures images of squalor, starvation, disease, and death. The teeming masses of humanity overpower you to the point of suffocation. You can't move without forging a pathway through currents of dark skinned Indians; Hindus in loincloths, turban topped Muslims in business suits, government workers in cotton spun saris, laborers dressed in sweat-soaked burlap, and grimy, rag-tag beggars.

"The day in question dawned hot and muggy. I had flown into Dum Dum airport at six AM to check on the preparations made by the advance team. After inspecting the two scheduled speech sites, I returned to the airport to meet Rajiv.

"His jet landed on time, just before noon. A man of incredible stamina, Rajiv would nap and shower on flight, appearing fresh and confident at campaign stops. On this particular day all seemed to be going smoothly. His helicopter took the two of us from the airport, across the bustling city below, to the downtown speech site. We unloaded, the crowds cheered, and the speeches began.

"Repetitious activities can lull one to complacency. I suppose even a brain surgeon, if forced to perform the same delicate procedure day after day, might find the routine becomes dull and repetitive. So can it be with bodyguarding. The speeches rarely vary. The crowds and cities all blend into homogeneity. On hot humid afternoons it would be easy to relax and let your mind wander.

"And it would be fatal. I scanned the crowd constantly, like a security guard with a horde of teenage shoplifters in his store. Might there be ten listeners or one million, as it surely seemed that day, I kept constant vigil. The crowd seemed docile, occasionally clapping and cheering, mostly standing around quietly as Indians tend to do.

"I noticed two men with turbans pushing their way through the crowd, approaching from the outskirts. They demonstrated the determination of the fanatic, knocking aside several stubborn bystanders.

"I edged forward, finding a spot just behind Rajiv and to his left, the side the attackers had chosen. I looked straight ahead now, marking their progress with my peripheral vision. Slowly and steadily they plowed a path forward.

"I babied my pistol out of its holster, holding it slyly hidden behind Rajiv's leg. When the two assassins reached the base of the stage, they jerked out their guns, screaming in Bengali. One jumped up on the platform, swinging his pistol toward Rajiv.

"Without even pushing Rajiv to the side, I shot the fellow through the chest, sending him flying back onto the crowd. I pulled the podium over on top of the other. The single shot was all that was needed. The crowds pummeled both corpse and wounded until both were carried off by the local police.

"Rajiv hardly paused a moment. Retrieving the microphone, he went on with his speech as if nothing had happened. I asked him later what he thought when I fired my gun a mere two feet from his head. Had he been frightened? He told me no, not really. Just annoyed. For the rest of the week he couldn't hear a thing from that ear."

After Bill's tale ended the quiet sea sounds again took hold. Tricia's sense of admiration for this remarkable man swept through her with dizzying force. Handsome, bright, resourceful, adventuresome, and chivalrous; he seemed a man out of a storybook. She sipped the last swallow from her wine glass and accepted Bill's offer of a refill.

Tricia compared this man to Mel. *Of course I know so very little about Bill. Even so, one has to trust one's instincts, doesn't one?*

Mel plodded, placing one clumsy step in front of the next. He certainly was kind and gentle, and, if you enjoyed a certain crass level of humor, rather entertaining. But he couldn't dress and he abhorred high society. Mel was like a stray mutt, slobbering in friendliness but untrainable.

Bill, on the other hand, had the class of a thoroughbred. Suave and exciting, he fit in comfortably in tuxedo or, as now, cutoffs and ragged tank top. Tricia admired his ample muscles as they flexed and strained, working the anchor as the bay glistened in the light from the rising half moon. With a jerk the anchor caught. Laconically, Tricia twisted her head, noting that he had anchored a half mile offshore. She watched an occasional car light wink its way along the palm tree lined Ocean Drive.

Sleep tickled her mind. She remembered she was supposed to ask Alma something, but couldn't remember what. Tricia contemplated asking Bill where he had met Lupè Garcia before — and why Lupè had called him "Nate?" Instead she allowed the roll of the waves to deliver her into slumber.

The hours passed. Tricia startled to wakefulness. Her nightmare of being held down and raped glared in screeching agony. Sweat beaded upon her body. She choked back her scream.

She lay still on the rocking boat, staring up at the half moon above. The night air felt comfortable, offering the lightest of breezes. Yet the boat rocked hard. Then she heard.

"Oh. Oh. Oh. *Mia Dios! Vamos! Veno, veno, veno!*"

Tricia recognized Alma's voice, her muffled expressions of passion pouring from the cabin like lava flow. Revulsion roared up within Tricia with bitterest bile. Carefully she lowered herself over the side of the boat, enjoying the feel of the warm bay water. She swam to shore with a strong stroke, climbing up on open shorefront to the road.

Her watch read three AM.

It's too far to walk home from here, and my car keys are still on the boat. I need a friend. Now who do I know who lives around here?

A short walk brought her to the Smyth mansion on Ocean Drive. She fell fast asleep in their guest room.

Tracy's Tidbits
by Patricia Tracy

Corpus Christi Caller Times
Tuesday, September 13, 1994

Mayor's Reception; Have a Coke?

Fluttery birds of a feather flocked together at Mayor Arthur Andrews' campaign fundraiser last night. Glittering gorgeous gowns draped decorously on sparkling socialites. Blonde buxom beauties belonging to boisterous businessmen paraded proudly, bantering political banalities. Campaigning conservationists canvassed powerful politicians, who preferred listening to laughing lobbyists.

Mayor Andrews' reelection is as certain as a heat wave in September. His six years of uniting Anglo and Hispanic interests have paid off with city wide admiration. His tenure has provided a new high school, two parks, and the opening of the Padre Island Expressway. The police force has been increased, teachers have had raises, and commerce is booming. What's not to like?

Our shining city by the sea brings in tourists, oil tankers, grain transport, and ... cocaine. Drs. Carl and Debbie Carter from the Carter Drug clinic tell me that this discretion of the rich flows in cornucopian supply. Cocaine burns as bright as a flare, heightening pleasures, but then, like the flare, leaving the user sitting in the dark tasting ashes. To get more, what won't he do? Hock his car. Abandon his job. Steal from his neighbor. Perhaps even murder his wife.

Now, riding the high of successful political capital, Mayor Andrews has an opportunity to develop a task force to fight this modern plague. The needs are multiple; more narcotics agents, educational programs in the community, and, most importantly, a heightened presence at our docks. A bit more port authority will cork this leaky flow, saving untold lives.

8

Coming downstairs for breakfast, Tricia found her friend Becky Smyth sitting at the table, hard at work on a crossword puzzle. "What's a five letter word for 'domicile'?" Becky asked, as Tricia came through the kitchen door. Becky tossed her head, sending her bleached blonde trusses twirling.

"House," Tricia said, settling into a chair next to Becky. Accepting a steaming mug, she smiled up at Martha, Becky's maid. She sipped the chicory flavored coffee, gazing out the large picture window into the back garden. Late summer foliage of chrysanthemums, crape myrtle, and a flock of birds of paradise waved in the gentle breeze. Somewhere deep in the house a grandfather clock struck ten deep tones.

Martha set a plate of *huevos revueltos*[1] with cornbread at Tricia's place, which she ate with gusto.

"You always have such exciting adventures," Becky said, pushing her newspaper away. "What brought you here in the middle of the night?"

"I swam ashore. I had to walk two blocks in my soaking wet clothes at three AM. It's not an adventure I'm eager to repeat, I'll tell you that."

"Oh, I'm all ears, Tricia. How did you get in this situation? Escaping from pirates? Parachuting over the gulf? Crashing your hang glider on an off shore oil derrick?"

Tricia laughed with her.

"No, Silly, nothing so dramatic. I fell asleep on a boat with Alma Trevino and her date. When I woke up I heard them making love. Well, naturally, I couldn't stay on board with that going on."

Becky clucked her tongue. "How rude! But gosh, that was dangerous! I mean, swimming in the bay in the middle of the night? You could have been bitten by a shark, or lost your way in the dark and drowned."

"I can take care of myself. Anyway, I couldn't stay with that going on."

Becky smirked. "I bet I can guess how you felt when you realized people were having sex near you!"

Tricia flushed as Becky's suggestion hit a sensitive nerve. "The world would be much healthier if people observed a higher level of morality. I don't believe in premarital sex."

---

1   Spanish scrambled eggs

"Oh? So you and Mel have remained chaste?"

Tricia turned away, fixing her attention on the garden. "Well, almost."

"Then tell me, doesn't it feel scrumptious? Can you honestly say you don't enjoy sex?"

"Not too much, really. I get so nervous. You like sex?"

"Do I like sex? Ha! I love to screw! God gave women an unlimited capacity for sexual sensation, endurance and enjoyment. Now I'm not one to run around, Dear. But I certainly don't believe in depriving myself of the good feelings either. Tell me, if I might be so presumptuous. Is Mel the only man you've ever been with?"

Tricia nodded. "Except for a little petting in high school."

Martha Gonzalez, Becky's housekeeper, waddled into the room with the coffee carafe. Tricia wondered how Martha and Becky could both eat Martha's delicious cooking, yet only Martha gained the weight. Tricia acknowledged the refill with a smile. While Martha cleared off the breakfast dishes, the two friends sat in companionable silence. Tricia played with the topic in her mind, wondering whether her sexual reticence deprived her of untold pleasures.

After Martha left Becky said, "Tricia, all I'm trying to say is that you're only young once. When we get old and fat like Martha, I'm not going to look back on these years with regrets for pleasures missed. Different men teach you new things. Mel is a nice guy. But really … he's such a geek."

Tricia thought about Mel. Their occasional attempts at making love had been brief and uncomfortable. What if she just needed a different lover? That William Tucker; surely he'd know how to lead a woman to new and exciting passions. Based on Alma's outbursts of the previous night, untold delights lay just beyond Tricia's imagination.

"Alma, Pam and I are going out to The Cannery Thursday night," Becky said. "Why don't you join us? Try out some young men on the prowl instead of those old fogies at those socialite parties."

Tricia nodded slowly. "Maybe you're right. Sure. I'll join you."

"Great. We're meeting them at seven. How about you pick me up at six thirty? We'll have a round of drinks here before we leave."

The melodic song of the doorbell echoed through the house. A minute later Martha lumbered into the room.

"It *Señors* Sweeney and Byrd, *Señora*. *Señor* Sweeney say he want to talk to me about my niece."

"Mel's here?" Tricia asked in surprise. "Say, that's great. Ask him to come in!"

As directed, the detective came to stand in the doorway. His six-foot figure looked especially lanky in a red and white vertically striped too large dress shirt and baggy green and black checked pants. Dusty brown loafers peeked out from below thread worn cuffs. He raised his giraffe arm in greeting.

"Howdy! Are we friends again, Tricia?"

She went over and gave him a hug and light kiss. "More than friends, Sweety. What brings you here, oh darling daring detective of Corpus' criminals' capers?"

Accepting Becky's invitation to join them at the table, he sat with a leg folded under him, the other sprawled out like a bird's broken wing. Martha brought orange juice and a plate of Mexican *postres*[2].

Between bites he answered, "Here to interview Martha. Won't take long. You need a ride? I didn't see your hot rod banana out front."

"Right again, super smart sleuth. You never miss a clue. I do need a lift downtown to the bay front docks. It's a long story, but I left my Ferrari sleeping there."

Mel gulped the last of the juice and snapped back to his feet. "Sure thing, Sweetheart. I'll be with you in a jiffy. As it happens, Sam and I came in separate vehicles. He'll take the cruiser back to the station and I can drive you to your car in my jalopy.

"Is there a room we can use to talk with Martha, Mrs. Smyth?"

---

2   desserts

9

Interview:	Martha Gonzalez
Date:	Tuesday, September 13
Location:	Smyth home, Ocean Drive

Sweeney: Martha, as I just said, I'd like to tape this interview if that's all right.

Gonzalez: *Por supuesto.*[1]

Sweeney: Thanks. For the record, present here are Martha Gonzalez, housekeeper for Becky Smyth, Mel Sweeney, detective, and Samuel Byrd, police sergeant. Today's date is Tuesday, September thirteenth. Martha, how have you been? It's been several months since I last saw you.

Gonzalez: *Bueno suficiente*[2], *Señor, gracias.* I cook, I clean. With only *Señora,* keeping house clean much easier.

Sweeney: I remember the last time I was out in this neighborhood. It was about a month ago. I was following up a clue about a man accused of molesting his niece. Turned out the niece had some unsavory history herself. Speaking of nieces, that's why I'm here, of course. When did you first realize your niece, Maria Garcia, was missing?

Gonzalez: We plan on family visit in McAllen for holiday, Labor Day. We supposed to meet at

---

1   Of course

2   Good enough

bus stop Saturday *por la mañana.* She not show up. I go without her. When I get back *fui á su casa.* She no there. I call you.

Sweeney: Right. You called Tuesday, I went there that evening. Tell me how you are related to Maria, please.

Gonzalez: Her mama, Juanita, she my older sister. Juanita have two children. Maria is her *niña,* sweet baby. Juanita *tenia* forty years *cuando* Maria born. Mama gave her everything. She spoil her. You think Maria grateful? *No, nada!* She wild thing. She drink, and smoke, and run with *caprones malos.*[3] *¿Comprende?*

Sweeney: Sure, I understand. I see girls like that all the time.

Gonzalez: When she marry Lupè it break her mama's heart. Juanita die four years later.

Sweeney: I understand Maria married young, didn't she?

Gonzalez: Umm. 1981. Maria, she sixteen years old. She and Lupè fight all the time. Maybe that why they never have children, *¿si?*

Sweeney: What did they fight about, Martha? You have any ideas?

Gonzalez: *Si, yo se.*[4] She wild girl. I say that, *¿si?*

Sweeney: Yes, you did. Did Maria ever express fear of Lupè to you? Did she ever tell you she

---

3   Very bad men. Understand?

4   Yes, I know.

was afraid he was going to hurt her or kill her?

Gonzalez: No. He beat her *muchas veces.*[5] Lupè drink too much. *Pero,* she not afraid. Say he love her. You going to arrest him, *Señor?*

Sweeney: I tried that, Martha, but the judge set him free. Have you known Lupè long?

Gonzalez: He nineteen when marry Maria. Go to prison once. Stab someone, *creo*[6]. Maria move back with Juanita 'til he out. Lupè *loco.*

Sweeney: Loco Lupè, huh? I like that. It's got a ring to it. It reminds me of a couple of con artists, Weasel Willie and his sister Wandering Wanda. They used to wiggle their ways into deals all over town. One time he and his sister sold a truck load of dirt back to the same company he had been paid to haul it away from. Tell me a little about your sister Juanita.

Gonzalez: She work hard. She seventeen, start work for Tracys.

Sweeney: Excuse me, Martha. Did you say Tracys? Which Tracys would that be?

Gonzalez: *Señorita* Tricia's grandpa, *Señor* Herbert Tracy. *Su esposa*[7] die when two babies young. When she die, Herbert get Juanita *por ninos.*

Sweeney: I didn't know Tricia had any uncles or aunts. She told me that both her parents

---

5   Many times

6   I believe

7   His wife

were only kids. Besides Richard, who was the other child?

Gonzalez: Baby sister, Beverly. She Juanita's favorite. Juanita tell me Beverly send *muchos* letters.

Sweeney: I have a box of letters that I took from Maria's house, thinking they might have a clue to her disappearance. I didn't think much of them, since they were all pretty old and none of them addressed to Maria. I guess Maria kept them because they reminded her of her mom. There was a rosary and some old photos in there too. Would you like the box?

Gonzalez: *Si, por favor.* Family letters *son buenos.*

Sweeney: Of course. I'll bring them over later in the week. Maybe I'll have a chance to go through them one more time. How long did Juanita work for the Tracys?

Gonzalez: *Por mucho tiempo[8].* Umm. She start when she seventeen, that be 1942. She stay until old *Señor* Tracy die. That be 1956. *Un año bueno para Juanita[9].* She get new job and marry nice man. Hector, *su hijo[10],* he born next year. Maria nine years later.

Sweeney: What kind of job? Did she work for another family?

Gonzalez: *No Señor.* Work for *Señor* Randolph. Clean and cook, *como yo[11].*

---

8   A long time

9   It was a good year for Juanita

10 Her son

11 Like me

Sweeney: Bob Randolph, the editor?

Gonzazlez: *Si. Esta.*

Sweeney: What happened to Juanita's husband?

Gonzalez: He die in car accident. *Que triste*[12]!
                Juanita *tenia pega*, bad luck.

Sweeney: And Hector, her son?

Gonzalez: He … how you say? He like boys. He die of
                AIDS. Juanita dead already.

Sweeney: So Maria was the last of her family. That's
                a shame. I come from a real large family
                myself. Did you know I had eight brothers
                and sisters? Yep. We all helped around the
                house. My oldest sister Katie Rose used
                to cook all the time. She could make some
                really good cookies. Almost as good as
                yours, Martha.

Gonzalez: *Muchas Gracias, Señor.* You want more cook-
                ies? *Estan* fresh.

Sweeney: Why that would be nice. Thanks.

Pause

Gonzalez: *Aqui, Señor.* Help yourself. You too, *Señor*
                Byrd.

Sweeney: Thanks, Martha. Umm, these are great! Let's
                see, where were we?

Gonzalez: You ask about Maria's family.

---

12 How sad.

Sweeney: Right. So you were the closest relative
                she had, is that right?

Gonzalez: *Claro*. In McAllen are many cousins. But
                Juanita and *yo somos aqui solos*[13]. Maria,
                she talk to me sometimes. *Pero, estoy
                vieja, Señor*[14]. Next month be sixty-four!

Sweeney: Do you know anything about Lupè's family?

Gonzalez: *Solo que es pequeña*[15]. They from Robstown.
                Rough people.

Sweeney: Her neighbors tell me that Maria didn't
                get out of the house much. They said she
                didn't have a job.

Gonzalez: *No esta verdad*. She work *a veces*. She work
                for *Señor* Randolph after her mama die. I
                think she get money other place too.

Sweeney: What other place? You're shaking your head.
                You won't tell me?

Gonzalez: No.

Sweeney: I'll have to think about that one. Did you
                know if she went out without Lupè some-
                times? Did she have friends?

Gonzalez: *No se, pero creo que no*[16]

Sweeney: Okay, is there anything else you want to
                tell me about Maria or Lupè? Anything

---

13   She and I are the only ones here
14   But, I'm an old woman
15   Only that it is a small (family)
16   I'm not sure, but I believe she didn't.

else you think might help me solve her
disappearance?

Gonzalez: *Si, Señor.* Maria, she wild thing. She may
have run off with *un hombre. Pero,* if
Lupè kill Maria, you put him in jail, *por
favor.*

Sweeney: I'm working on it, Martha. Thank you.

End of recording.
MS/sb

10

Mel's old Chevy rattled down the highway, traffic noises washing in the open windows. Besides the dysfunctional air conditioner, the radio wouldn't sing. The back window wouldn't close. The heater didn't heat. The gas gauge perpetually boasted full. The back left door wouldn't open. The seat covers sported large threadbare patches over loose springs. The one remaining carpet mat had only small island tufts of rug. With each minor bump the back bumper clanged against the car's frame.

"At least the horn works in this old hunk of junk," Tricia groused.

"Of course the horn works," Mel replied. "A car without a working horn would be illegal."

Tricia braced herself against the dashboard as the green machine lurched to a stop at a light. After the light changed the car banged along until reaching a steady rocking speed. In order to be heard, the two occupants half shouted at each other.

"Say, Tricia, I never knew you had an aunt."

"Don't. Never did. I know I told you that both my parents were only children."

"I remember. But Martha just told me that her sister used to work for your grandfather taking care of two kids. She says your father had a sister named Beverly. You've never heard of her?"

Tricia looked at him in surprise. "No. This is the first I ever heard anything like that. She must have been a black sheep or something. What did Martha tell you about her?"

"Not much. Who do you think would know about her? You have any old family albums or old letters hidden in trunks in the attic?"

"Why are you so interested? It's my family after all."

"Just a loose end. Following the loose ends often leads to amazing results. I remember one case where a fellow's aunt's brother's partner gave me the clue I needed."

"I suppose that if you want more information about our family, you best try the Iron Maiden at the castle. You know; my mom. Meredith."

"Why do you call her the Iron Maiden? That has a nasty medieval connotation. It reminds me of a knife wielder I knew we called Lancelot Larry. Get it? You see, knife cuts, lance a lot? Never mind."

"Besides Meredith's social coldness, inside she's a suit of nails. Well, you'll see."

The car jolted and banged around a corner, temporarily silencing the duo.

After the cacophony quieted, Tricia asked, "Mel, have you ever had another woman?"

He turned quickly, alarm registered across his features. "What?"

Her expression serious and tense, Tricia repeated the question.

Mel directed his attention to the road ahead. Shaking his head he replied, "It's really not something we should talk about, Tricia. What possible difference could it make what we've done before we met? What's important is that now it's just us — two destined souls locked together in eternal love like Romeo and Juliet, Sonny and Cher, Simon and Garfunkel."

"Mel, every couple you mentioned ended their relationship on a sour note, Romeo and Juliet the worst. Don't evade the question, please."

"Gosh, I'd really rather not. It would just make you mad."

"So you have!" Tricia felt angry and somehow betrayed. "So, how do I compare?"

Mel laughed nervously. "Really, Tricia. This is a very delicate subject. Can't we talk it over later? How about I take you out for dinner tonight?"

"Where did you have in mind? Whataburger? You won't take me anywhere nice and you won't dress up when I invite you out. I'm embarrassed to be seen with you in your mismatched clothes and your junk heap car. Maybe it's about time we started dating other people."

Mel pulled off the road and turned to face her. Seeing his dismay, Tricia's compassion rose.

"Patricia Tracy! Please. Think of what this means! You and I are good for each other. I love you, Tricia. You've told me you love me too. I know I'm not the most suave man around. But I'm fun and sincere. Don't do this."

He faced her, his mouth clenched in tense sorrow; tears forming in his eyes. One salty packet traveled down his left cheek. He caught it halfway down with his sleeve.

Tricia turned away, her aching made it impossible to continue looking at him.

"Look, Mel. I'm not saying I never want to see you again. I just feel like I need to get out a little more. I'm only twenty-four years old. I need to experience some things for a little while. You were right. Now's not the time to talk about it. Look, we're only a block from the 'L' head pier. Please, drop me off at my car and we'll talk about it tonight. I'll call you, okay?"

Mel reached out and gently turned her head toward him. He stared into her face, his eyes searching for her heart.

"You promise you'll call me tonight?" he implored.

Tricia promised. In silence they rode the remaining short distance onto the 'L' head. Mel recognized the yellow roadster easily, pulling up behind it. As Tricia climbed out Bill called out from his boat.

"Hey, My Beauty! I was wondering when you'd show up."

Despite his slight limp, he jumped lithely from his boat onto the pier, using his cane to help absorb the force of landing. He crossed quickly to Tricia's car, his welcoming smile melting Tricia's heart. Bill extended his arms in offering of a greeting hug. Tricia took hold of each hand, converting the motion into a double handshake instead. The black cane hanging on his wrist swung lightly in the sea breeze.

"Boy, am I glad to see you," he said. "When I came up on deck at dawn and found you gone it gave me a bit of a shock. Alma assured me that you probably just went for a swim. What happened?"

Tricia blushed. Without turning she loosened one hand and pointed behind her.

"Bill, I'd like you to meet a good friend of mine; Mel Sweeney. Mel, this is William Tucker."

Bill let go with the other hand as well, extending the right hand in offering of a shake. Breaking into a smile he approached Mel.

"Any friend of Tricia's is a friend of mine. Nice to meet you, Mel."

Mel snubbed the outstretched hand. Staring past him at Tricia, she felt his glare boring into her head. She turned to face him, defiance set into her features like a post office "Wanted Poster."

"Now I see what this is all about," Mel growled. "Some swashbuckling pirate comes along with a ship and a story and the next thing I know he's turned your pretty head. I really thought you were deeper than this, Patricia Tracy. Okay. I get the picture."

Turning to Bill he snarled. "You've made an enemy today, Buddy. That girl was the best thing that ever happened in my life. Maybe you're not at fault. But then again, maybe you are."

Bill looked on in astonishment. "Hey, fellow, you've got it wrong. I didn't touch her last night, I promise! I don't know what Tricia told you, but I was with another lady."

Suddenly a change came over Mel's features. The anger turned into puzzlement. He looked at Bill askance, like a bird studying a worm hole. The sailor half turned toward Tricia, keeping his one eye on Mel.

"Is he all right?" Bill asked her. "He's acting awfully strange."

Mel said. "You look familiar. Do I know you?"

Bill shook his head. "I really don't think so. I've only been in town a few weeks, though I suppose you may have seen me somewhere in that time."

Mel studied him closely. Slowly he shook his head, his face twisted in concentration. "No. I recognize you from somewhere, but I just can't place it. It's the eye patch that seems out of place."

Bill smiled and shrugged his shoulders. "I've had this patch for years. I'd be happy to tell you about it. See, this story takes place many years ago. I was in Nairobi at the time. Have you ever been there?"

Mel shook his head. "I'm not interested in your sailor yarns, William Tucker, or whatever your name really is." He turned to Tricia. "I guess this is farewell. When this charlatan has finished with you, remember that you still have a faithful friend."

He turned quickly and strode back to his car. Avoiding looking at them again, he backed up and exited the docks, the rattles fading quickly in the distance.

Tricia walked up beside Bill as the two of them watched Mel's car turn onto Shoreline Drive and disappear in the traffic.

He turned to her and asked "What was that all about? I'm sorry if I caused problems between you and your boyfriend."

She sighed. Biting her lower lip, her brows clenched together to hold her face in resistance of crying. Tricia shook her head, as much in denial of Bill's statement as in an attempt to dispel the heaviness in her heart.

"No, it's not you. Or, at least, it was mostly me." For a moment longer she continued gazing toward the spot of Mel's disappearance. With a spin, and a stance, and a defiance in her voice, she made the break.

"Okay, then. I guess that's it for now. How about I come on board and retrieve my stuff." She strode quickly toward Bill's boat.

"Have you had lunch?" he asked. "Come join me below for a tuna salad."

On reaching the boat she turned and waited as his slightly slower step brought him near. Using the duck's beak on his cane as a hook, he pulled the boat close enough for an easy reach. He stepped aboard first, holding a hand out to help Tricia cross.

Bill had put her dress, purse, and keys together in a brown bag which he retrieved for her. Peeping into the cabin after him, she saw that he had set out a can of tuna and fresh celery stalks.

"No, thank you," she answered. "I had a late breakfast. Besides, I'm sort of eager to get over to the office. I'm working on an important story." She wondered if that Dupree woman had called her back. Now that it came to her mind, she regretted not having called in from Becky's home. Well, never mind, she'd be back at the office soon enough.

"Ah," Bill observed. "A woman who enjoys her work. That is indeed a pleasant situation. I have never quite found my niche, I suppose. I've traveled the world over, sailed wild seas, climbed rugged mountains, foraged native forests. I've enjoyed my many adventures and have few regrets about my life. Still, I have never found an occupation that I thought would satisfy me enough to warrant settling down. Life has always seemed too short and too promising of new thrills to limit myself to one field."

Tricia, who had been about to step off the boat with her package, turned instead and sat on the boat's deck. She'd never met a man of such independent lifestyle. She loved to study his face. It seemed to Tricia that something magical had occurred when she first set eyes upon him, as if they were soulmates.

Her thoughts turned to Becky's comments and Alma's cries of passion from the previous night. She felt jealous; and yet, ashamed for feeling that way. Perhaps it wasn't jealousy, but envy.

"Bill, could I ask ..." she began, but then quickly stopped in embarrassment.

He looked at her with surprise. "Of course, Tricia, ask me anything. You needn't be shy."

"Well," she started. "It's a very personal question. I ... I'm really surprised at myself for even considering asking. No. Forget it." She shook her head and felt her cheeks flush.

Bill, who had been standing holding onto some lifelines, squatted down in front of her. He used his cane to balance from the slight rocking of the boat. Hovering a few inches from her face, his bright handsome eye sought out hers with insistence.

"Please, Tricia. I'd love to know that we are friends. Feel free to talk to me honestly and sincerely."

Hypnotized, Tricia stared into the sailor's eye. He reached into her soul, gently calming her heart. Her shyness faded.

In a quiet even voice she asked, "How many women have you loved?"

He continued to stare into her eyes, rocking gently with the boat's rhythm. They rested there, communicating with their eyes, their thoughts and feelings riding the mists of ocean spray.

When he spoke, Tricia found his rich baritone entrancing. "I have known many women, Patricia Tracy. There have been those times in my life when I desired companionship; intellectual, physical, or spiritual. Ladies of many cultures have taught me eccentric mysteries, impassioned sensations, and soulful nourishment. But I still search for that woman with whom I will have true love.

"In you I sense something special — something fantastic! Though I just met you, my beautiful Texas belle, I somehow feel that I have known you forever.

I sense that I understand you intimately, as if we were destined for each other. Somehow my whole life, my travel all over the planet, has brought me finally to the woman for whom I have always sought. Do you feel it too, Tricia? Do you feel the magic?"

His voice quieted. Clinks and clanks of rigging mixed with the whiffing of the riggings. The incessant waves lapped on the hull. Behind her a couple of saucy seagulls taunted each other.

Slowly she leaned her head forward as he, on cue, came forward to meet her. She closed her eyes. Their lips met. Electric sparks of ardent passion surged through her. Her nipples hardened. Her groin ached. The thrill of the delicious intimacy made her feel faint.

She pushed away and stood up. He stood also, proud and serious.

"Patricia, you are magnificent. Please. Stay here with me."

"No!" she whimpered, frightened of her desire to say yes. "No, no, no. I must go before.... I must go."

She turned and climbed quickly off the boat, clutching her bag tightly to her chest.

"Wait, please," he called out to her back. "Dinner! You must have dinner with me."

Tricia rushed to her car, yanked her keys from her bag and shoved them into the door lock. Instead of opening it, she leaned against the canvas roof. She stood quietly for several seconds, struggling with her desire.

"Please," he called. Bill walked up to stand behind her. Gently he placed his hands on each side of her face. His eye glowed like the fire of the setting sun on the gulf. She leaned into this kiss, clinging with urgent passion.

An eternity passed.

Bill released her and took one step back.

Tricia breathed deeply several times, uncertain as to whether she had breathed at all for the past lifetime. With a trembling voice she said, "Yes. Dinner. How does seven sound?"

"Too late. When will you finish with work?"

"Mid-afternoon?"

"I will wait with baited breath until My Beauty returns. Please plan to show me your favorite spot in town."

Tricia nodded her assent. She climbed into her car, started the engine and lowered the top. She gazed at him, leaning on his cane a few feet away. She yearned for one more taste of this wonderful man. She dared not. She drove slowly from the lot, a speed she had never tried before.

11

Interview: Meredith Randolph Tracy
Date: Tuesday, September 13
Location: Tracy Mansion, Ocean Drive

Sweeney: Good afternoon Mrs. Tracy. I appreciate you giving me this opportunity to talk with you. As I just mentioned, with your permission, I'd like to tape this interview.

Tracy: As you wish, Detective. I can only spare an hour. I have a garden club dinner this evening.

Sweeney: Well, no doubt you're the president. I've never seen such fabulous flowers. What are these called?

Tracy: That particular plant is an African violet. They make good household decorations. Surely you didn't wish to consult me about plants?

Sweeney: No ma'am. For the record, today is Tuesday, September Thirteenth. Present today are Meredith Tracy, community leader, Mel Sweeney, detective, and Samuel Byrd, police sergeant.

Tracy: Mel Sweeney. I seem to recognize that name. Have we met before?

Sweeney: No ma'am. Probably your daughter talks about me often. We're … that is, we were real close friends.

Tracy: You're a friend of Patricia's? Maybe she did mention your name once.

Sweeney: Only once? Son of a gun. Well, on to the task at hand. You see, I'm working on the disappearance of Maria Garcia. Maria's aunt, Martha Gonzalez, told me that Maria's mother, Juanita Gonzalez, used to work for your late husband's family. Do you know anything about Juanita Gonzalez or Maria Garcia?

Tracy: I know of Juanita only in that she shows up in some of Richard's old family photographs.

Sweeney: Yeah? I'd really appreciate seeing them.

Tracy: Sorry. They're all packed away in boxes in the attic.

Sweeney: All of them? You mean you don't have pictures hanging on some wall somewhere?

Tracy: No. That would be rather plebeian.

Sweeney: Well, gosh. In the Sweeney household there are family pictures everywhere. Of course, there are lots of family members to take pictures of. I have eight brothers and sisters. Sometimes there were as many as twenty people stuffed into my home at any one time, what with visiting cousins and friends moving in and out. You got cats around here? You sort of seem like a cat person.

Tracy: I am a certified daughter of the American Revolution. The Randolph family name has a long and sacred tradition. No, no cats.

Sweeney: Sorry, I didn't mean any offense. But as I was saying, in the Sweeney home we have dozens, maybe a hundred photo albums. Every kid has his own set. Any time someone comes back to visit we pull out the latest book and do show and tell about where we've been and what we've been up to. Don't you ever look through old albums?

Tracy: I prefer to live in the present. Look, Mr. Swenson …

Sweeney: Sweeney, ma'am.

Tracy: Mr. Sweeney. Could you please come to the point, if you have one.

Sweeney: Well, I'm really just trying to get information. I'd appreciate you getting out one of those albums for me.

Tracy: And if I don't?

Sweeney: Mrs. Tracy, I really feel that I need this information as part of my murder investigation. I sure wish you would.

Tracy: Oh, very well. You and your man may accompany me upstairs to move around boxes.

The recorder was turned off at this point.

Sweeney: I've turned the recorder back on now. Thank you for going to all this trouble for me. Boy these pictures are really old, aren't they? Who are these people?

Tracy: Those are Herbert and Constance Tracy. Patricia's father's parents. This was taken soon after their wedding in 1930.

Sweeney: Constance was a beautiful woman. I can see a lot of Patricia in her. Herbert looks older than Constance, doesn't he?

Tracy: Herbert was twenty-seven at his marriage, Constance eighteen. It's not uncommon for the man to be older than the woman. Richard was twelve years my senior. If I'm not mistaken, you have a few years of maturity over Patricia, don't you?

Sweeney: Eight. You've got me there. So here's a picture of Richard as a baby, huh? Wait, who's this?

Tracy: That would be Beverly, Richard's younger sister. She was born three years after Richard, in 1935.

Sweeney: Martha Gonzalez told me that Richard had a sister. But Patricia had told me that neither you nor her father had any siblings.

Tracy: Either you misunderstood or she was mistaken. Though, for all practical purposes, that statement would be correct.

Sweeney: Why? Did she die?

Tracy: Here's a photograph of her at Richard's birthday party. 1939. That would be Richard's seventh birthday. On Richard's left sits his sister Beverly, and on his right is my cousin, Robert. He would have been six at this time.

Sweeney: Robert Randolph? Bob Randolph, the editor, he's your cousin? You could sure pick him out in a crowd, huh? Only six years old and already knows how to eat! So Bob and Richard were good friends growing up?

Tracy: Of course. People of our class naturally
            congregate. Look. Here's a picture of that
            Juanita Gonzalez you were asking about.

Sweeney: It looks like a family portrait, without a
            mom. Was Constance taking the picture?

Tracy: No. Constance died during childbirth com-
            plications in 1938. The infant died as well.
            That's why Herbert hired help. Though, of
            course, in those days it was common for
            people to have hired help. Not like now.
            In those days, before our current welfare
            state, people were eager to work. Reliable
            help could be hired easily.

Sweeney: 1938? So Juanita came to work for them when
            Richard was … let's see, six and Beverly
            was only three?

Tracy: No. Juanita wasn't their first nanny. I
            suppose they called her that. Look. The
            date on the photograph is 1942. Richard
            would have been ten and Beverly seven. You
            can see how young Juanita looks here. She
            couldn't have been more than seventeen.

Sweeney: Let's keep going. My there are a lot of
            pictures with Juanita and the kids.

Tracy: Yes. Richard was very fond of her. I sup-
            pose she was like a surrogate mother.
            Richard told me once that Beverly was even
            fonder of her.

Sweeney: Look at this picture. Juanita looks quite
            proud of Beverly in that ballerina outfit.
            Hey. Here's Richard's high school gradu-
            ation picture. 1950. There's Herbert and
            there's Juanita. My, Juanita looks awfully
            sad doesn't she? Where's Beverly?

Tracy: I believe that was the year Beverly ran off.

Sweeney: Ran off? She'd only be fifteen then. Why did she run away? Did they look for her?

Tracy: I believe not.

Sweeney: Excuse me? I'm sure if I had a fifteen year old daughter who ran away I would surely look for her.

Tracy: Maybe you would, maybe you wouldn't.

Sweeney: Why wouldn't I?

Tracy: Well, Mr. Swenson, you figure it out.

Sweeney: It's Detective Sweeney, ma'am.

Tracy: Sweeney, then. In any case, they knew where she was. Richard told me once that Herbert tried to send her money and tried to get her to come home, but she refused to have anything to do with the family ever again.

Sweeney: What's this? A funeral?

Tracy: Yes. Herbert died in 1956. He was only fifty-three. Like Richard, he died suddenly of a heart attack at a young age. I'm afraid the Tracy family has bad heart genes. Perhaps they have high cholesterol. Juanita must have been about thirty then, though she looks much older in this snapshot.

Sweeney: So is that when Juanita began working for your cousin?

Tracy: Yes. Richard took over this home when his
              father died and Juanita's position was
              terminated.

Sweeney: So you never met Juanita or Beverly or
              Maria, is that right?

Tracy: No, not quite right. Corpus Christi isn't
              that large a town, Mr. Swenson. One time,
              I believe it was just before Richard's
              sudden collapse, he and I were out for
              an evening stroll in the park. He became
              quite excited and ran across the field like
              a little boy. Most uncharacteristic. He
              caught up with this stooped Mexican woman
              and brought her back across the grass to
              introduce me to Juanita. I found it to be
              a rather embarrassing exchange. He still
              seemed to have very fond feelings for the
              old lady. She must have been almost sixty.
              Strangely enough, she didn't seem as happy
              to see him.

Sweeney: And you've never heard from Beverly? In
              all the years you were married to Richard
              she never wrote to him nor he to her?

Tracy: No.

Sweeney: Why did you hide all this from Patricia?

Tracy: Do you have anything else you wish to ask
              me, Mr. Swenson? I have an engagement for
              which I must get ready.

Sweeney: Sweeney. It's Detective Sweeney, ma'am.

Tracy: Sweeney, then.

Sweeney: No ma'am. I guess that's all. Thank you
              for your time. Could I borrow this pic-

ture, this one with **Bever**ly and Juanita together? Thanks.

Tracy: Oh, by the way. The next time you see Patricia please tell her that I had my attorneys send that information to her new lawyer as he requested. She probably already knows, as I sent her a note.

Sweeney: Her new lawyer? Tricia didn't mention any-thing to me about a new lawyer. What is the new lawyer's name?

Tracy: A Nathan Kahn or some such nonsense. It's just like her to finally leave that Mexican woman and then choose a Jew. Not that all Jews are cheats, you understand. Some Jewish lawyers are very bright. But still, with her upbringing and wealth she should be with a well established firm such as mine.

Sweeney: Would you mind telling me what information she requested?

Tracy: I sent the request on to my firm, Carothers and Matthews. I believe her lawyer requested copies of her trust agreement and my will. What possible bearing could this have on your case, Mr. Swenson? For that matter, what bearing does any of this have?

Sweeney: Probably none, ma'am. Would you mind if I looked over those papers?

Tracy: Truly, Mr. Swenson, you are becoming quite tiresome.

Sweeney: Please.

Tracy: As I just explained, I don't keep those
                papers here. You'll have to contact my
                attorney, Bryan Matthews.

Sweeney: Of course. Thank you. I'll go by some time
                this week since I have your permission. I
                appreciate your time, Mrs. Tracy, and I
                promise to take good care of your picture.
                I'll be sure to get it back to you as soon
                as possible.

Tracy: As you wish. It has no meaning to anyone
                any more.

End of recording.
MS/sb

12

The newspaper office undulated with its usual background clatter. Machines hummed. Word processors clicked. Phones rang. Gossips prattled. On the way to her work station, Tricia stopped at Luke Merino's desk. The sports writer balanced precariously on the hind two legs of his hard backed wooden chair, a beat-up relic from the fifties. Engrossed in his *Sports Illustrated*, his feet were propped up on his desk. A country and western station sang regrets from a clock/radio. Tricia gave him a light touch, but he managed to regain his balance.

"Hard at work, are we?" Tricia asked sweetly.

"Research. Very important." He placed the open magazine on his desk. "What's up Tidbits? Or are you just pestering me for the hell of it?"

"I liked your article about the city's tennis team. What do you call them? The Tornadoes?"

"Tornadoes? You think this is Kansas, Dorothy? No, child. They're the Hurricanes. But thanks for the compliment. It's really a silly-ass sport but the public likes upbeat stories. It's a silly name, too. Remember when they had the contest to name the team? I suggested 'Corpus Delecti'. You like the idea?"

"Speaking of articles, yours had its usual weird flair. What gives you the right to tell the mayor how to run the city? And where did that crap about cocaine come from? You need some snow, 'ol Luke will fix you up. You want to meet me at my place after work? We'll have our own private party."

Tricia shook her head and clucked in disapproval. "You're nothing but a pitiful cynical leech. How is it that your articles turn out positive? Does it hurt you to write that way, so foreign to your nature?"

"Nah. It's all part of the game. My team against yours, getting the paycheck, scoring the winning goal. I write happy, it makes people happy. That makes the man smile. I get my money. It's a living. And look. I get paid to sit here and read *Sports Illustrated*. Where's the payoff in bitching?"

"I never realized you were such a pragmatist, Luke."

"A whatzit?"

"Pragmatist. Someone who does what is expected of him rather than what he believes in."

"You like big words huh? How about nepotism, as in 'Not all of us have nepotism in our favor.'"

Tricia glared at him. "My degree in journalism earned me this job, Luke. What earned you yours?"

Luke laughed. "It's not what you do, it's who you know. Are you done bugging me? I've got some serious research to get back to."

"I wanted to ask you if you've seen Jesus Morales around? I need to talk to him."

Luke motioned toward her desk on the other side of the cork wall. "Yeah, Poor K was here a little while ago looking for you. He left a note somewhere I think. Are you two a hot item? Can I start the rumor mill churning?"

Tricia aimed a kick at his shin which he avoided. "Imbecile. Some people around here actually do a little work."

Luke pointedly examined his watch. "Why yes, I see how devoted these twelve o'clock scholars can be. Wait, don't tell me. You've been slaving away all morning researching your latest column. I can see the sweat stains now. Take my advice and lay off a bit, Tidbits. Otherwise, you're going to go prematurely gray and wrinkled. Yeah, I see that scares you. Why don't we take off early and head up to my apartment? I've got a bottle of rot gut tequila with your name on it."

"Cretin."

Tricia turned her back on him and sashayed to her desk. Settling into her chair she picked up the small stack of memos and letters from her "in" box. Alma had called, and Jesus had left a note as well.

Alma answered on the third ring.

"Hi, Alma, it's Tricia. What's up?"

"What indeed, Weirdo? You trying to scare the beejeezus out of me? I was about to call the Coast Guard to dredge for your body."

"Oh, don't go off the deep end. I just decided to take a late night swim, that's all. Say, I'm glad you called. I wanted to find out what papers you wanted from my mother?"

"Once again, my friend, you speak in riddles. I haven't talked to your mother in a year, since we ran into her at that wedding."

Tricia nodded. "I figured this was all some silly mistake. Well, I'm okay. Say, Becky invited me to go out with you girls on Thursday."

"That'll be fun. I'll look forward to seeing you then."

"See you then."

Jesus' line was busy on the first few tries. The librarian had sent her a few references about the Dupree Development Company that Tricia skimmed for a few minutes before trying Jesus again. This time he answered right away.

"¿Hola?"

"Hi, Jesus. Tricia here. What's up?"

"Ah, I am glad you have called. I tried to reach you at home, but, alas, *por nada.* You are here, *¿si?* Good. We must leave soon for our interview. I will check out a camera."

Tricia shook her head in puzzlement. Either she had missed a page or Jesus had skipped ahead without her. She certainly didn't remember any interview appointments. "What are you talking about, Jesus?"

"Barbara Dupree, *por supuesto.* She is very honored that you wish to interview her for your column. We have an appointment at her home at one o'clock. We'll take your car, *¿si?*"

On the way Jesus shared the results of his investigations. The perking report involved the part of the development known as Westchester Acres which bounded on the Nueces River. The denial was based on an anticipated contamination of the city's water supply. According to Jesus, his check at the county office showed that all of their records showed all inspections had received passing certifications on their first try.

The Dupree mansion glared with tasteless ostentatiousness. Keeping lawns green in dry Corpus Christi took extraordinary measures. This household had solved that problem by paving the whole front yard. On either end of a dull black metal picket fence, a cupid adorned swinging gate opened onto a circular drive. In the courtyard sat a mammoth bright pink fountain, complete with three dolphins spouting water in perpetual regurgitation. A new gold Lincoln Continental rested in one corner of the driveway.

Flat and plain, the house looked as if someone had said to the architect, "I have X dollars. Build the biggest building you can construct, and don't worry about looks." Its boring Masonite siding had been painted dull gray, apparently by low bid painters who had left splatters of color on window panes and graveled easement.

Tricia waited at the house's entrance for Jesus to gather the camera and join her. The big chunk of wood serving as the house's door had only two ornaments, a peep hole and a cheap brass knob. Along its bottom, the edge was rather splintered.

"What do you think of this house?" Tricia asked her comrade as he approached.

Jesus stopped a dozen feet away, then stepped back and surveyed the dwelling. "It's very big. *¿Porqué?* Why do you think she needs all this room?"

Tricia was slightly exasperated that he had missed the point of her question — the ugliness of the structure. She shrugged and tried to answer his. "She probably thinks that big is better. I doubt if she uses half the space. Perhaps we'll see."

She turned and pressed the doorbell. Loud garish four toned chimes sang out in sixteen note chorus.

Barbara Dupree threw the door open wide. Overly rouged thin lips stretched across a wide mouth. A long hook nose propped up black plastic framed glasses, greatly magnifying the pair of bloodshot pale blue eyes beyond. Thick black eyebrows held up a brow heavy with worry lines.

"It's a pleasure to meet you, Mrs. Dupree," Tricia said, extending her hand. "This is my photographer, Jesus Morales."

"Well, howdy doo. Come on in and set a spell. And please call me Barbara." She smiled widely, displaying a crowd of eager teeth. Tricia developed an image of the coarse woman spitting in her hands, rubbing them together, and extending one for a vigorous shake. Fortunately, it was only a fantasy.

Barbara led them into a sitting room furnished solely with a well worn love seat and two chairs, set around an imitation wood coffee table. Tricia watched Barbara's stooped walk, her shape thin at the top and ballooning at the hips. She wore layered bright colors, dress, blouse, and chemise, accessorized with pink scarf, a wide plastic green belt, dangling Starship Enterprise earrings, and a Chinese hairpin.

"You want some cola or tea?" Barbara asked.

"Iced tea would be nice," Tricia said.

"Water, *por favor*," Jesus answered.

When she left, Tricia settled into one of the chairs and examined the room. A floor to ceiling bookshelf decorated one wall, one third full of paperbacks and two thirds full of knickknacks. Mysteries, science fiction, and romance titles seemed to be in even mixture in the well worn book section. The only other decorations in the room hung on the opposite wall where photographs of two different girls represented throughout their maturity made up a rogues' gallery panorama. The room sparkled with cleanliness — almost sterility.

"You want extra sugar, Miss Tracy?" Barbara asked, returning with plastic mismatched glasses and a blue Tupperware bowl two thirds full with grapes. Tricia appreciated the tea, the big house's air conditioner being inadequate to the Texas September sun. Tricia placed her tape recorder on the table, its little microphone on a stand pointing so that it would pick up both their voices.

"Yes, please. Two teaspoons. Please call me Tricia."

"You could have knocked me over with a peacock feather when I got your call yesterday asking for this interview," Barbara gushed in her nasal tones. Tricia struggled to keep her face pleasant and appreciative. Peter Kriten's description of her as obnoxious and abrasive leapt to her mind.

Barbara pushed her glasses back up on her nose, a gesture she repeated every few minutes. "I read *Tracy's Tidbits* every day, I swear I do. It's sort of like a morning ritual, you know what I mean?" Here she stopped to laugh loudly, the hairpins in her gray-streaked hairbun shaking. "Get up, pee, make coffee, read *Tracy's Tidbits*. Of course, I always read the comics first. But you're second!"

"Why don't you tell me a little about yourself?"

Barbara sat back a moment, munching on some grapes and considering the question.

"What do you mean? You want to know about my childhood? Or what I'm doing now? Or is this some sort of qualifying question; like why I think I deserve to be featured in *Tracy's Tidbits* in twenty-five words or less?"

Tricia smiled at the joke, though she wasn't certain that Barbara was joking. "Oh anything's fine. I'd just like some background information first. Then I'd like to hear about some of your developments; those past and any pending. My column isn't about verbatim interviews."

Barbara chortled. "I should say not! I loved the one last week where you compared that policeman to a bulldog." A worried look came over her face. "Say, you aren't planning to say mean things about me, are you?"

"I don't think so. You aren't planning to give me a speeding ticket are you?"

Barbara guffawed, slapping her knee in merriment. Tricia thought *it wasn't that funny.*

Barbara took a long drink of tea. "Okay. Sure. I can talk about myself. I mean, after all, who couldn't? I'm the older of two children. My parents always liked my brother best. For him they went to debate tournaments. For him it was new suits and a fancy school. For him it was an all expense paid trip through Baylor Medical School. Not so for big sister Barbara. So, I showed them I could be a success. Of course, it took me awhile. Life is always full of detours. You know what I mean? I had to go through one rotten husband and two fantastic daughters first. You see those pictures over there? Briana, she's thirty-one now. I had her when I was seventeen. Can you believe it? Then Jasmine, she's twenty-nine. Wow, how quickly time flies. Neither one of them has kids of their own yet. Well, I suppose that's the way to go. I didn't start my career until I had them both off in college. Those two are too busy with their careers to be encumbered with kids. Plenty of time, sure. I just sometimes wish there were little kids around. I miss them so. Or anybody for that matter. Now don't get me wrong. I do a very good job living by myself and taking good care of everything. But sometimes you want someone to talk to instead of the old TV, you know what I mean? So, I've got to keep myself busy anyway. That's why I got into real estate development. There's plenty to do there, I guarantee. I'm pretty much a one woman company. Dupree Development Company, that's me. First I get an option on a piece of land. Then I've got to round up the investors.

The first time was the hardest, of course. After the bankers saw what I could do, they practically begged me to take their money. Can you imagine? Well, I'm not one to turn down money. Who would, after all? So I get a good grub-stake going and then I get the surveying team out there. There's this cute little architectural firm I work with. Really, only two gay guys. But they do a good job and, heck, they're cheap. So then I've got to get the utilities in and the lots perked and the roads built. I tell you, you've got to be there or they'll make a mess! I've learned a lot of lessons, that's for sure. You know, if a guy in a bull-dozer accidentally hits a tree, he'll just take it right out and pretend he meant to do it all along. Can you believe it? I put together the subdivision that this house is in. Did you know that? Yep, this is my second one, Remington Heights. I got the name Remington from the guns. My ex-husband used to love guns. Can you believe it? Yuck. Anyway, there used to be a little hill out here. What, a hill in Corpus Christi you ask? Yep. Of course, we bulldozed it away. But the name 'heights' stuck. Before this one there was Remington Grounds. And after this one I built Westchester Acres. Cute name, don't you think? Westchester was the name of my high school in Houston. It's closed now. They built it when the place was surrounded by cheap apartments, but they all were torn down. The school only had a dozen graduating classes in all. They use it for adult educa-tion now I think. Anyway, my next development is about two miles northwest of Cal Allen. We're going to call it Jasmine Township. It won't be a real town-ship in a legal sense. But you can name your development anything you want. You know what I mean?"

Tricia just nodded and smiled at the appropriate times as the interviewee rambled on and on. The columnist remembered how she had developed an almost instant dislike when hearing about this woman at the meeting yester-day. On seeing the tactless house, her loathing had intensified. But now all she felt for her was pity; pity for her loneliness, pity for the unremitting drive that drove her husband and children away; pity for this woman's fruitless attempts to prove herself over and over without anyone to prove herself to.

As Barbara's monologue continued, Jesus circled her snapping pictures. At first Barbara tried to keep her best side toward him, pausing momentarily and smiling when she thought he was about to take a photo. Eventually she just ignored him. After about twenty minutes he put his equipment away and stood quietly, watching Barbara with polite interest.

Tricia kept expecting Barbara to wind down. At the thirty minute mark she turned her tape over, but Barbara didn't even pause during that activity. After another ten minutes Tricia decided it was time to make her move. She took out a copy of the perking report from her purse and handed it to Barbara. As soon as she saw what it said she stopped chattering in mid word. For the first time in almost forty-five minutes, silence reigned in the Dupree household. Tricia's ears rang.

Barbara studied the paper before looking nervously into Tricia's eyes. "Where did you get this?"

Tricia shook her head. "I'm sorry; I could never reveal my sources."

Barbara glared at her for a moment. Then her eyebrows rose in understanding. "Oh, I get it. That black man who bought my old car must have found it under the seat or something. Well, well, well. People should just mind their own business or they may just get into trouble. You know what I mean?"

Tricia stared at the woman coldly. "I don't like threats, Mrs. Dupree. Tell me about this report."

Barbara laughed again, this time the sounds came out hollow and nasty.

"It doesn't mean anything. If this is why you came out to see me, you've wasted your time — and mine too. This first perking report was wrong, that's all. It's all a matter of public record."

Tricia looked steadily at the brazen woman. The words sounded right, but the tones lacked sincerity. Though Jesus had confirmed the public records in order, Tricia felt certain they hadn't gotten that way honestly.

Barbara stood. "Look. I don't mean to be rude, but I've got some other things to get done today."

They followed her to the door and Barbara held it open for them. "I hope you can find something nice to say about me. I think I've been a good person; good for my daughters and good for the city."

She waved good-bye from inside the doorway, and shut it solidly behind them. As Tricia climbed into her Ferrari, she looked back to the house. She spied Barbara watching them from a window, peaking out from a towel acting as drapery. Tricia pointedly ignored her as she started the engine, and when Jesus had clicked his seat belt, she sped off.

13

Interview: Robert Randolph
Date: Tuesday, September Thirteenth
Location: Caller Times Building

Sweeney: Thank you for allowing me to tape this interview, Mr. Randolph.

Randolph: Always happy to help our men in blue, Sweeney. When I was a cub reporter I used to hang out in the police station all the time, trying to get a lead on a good story. News doesn't change much, not really. It's all about the five Ws and the H. You know the five Ws, Sweeney?

Sweeney: I guess so, Mr. Randolph. Who, what, which, where, and why?

Randolph: Right on the money, Sweeney. And the most important of those is "Who." I tell my reporters all the time, "Names." Get a name and you got a story. Without one, it's just a rumor.

Sweeney: For the record, today is September thirteenth. Present at this interview are Bob Randolph, city editor, Mel Sweeney, detective, and Sam Byrd, sergeant. I hate to take you away from your business, Mr. Randolph.

Randolph: Don't worry about it, Sweeney. Most of the important stuff is done early in the day. I'm just hanging around now in case something happens or someone needs my advice. I've been in the news business a long time, know the ropes. My kids are always coming up and asking for help. What can I do for you today?

Sweeney: I'm investigating the disappearance of Maria Garcia. Patricia Tracy wrote about it in her column yesterday. According to Meredith Tracy, you knew Maria's mother, Juanita.

Randolph: Yep, sure did. Sweet old lady. Good worker, too. Never heard any complaints about her. I guess Meredith told you that Juanita worked for me after she quit at the Tracys?

Sweeney: Quit? Why did she quit?

Randolph: She never told me, Sweeney. I think she didn't particularly like Richard for some reason. She went through a lot of changes that year, Juanita did. Got married, too.

Sweeney: What did she do for you?

Randolph: Cleaned my house. I'm a confirmed bachelor, Sweeney. Newspaper's been my life, never had time for a wife. Hey, like that rhyme? I come up with things like that all the time. Natural poet, I guess. Any-hoo, Gonzalez would come clean for me about once a week, scrub the toilet, do my laundry, that sort of thing. Did a good job for a long time. After she died her daughter took over.

Sweeney: Maria? Maria Garcia was your house cleaner?

Randolph: Well, for a little while. Not nearly as good as her mom. She wasn't reliable and I noticed things were missing. So I let her go after a couple of months. She still comes over every now and again. I've got a service now. Mighty Maids. Ever hear of them? They're bonded.

Sweeney: What kind of things were missing? Minor things like cups and cans of soup? Or more valuable things like jewelry?

Randolph: What use would I have for jewelry, Sweeney? But you don't want a thief in your midst. If a person doesn't have integrity, no telling what they might do next.

Sweeney: I agree with you there, Mr. Randolph. I know a lawyer in town named Harry Harper. Know him? Yes, of course you do. Everyone seems to, and therein lies his problem. He'll say things that turn out to be untrue. By the way, I found this at Maria's house. Do you recognize it?

Randolph: Let me see. A broach, huh? Very pretty. Am I supposed to recognize it, Sweeney?

Sweeney: Fred Scouras thought you might.

Randolph: Scouras is it? Well, now that you mention it, it does seem to have a familiar look to it. So you think Maria stole this from me, do you Sweeney? Seems likely enough. Just as you said, people aren't always on the up and up, now are they?

Sweeney: Did you give it to her or did she steal it, Mr. Randolph?

Randolph: I may have given it to her. Yes, probably did. She showed it to me one day and oohed and ahed. I suppose I'm an old softie that way. Like letting her come back to the place every now and then. Poor girl needed to get out of the house once and awhile. Any-hoo, I guess you think she's dead, now, huh? That's what Tracy said you think.

Sweeney:	I'm worried about her, I'll say that for sure. Do you have any idea about what might have happened to Maria?
Randolph:	I can't say I knew she had disappeared until Tracy wrote up that article yesterday. You think this is going to be a big story? You want me to assign a reporter to dig into it?
Sweeney:	Really, I'd rather you not do that, Mr. Randolph. You remember that Blakmum case last year, the one you had the reporter digging into? He damaged evidence and ended up compromising witnesses. Eventually we had to convict the guy on totally different charges. Got away with murder, you see.
Randolph:	Yeah, well, we fired Pilsner after that mess up. I don't tolerate that kind of stuff from my kids.
Sweeney:	Since you know Maria, do you know Lupè Garcia too?
Randolph:	I know a lot of people in this town, Sweeney. It's a newspaper man's job to know! There was a time when I could walk down the street and name everybody I passed, and tell you about their daddies and their granddaddies, too. Makes a difference when you grow up in a place. Of course now, the city has gotten so big, and so many new people. There's been a huge growth in the Hispanic side, especially. I still know the bigwigs. Senator Sosa and I go way back. You know his daughter, Trevino?
Sweeney:	Yep, Alma and Tricia are good friends. Speaking of knowing people, tell me a bit more what Maria was like. Did she get along

with people? Her aunt told me that she was wild.

Randolph: Yeah, she was a wild one okay. At the Lonesome Coyote she'd pick up guys right in front of her husband. Garcia'd be so drunk he wouldn't notice. Used to call her *puta*, though. That's Spanish for whore.

Sweeney: How do you know that she'd pick up men? Did you see that happen?

Randolph: Ha, Sweeney. Never ask a newspaper man for his sources. I'd go to jail before I'd squeal.

Sweeney: No, wait a minute. Someone told me yesterday that a newspaper man named Bob goes to the Lonesome Coyote on Fridays. Would that be you by any chance?

Randolph: Well, I suppose that might be me, after all. I like a little libation and a bit of camaraderie after a hard week's work. How about you, Sweeney? You like to relax with a cold one every now and then?

Sweeney: No, I'm not a drinker. If you hang out at the Lonesome Coyote on Friday nights, you must know Lupè pretty well. Did you talk with him while you were there?

Randolph: A good newspaper man talks with everyone, Sweeney. That's how you keep the pulse of the city, talking with its citizens. You can find out a lot of information in a bar, fellow. You might try it someday. A couple of beers wouldn't do you any harm. Get some new perspective on life; how to dress, how to fraternize. Not that you need to change your taste in women, mind you. Tracy is a fine one.

Sweeney: Agree with you there, Chief. Did Maria talk
             about running away? Do you think she would
             have left Lupè and not told anyone? Not
             even her aunt?

Randolph: As I remember it, young fellow, the last
             time I talked with her, she was excited
             about a trip she had planned. Yes, she
             said something about a holiday with the
             family.

Sweeney: Martha Gonzalez told me that she had
             planned to go to McAllen with her for the
             Labor Day weekend.

Randolph: Yep, that's right. Say, you wouldn't be
             such a bad reporter, Sweeney. You get those
             facts.

Sweeney: So, were you at the Lonesome Coyote on
             Friday, August 26th, 3 Fridays ago? As near
             as Lupè can remember, that was the last
             time Maria was seen alive.

Randolph: I believe I was, Sweeney. What do you want
             to know?

Sweeney: Tell me everything you remember about that
             night.

Randolph: I didn't spend much time with the Garcias
             that night, Sweeney. I met an old buddy and
             we celebrated old times off in a corner. I
             did notice Lupè was quite plastered.

Sweeney: You seem to have known Maria and Lupè bet-
             ter than anyone else I've talked to yet.
             Give me your honest opinion, Mr. Randolph.
             Do you think Lupè killed her?

Randolph: Well, he loved her, but she'd make him so
             mad with the things she did, he'd hit her
             just out of frustration. It doesn't sur-

prise me that she ran off. She may just turn up somewhere, Sweeney, and Tracy'll have to publish an apology.

Sweeney: Thanks for all your help, Mr. Randolph.

Randolph: My pleasure. Give my regards to your girl friend, Sweeney. Young love. Ha. Reminds me of when I had all my sexy hair. Those were the days. Say, can I keep this broach?

Sweeney: I'd prefer to keep it for evidence for now, if you don't mind.

End of Recording
MS/sb

14

Tricia and Bill stood together looking out over the bay at Cole Park. The early evening air sat heavily with the afternoon's legacy of heat and humidity. The sun behind them held dominion, a majestic king overlooking his realm. The park's sparse crowd sang out with children's joyful laughter. Tricia let her hand swing out slightly, lightly brushing Bill's at her side. He grasped hers, cuddling it in a loving embrace.

"I love the sea. When I get my inheritance next year my first purchase will be a home overlooking the water." Tricia spoke quietly, almost wistfully. She thought of Bill's life, lived to the fullest on land and sea.

In a dreamy voice, Tricia reminisced. "When I was a child my father would take me out on his sailboat. I don't remember it well. I must have been eight or nine when we started. Dad's work left him so busy with traveling, negotiating, contracts, supervising acquisitions; oh, all that stuff. So the times we had alone together were special.

"I remember his boat looked very much like yours. I loved the thrill of sailing to victory in the yacht race, with the wind whipping through my hair. Sometimes we'd take the boat out to an island or spend a night on the yacht."

Tricia stopped talking, her eyes unfocused as she dwelt in her past.

Bill shook her shoulder. "Tricia? Are you okay?"

For a moment Tricia stared into his eye, her face open and exposed in wonder and confusion. With a flip of her lovely auburn hair, a school girl smile broke upon her countenance.

"Where in the world did you go?"

"Oh, I forget," she said with a laugh. "Old memories flit in and out of your consciousness like a finch living in a parrot's wide barred cage. Come on, I'll race you to the pier!"

Squealing in glee, Tricia took off sprinting. Half way to the assigned goal she glanced back. She realized her *faux pas* as she caught sight of Bill loping along with his cane. She waited as he caught up, accomplishing a good pace if not really a run.

"No fair, My Beauty. You took too much of a head start. Ah, but since you won, we'll have to decide on your prize. Let's see now — what could I offer that might please you?"

For a prize, an image of their earlier kisses brought a warm urge chasing through her body. She blushed and turned away. Spying a man selling ice cream from a cart behind them, Tricia pointed out her claim for reward. The two walked across the park to the vendor, each picking out a treat.

They strolled hand in hand; Bill entertained her with stories of his adventures. Tricia talked of her many local friends and dreams of the future. As the evening aged the park became crowded with families bringing picnics and blankets, young men throwing plastic saucers, and people of all ages jogging and strolling together. In various spots musicians sat with their guitars or horns and open cases, catching scatterings of coins. Just behind the amphitheater the two came upon a large group gathered around a flute player and dancer.

"Oh!" Tricia exclaimed in delight. "I had forgotten that Dovie told me she'd be out tonight. Come along, magical mystery man. Come watch my friend dance."

Tricia led Bill to a thinner part of the circle that had formed around Dovie and Turtle. Turtle, sitting cross-legged, played a medium speed tune. The high clear notes provided a stairway of musical steps, as Dovie improvised a graceful prancing dance. Glancing into the carved wooden box laying open beside Turtle, Tricia noted several crumpled dollar bills as well as a generous landscape of coins.

As Turtle changed the music to a fast paced Irish jig, Dovie's movements took on the melody's urgency. Her legs began to pump, her dress sailing out with her spins and twists. She danced with the excited energy of a busy park chipmunk, storing up the fallen nuts for the winter. Turtle brought the music to a slow mournful tune, as if sensing that Dovie needed a breather. The crowd, which had been clapping in rhythmic excitement, broke into an overall rowdy applause, adding a tidal wave of money to the performers' collection.

Tricia called out, "Wonderful, Dovie!"

The dancer scanned the crowd. On finding her friend's face, she threw Tricia a wave and a smile, not breaking the rhythm of her steps to do so.

The music stopped abruptly in mid note. Everyone turned to look at Turtle who, Tricia saw, stared toward her. He dropped his gaze, and began packing away his flute.

"Go," he growled at Dovie.

She looked at him in astonishment. "But Turtle, Sweetheart. What's wrong? It's not time to go. We have such a nice audience."

Without answering her, he finished storing the instrument and closed the wooden box. With the cessation of the performance the crowd quickly dispersed. Turtle strode toward the city, taking the park slope like Sam Houston sweeping over the Texas countryside in search of destiny. Dovie looked after him in consternation.

"What happened?" Tricia asked, stepping up next to her friend.

Dovie, biting her lower lip, shrugged. "Damn. It's been such a long time since he stopped in the middle of a show like this. Something spooked him I guess."

Tricia reached out and took Dovie's hand, gently squeezing it. "What do you mean, 'spooked him'? He sees ghosts?"

"Ghosts? Yes, that's probably the right word. Post traumatic stress disorder, they call it." Dovie sighed. "I understand the army started out real proud of him, a Green Beret or something. He even has some medals. Then he had a nervous breakdown. They had my poor Turtle in the hospital for over two years. When he got out he hid in a haze of drugs and alcohol. His life consisted of eating, breathing and sleeping. I better go after him."

Tricia restrained Dovie's flight.

"Wait a moment, Dear," she said. "There's someone I'd like you to meet."

Tricia turned to look for Bill, but couldn't find him. The milling crowds and setting sun made it impossible to see much.

"Who are you looking for?" Dovie asked. "Tell me what she looks like and I'll help you look."

"Sorry, Dovie, he must have gotten lost in the crowd. Well, I guess we're both without a man. Have you eaten? I'll treat you to dinner."

Dovie hesitated a moment. She looked toward the town, in the direction Turtle had disappeared. Tricia knew their house sat only four short blocks up the road, an easy walk. Dovie shrugged and smiled at Tricia.

"Well, I guess there's no sense in going home with an empty stomach. Turtle will probably be fine. Where do you have in mind?"

Tricia grinned. "My favorite place. September has an 'R' in it. Though the season is still a bit young, let's see if Christof's can provide some decent Oysters Rockefeller."

Over dinner their conversations ran to mutual friends and past experiences. When Dovie asked about Mel, she told Dovie that she and Mel had a little fight.

"What did you think of Mel?" Tricia asked.

"You only brought him by my house once, I think. I liked him. He made me laugh."

Tricia nodded. "He's easy to laugh at, all right. I've met someone new. That's who I was going to introduce you to at the park just now. His name's Bill and he's a sailor."

"My, my, Tricia. Your cheeks are flushed and your eyes are absolutely glowing. How long have you known this guy?"

"Just met him last night, actually. How long does one need to know someone when the chemistry clicks? When you met Turtle, was it love at first sight?"

Dovie shook her head with a laugh. "Hardly. I was volunteering at the Naval Hospital. He needed a place to stay and seemed so gentle and needy. I felt like I was giving a home to a stray puppy. He just sort of grows on you, don't you think?"

Tricia shrugged. She had never thought much of Turtle, seeing him as a loser. She felt, with a bit of effort, anyone could have a successful life. Turtle wallowed in uselessness simply due to his lack of character.

"People have to grieve, I admit that," Tricia said. "But in twenty years you should be able to get over almost anything."

In a quiet voice, Dovie murmured, "No. Some people never get over their tragic life events."

Tricia cocked her head. "What do you mean?"

Dovie smiled weakly at her friend, a brief glimmer of a smile, like foam appearing for an instant on an off shore wave before disappearing into the flotsam of the ocean. She sipped her drink before continuing.

"You know I have a child? Yes? Sundev couldn't comprehend my life choices. He chose to live with his closed-minded father when he turned ten. I embarrassed him."

She stared into her drink as if it were a gypsy's magic ball swirling with the answers to life's questions. Tricia maintained a sympathetic silence.

"I'll never get over the loss of my son's love, Tricia. Abandonment by my husband I can forgive and forget in a flash. But my son's rejection haunts my dreams. Maybe that's why I've picked up Turtle, do you think? Although a man, he's like a child in so many ways."

Tricia considered that she might be right. In many ways the huge forty-seven year old did act like a child, a sullen teenager.

"Well," Tricia said. "I suppose I'm one of the lucky ones then. I've never had that type of life event to shake me to the core."

Dovie raised an eyebrow in surprise. "Tricia, dearest, did you really mean to say that?"

Tricia looked surprised in her turn. "Of course. Why do you sound so doubtful?"

"Well, please forgive me. But I know better. The loss of a parent has no equal in childhood trauma, particularly such a loved one as the relationship you had with your father."

Tricia felt a tear form in one eye, turned away and lifted a napkin to catch it.

Dovie reached across the table to take her friend's hand. "There, there, now, sweet girl. Crying is okay. Go ahead and grieve."

Tricia shook off Dovie's hands. "No, no. I'm being silly. That was ten years ago. I'll be twenty-five in January, after all. I've put that behind me, I assure you."

Over dessert, Dovie asked Tricia about the paper Turtle had found. "Did it turn out to be important?"

"I think so. I showed it to Barbara Dupree today, and she denied it meant anything, but I think she was lying. I'm still checking into it. Hey, read my *Tidbits* tomorrow. I mentioned your paper in it."

After their dinner, Tricia drove Dovie home. Finding the place dark, Tricia accepted her friend's request to come in for a minute.

"At least he's been here," Dovie said, pointing out their wooden money box and his flute case on the table. She checked the garage. "The Lexus is gone. I can't imagine where he's gotten off to?"

It was almost ten o'clock by the time Tricia finally got back to her townhouse. Although Lakewood Village offered assigned spots behind each building, Tricia preferred the ease of departure provided by a space in front of her home. The yellow Ferrari settled down, falling off to sleep as Tricia patted it good night.

She kept her keys in her hand on the short walk from car to door. Tricia cried out when a man stepped out from the bushes to block her path.

"Hey ugly *puta*! You remember Lupè? I told you I'd remember your *auto pequeño.*[1]"

Tricia's blood turned to ice. She fought the urge to scream.

"You leave me alone, Lupè Garcia. Go on, get out of here." Tricia squeaked.

He laughed harshly, his head rolling back and his fat belly shaking. As abruptly as the laugh had started it halted, leaving an eerie penetrating silence. Lupè turned his head to one side and spat on the ground.

"You owe me, you ugly *puta*. Your story in the newspaper cost me my job. *Tu eres un diablo, puta!*[2] I make you pay tonight!"

He took two steps toward her, but paused when she didn't retreat. Now only four steps away, the fetid alcohol on his breath nauseated Tricia, nearly caus-

---

1   little car

2   You are the devil, whore!

ing her to swoon. She focused her energy on being angry, drawing on her self confidence and sense of invulnerability.

Her voice came out strong and vibrant. "You fat scum. I didn't cost you your job. You lost it when you killed your wife. Go ahead. You tell me you didn't kill her. Go ahead. Just tell me that. Well? What are you waiting for?"

Lupè looked confused. He staggered back from Tricia, staring into her eyes. He lowered his gaze to the ground, and began mumbling.

"*No se.* I don't know. I just don't know. I don't remember killing her. Did Lupè kill his wife? *No se. No se.*"

He continued mumbling as he turned aside and slowly ambled off. Tricia saw that his right arm was in a cast up to the elbow, held chest high with a sling. Her heart pounding, she stood watching his retreating back until he disappeared around a corner.

Tricia managed to control her trembling enough to unlock both the deadbolt and the doorknob, quickly locking the door behind her. For a moment she thought of calling Mel; she had given him a set of keys last month. Instead she pulled out a bottle of Jack Daniels whiskey from below the sink. The sweet fluid soon had its desired effect. She tumbled into bed fully clothed, a sleep of exhaustion enveloping her.

Corpus Christi Caller Times
Wednesday, September 14, 1994

Masked Varmint

Have you ever noticed how some people remind you of animals? Yesterday I interviewed a prominent land developer of this town, Barbara Dupree. With her stooped figure, active hands, and large glasses, she makes a remarkable portrayal of a raccoon.

I remember as a child staying at my father's home in the country. A determined raccoon kept raiding our garbage cans. My father tied down the lids. The creature untied them. Dad attached bungee cords. The next morning the shredded pieces decorated the porch. Dad built a large wooden box with a heavy lid. Darn if the raider didn't figure out the sliding door mechanism.

Barbara Dupree showed this same determination in developing three subdivisions in this city; Remington Grounds, Remington Heights, and Westchester Acres. Though some architects have complained about the boring uniformity of their straight streets, copy cat houses, and postage stamp yards, they perfectly illustrate Dupree Development Company's juggernaut. Let no tree stand in her way. Let no hill disrupt the pattern of her roads. Let no creativity disturb the monotonous sequencing of the houses.

As I talked with Barbara I wondered what it might take to thwart a creature of such determination. Instead of animal control officers and cages, cities handle their human scavengers with inspectors and regulations. I presented Mrs. Dupree with a city perking report denying her building permission. In raccoon fashion she waved it away, just one more minor obstacle she had magically overcome.

One must admire the raccoons of our race. They accomplish so much with their industry and determination. Pioneers tame the wilderness. Miners gut our mountains. Developers carve real estate.

Yet people are not raccoons. We live not in a self serving vacuum, but rather in a mutually dependent society. By forcing her will over the countryside, Mrs. Dupree disregards the esthetic needs of the populace. We all love the cute raccoon, except when it's making a mess of OUR space.

15

Blam.

Wake up? No.

Dong. Dong. Dong. Dong.

Quiet again.

Dong. Dong. Dong. Dong.

There it is again. What? What is it? Doorbell?

Dong. Dong. Dong. Dong.

The ringing finally aroused Tricia. She swung her legs over the bedside and grabbed at her pounding forehead. A one eyed search for the clock discovered the time to be 3:43. She groaned and fell back onto her pillow.

Dong. Dong. Dong. Dong.

Reaching over she switched on the bedside light. On the way down the steps and to the front door she flipped on every light switch. She had almost reached the door when the visitor, seeing the lights come on, shouted through to her.

"Miss Tracy? Miss Tracy? Are you there? It's me, Miss Tracy. Sophie Silverman."

Tricia turned on the porch light as she opened the door. Outside the glass storm door stood Tricia's neighbor, old Sophie Silverman, in shawl and slippers. Her gray hair sat tied up in a hair net, surely an art taught in old people's night school.

"What is it, Mrs. Silverman?" Tricia asked, squinting away from the forty watt yellow bulb above the visitor's head.

"There's a fire, Miss Tracy. Come quick."

"Fire? The building's on fire?" Tricia's thoughts raced, wondering which precious items she should try to save. She looked behind her in terror, half expecting to see billows of smoke descending the stairs from the bedroom. She smelled acrid fumes.

"No, no, Miss Tracy. Out here; it's your car. Come quick."

Mrs. Silverman stepped aside, allowing Tricia to burst past her. All that remained of her once proud beauty was a black twisted frame; shattered glass, stinking flattened tires, and charred plastics and metals.

Surrounded by a small group of neighbors, someone asked, "Anyone know whose car it was?"

"Sure," someone else said. "Da pretty lady in 6205. I seen 'er park it 'ere 'undreds a times. Ain't she 'ere?"

Tricia shuffled closer. "Yes," she told them in a shaky voice. "I'm here."

The small audience melted away from her, leaving her an unobstructed view of her disaster. Putrid smoke drifted her way.

"What happened?" she asked plaintively. She felt dazed and stupid, overwhelmed by her encounter with Lupè, the stiff dose of whiskey, the interrupted sleep, and the enormity of this last shock.

"Didn't you hear it?" someone asked. "Gosh, my whole freakin' house shook. The explosion blew out a couple o' windows over there."

Tricia glanced behind her at this remark and saw two of Mrs. Silverman's windows glittering with jagged teeth of glass. Discoloring soot covered a good area of the sidewalk. The car sitting next to Tricia's ex-Ferrari had broken windows and buckled doors. Tricia realized she must have slept through an incredibly loud blast. Mrs. Silverman came up beside her, gently taking her hand in offered comfort.

A fire engine pulled into the townhouse complex, its red lights twirling in the eerie silence. With noisy efficiency the four men scrambled off their vehicle, hooked a hose to a nearby hydrant, and soaked both Tricia's car and the damaged one next to it. Tricia felt guilty about the other car. She couldn't shake the analogy of a terrorist attack where the other car was an innocent victim.

As the firemen put away their equipment, a police car turned onto the road. It, too, had its warning lights screaming in silence, this time in blue. The night duty cop shouted his request for an interview with the car's owner. Tricia tried to talk with the patrolman, a polite young black man who kept repeating his questions. She noticed he looked at her peculiarly and realized she was insisting that she had been wearing her seatbelt. Tricia wrote the tow truck driver a check for eighty dollars and he towed off the wreckage.

The sky was beginning to lighten by the time Tricia climbed wearily back into her bed. She unplugged the telephone and fell immediately into a deep sleep.

Police Blotter

Two automobile fires occurred last night. On Laguna Madre Drive in Flour Bluff a 1993 Lexus crashed into a retaining wall. The driver, who died in the vehicle, was tentatively identified as Sidney Jones, 48, of Naples Road in the city. The crash occurred sometime between 11 and 11:30 PM. Police request information from any witnesses.

A 1989 Ferrari exploded in the parking lot on Hidden Cove Drive. around 3:30 AM. No one was injured. Police estimate total property damage of $35,000. Although arson has not been ruled out, Officer Duncan suggested an electrical spark may have been at fault.

16

Interview: Anna Marie Dove
Date: Wednesday, September 14
Location: Her home; 445 Naples

Sweeney: As I just explained, I routinely tape
                my discussions. You said that was okay,
                right?

Dove: Yes, of course.

Sweeney: Thank you. For the record, today is
                September fourteenth. Present here in
                Mrs. Dove's home are Anna Marie Dove,
                Mel Sweeney, detective, and Samuel Byrd,
                police sergeant. Thank you for allowing us
                to come in Mrs. Dove.

Dove: Please call me Dovie, Mel. We do know each
                other, after all. I apologize that my home
                is such a mess.

Sweeney: That's okay, Mrs. Dove, uh, Dovie. It looked
                like this the time when Tricia brought me
                here. I've been in worse. I was interview-
                ing a sculptor one time. He specialized in
                a jungle theme. Stone trees, wooden carved
                animals, wild painted plants and vines and
                flowers hung everywhere. Hidden speakers
                ran a constant symphony of jungle sounds
                throughout our interview. I tell you, I
                wouldn't have been surprised if Tarzan had
                swung in through the window!

Dove: That's quite an entertaining story, Mel.
                My preference leans to the eclectic as you
                can see. Though my ex-husband accused me of

being a pack rat, I exercise marked selectivity in my accumulations. This item here, for example, was created by a good friend of mine who died of AIDS. Can you appreciate the deep rooted anguish expressed in the jagged lines here? Look at the colors he used! Doesn't this speak to your very soul?

Sweeney: Actually, it just looks like a lot of squiggles to me. Of course, I'm quite color blind.

Dove: Ah. That explains your clothing choices.

Sweeney: I do like the mannequin with the Indian headdress though. Did you apply the war paint yourself?

Dove: Sort of a Chinese effect, don't you think? I took a course in theatrical make-up once. You, for instance, Detective, would look philosophical with a light purple eye shadow. Would you like me to apply some, just to see how it wears?

Sweeney: No. No, thank you.

Dove: And what about you, Sergeant? How about some blush to lighten those hollow cheek bones of yours? Hmm? Silent type, aren't you?

Sweeney: Sam doesn't say much, but he's a reliable fellow. Anyway, we're here on business today. We have this address for Sidney Jones. Is that right? The other time I was here there wasn't anybody else around.

Dove: You didn't see him, but he was around. Mr. Jones has lived here with me for almost six years. He goes by the nickname 'Turtle' by the way. I'm sorry, though, he's not in right now. He left home last night and I haven't heard from him since.

Sweeney: You're not his wife then? He hasn't a legal wife or family somewhere?

Dove: Hardly. We're housemates. Turtle's a sweet man but not the marrying kind. And I, myself, have had some experiences I prefer not to repeat.

Sweeney: According to his driver's license, Mr. Jones … uh, Turtle? Yes. It says that Turtle's black, uh, African American. Is he light skinned?

Dove: Black as coal. Why, Mel? Are you prejudiced?

Sweeney: Me? No, not me. Turtle's a big fellow isn't he? What? Six foot four inches according to his driver's license.

Dove: Yes. And massive. Turtle's not the kind of fellow who you'd call 'nigger' to his face. Though he wouldn't hurt a cockroach, his very size is quite intimidating. I tell you, keeping a fellow like that fed strains the budget as much as it strains his belt line. He's a fine teddy bear.

Sweeney: Do you know where Turtle is now? Do you know where he went last night?

Dove: No. Actually, this is rather uncharacteristic. Turtle does make out of town trips on occasion in his business—but he always lets me know his plans.

Sweeney: And you? Where were you last night? I sup-
                pose you called around looking for him?

Dove: Where would I call? Turtle hasn't any
                friends and he doesn't hang out in bars. I
                was out with our mutual friend, Patricia
                Tracy. She can verify that when we returned
                last night about nine-thirty Turtle was
                already gone.

Sweeney: You were with Tricia, huh? How is she?

Dove: Just fine, Mel. I'm sorry you two had a
                spat.

Sweeney: Thanks. What is Turtle's business?

Dove: Cars. Turtle buys and sells used cars. He's
                really pretty good at it. You'd be sur-
                prised how eager some people are to sell
                their old vehicles. It's a crime how lit-
                tle the dealers offer in trade-in value.
                Turtle specializes in unusual models like
                Jaguar or BMW, though currently he's driv-
                ing a blue Lexus.

Sweeney: Yes. Mrs. Dupree said she had sold it to
                him. The tax office still had it under her
                name. I called her and she directed me
                to this address. I'm afraid there was a
                car accident last night, Dovie. That blue
                Lexus was destroyed.

Dove: Oh my God! Is … was Turtle killed?

Sweeney: There was a fatality I'm sorry to say. The
                victim matches Turtle's description, size
                and all, though we don't have a positive
                identification. This reminds me of a case
                I had a couple of years ago. A body was
                found in a burnt down house. We naturally

assumed it was the lady who lived there
… smoking in bed probably. But it turned
out later the woman had shot her ex-husband and burned the place down thinking to
destroy the evidence.

Dove: And is that what's happened here, Mel? Was
the car destroyed?

Sweeney: Yes ma'am. It looks like the driver may
have fallen asleep at the wheel. The car
crashed into a wall and burnt. Yep. That's
how it looks.

Dove: Oh, my poor, sweet Turtle. Poor, darling
man. What a tragedy. Oh my. I'm going to
cry.

Sound of crying.

Dove: Okay. Okay. I'm okay now.

Sweeney: I'm sorry Dovie. It's always tough to have
to deliver this news.

Dove: Something's not right though, huh?

Sweeney: What do you mean?

Dove: Well, you're a detective. I'm not familiar with police work, I know. But it seems
strange that a detective would come see
me, even though we do know each other casu-
ally. Is there something suspicious about
the accident? You said it looked like he
fell asleep and crashed, didn't you?

Sweeney: Yes ma'am. Well, I didn't mean anything
necessarily. Was Turtle a drinker? I
pulled his traffic record. He's never had a
ticket.

Dove: No. Turtle's driving is exemplary. Those
                 cars are his business. A long time ago
                 he used to drink a lot, but nowadays he
                 only does a little pot. Oops. I suppose I
                 shouldn't have told you that.

Sweeney: While driving? Did he drive stoned?

Dove: I told you, Mel. He's a very careful driver.
                 Turtle never drives while intoxicated. Oh
                 my. I'm going to cry again.

Short period of crying.

Dove: I'm sorry.

Sweeney: That's quite all right Dovie. It's a natu-
                 ral reaction. From what you're saying I
                 gather that he took good care of his car.
                 He wouldn't, for example, smoke in the car?
                 No. And he wouldn't be carrying explosives
                 or moonshine or gasoline or paint or any
                 type of combustibles?

Dove: Of course not. Oh, this is all so awful.
                 You're pretty sure it was Turtle who was
                 killed?

Sweeney: The car exploded and the body was badly
                 burned. We'll have to wait for the coro-
                 ner's report. Do you know where Turtle had
                 his dental work done? He did go to the den-
                 tist sometimes, didn't he?

Dove: Turtle was very shy, Detective. But I kept
                 after him to maintain his health. He went
                 to the Naval Air Station every year or
                 so.

Sweeney: Oh? Turtle was a veteran?

Dove: Oh yes. He had a medical discharge twenty
years ago. It's good for government medical care, so I made sure that he got his.
I wish I had the same deal.

Sweeney: Tell me about Turtle's war history and
about his medical discharge, would you
please?

Dove: Well, he was something of a war hero once.
He never liked talking about the war, you
must understand. But in the late sixties
Turtle was a Green Beret in Vietnam. He
kept all his medals in a box. Would you
like to see them? Yes?

Pause. Sound of footsteps.

Dove: Here they are. See this one? It's called a
purple heart. I can always identify that
one. He got that for being wounded in
action. He and his buddies were ambushed
and all three got shot. One died. Turtle's
wounds healed well, though. Look. Here's a
silver star. Someone told me once that it's
a big honor, this one. I don't know what
most of these are for. Turtle never liked
to look at them. He had some pretty bad
experiences in the war. For two years he
had to be hospitalized with post traumatic
stress disorder. Though lately he'd been
doing pretty well, sometimes he still got
spooked. Like last night, at the park. Oh
my. That's the last time I saw him. I guess
that'll be the last time I'll ever …

Sounds of crying

Sweeney: I'm grieved for your loss, Dovie, and apol-
ogize for having to keep asking you questions. Did Mr. Jones have any enemies that
you know about? Someone who had a real

serious grudge against him or threatened to kill him recently?

Dove: Of course not, Mel. You never met my sweet man, I know. But he was kind and gentle. He didn't speak much, hardly more than your sergeant here. You can't make enemies sitting in this house all the time. He was honest in his business deals, too. No, I can't imagine anyone wanting to hurt Turtle on purpose. Except … No.

Sweeney: Ma'am? You were about to say?

Dove: Well, I know this is going to sound ridiculous. I haven't read the whole paper yet, but did you read *Tracy's Tidbits* this morning? Turtle found something in that car that may have incriminated Barbara Dupree. I'm sure it's just coincidence. Oh, my poor Turtle. I miss him so!

Sounds of crying

Sweeney: Perhaps we'd better go. Here. This is my phone number if you need to reach me for anything. I'll be in touch once we've made a positive identification, probably tomorrow.

End of recording.
MS/sb

17

Tricia was dragging through her daily aerobics when the telephone rang.

"Tricia?"

Tricia recognized the sadness in Dovie's sultry voice. "Yes, of course, sweet Dovie. Is something wrong?"

"Oh my Heavens! Turtle's dead!"

A cold chill ran through Tricia. "How awful! My heart is bursting for you. What happened?"

Tricia waited patiently while Dovie sobbed. When her voice returned, it cracked and hesitated, an old beach car chugging along on mistuned points.

"That detective friend of yours, Mel Sweeney, just left. Turtle was in a terrible car accident last night. He crashed and the car blew up!"

"I'm so sorry. I'll come over right away to sit with you ... and bring some lunch. How about if I pick up Chinese food on the way? I'll get vegetarian."

Tricia waited quietly for Dovie's response, listening as she breathed deeply.

"Thank you. I'm terribly sad, Tricia. I won't be good company, and I doubt that I can eat anything. But a friend's shoulder would be a welcome crying board right now."

After Tricia hung up she realized she hadn't any transportation. She arranged for an open ended lease over the phone, and took a taxi to the airport to pick up the car. Tricia took an immediate dislike to the white Cadillac the agent had talked her into renting.

"It may seem like luxury to some folks," Tricia grumbled to herself, "but to me it drives like a cow; slow and stupid. If anyone hit me in this tank I wouldn't even know it for three days."

The trip back into town rolled along easily. The junkyards of outer Ayers Road gave way to the quiet businesses of the Hispanic half of town. Billboards in Spanish encouraged residents to smoke and drink. Storefronts proclaimed their names in Spanish: their window placards read in that language as well. Tricia chuckled at seeing one front with a small corner window sign, "We Speak English, Too."

Tricia tried to maneuver her machine behind Dovie's old yellow V.W. Rabbit, a car whose convertible top held together with Duck tape. The Cadillac jolted as Tricia klunked both right wheels into a gutter along the driveway's edge.

Wearing nothing but black panties, Dovie cracked the door open, her face sagging under puffy red eyes and tear streaked cheeks. Inside, odd shadow shapes and half seen colors peeked out through the smoke created by a dozen burning incense sticks.

Dovie fell into Tricia's arms with an accompanying release of tears. Tricia rubbed her back gently, softly cooing comforting words into her ears. Dovie pushed away and used a corner of Tricia's shirt to dab at her face. Tricia followed her into the single bedroom where Dovie slipped on one of Turtle's huge black tee shirts.

"You didn't talk to the police without clothes on?" Tricia asked, genuinely concerned.

Dovie laughed, not one of her enervating deep throated songs that brought a warm comfort and sense of peace, but a short staccato disharmony, an escaped convict of a cynical chuckle.

"No, I was dressed then. I took a warm bath after they left and never got around to dressing. Mel was very polite and professional. He asked about you."

Dovie led Tricia back to the kitchen, picking up the Chinese food bags deposited by the front door. She brought out plates, cups and a pitcher of iced tea. With chopsticks at the ready the two sat down to the nice smells and flavors. Tricia ate her lunch with gusto, watching as Dovie did little more than restir the stir fry on her plate.

"How can Death be so cruel, Tricia?" Dovie cried. "It's taken over twenty years for Turtle to cleanse his soul of the murders he committed in the war. Now, when he was finally beginning to smile and talk, to enjoy life again, Death snatches him up, burning him in a hell fire of damnation. Do you know they're going to have to use dental records to identify him?"

Tricia sat quietly, offering the sympathy of her presence.

"It's all so peculiar, Tricia. Turtle had been doing so well — you saw that yourself Monday. Then suddenly he drives off without a word and crashes his new car. It's so strange. He's always been such a careful driver."

The two sat in companionable silence as the overhead ceiling fan provided a gentle stir of the air. Back from the bedroom, the song of Dovie's canary brought an incongruous sweetness to the sad table.

"Mel seemed to think it was peculiar too. He asked me if Turtle drove around with explosives in his car. Why the very idea! What did he think? Just because Turtle had been a Green Beret in the war that he was a terrorist now?"

"How was Mel, by the way? Did he look well?" Tricia tried to sound nonchalant.

"Except for his mismatched clothing he looked fine. Mel's an awfully nice guy. You should try to make up. After all, life is too uncertain for unhappiness." Dovie burst into tears, holding a napkin to her gully gushing face. Tricia came around the table and gave her a loving embrace.

Later, after they had retired to the nest of a living room, the two relaxed as they sipped on their tea.

"I'll need to go on to work soon, if you're comfortable being alone?"

Dovie nodded. "It's so kind of you to visit. By the way, I saw that you drove up in a strange car. Is your Ferrari in the shop?"

Tricia shook her head sadly. "My loss is nothing compared with yours. The Ferrari caught fire last night. I rented a Cadillac this morning until I figure out what I want to do about a vehicle."

"At least you can get a new car." Dovie started to cry. "I'm sorry. That was so rude of me."

"No, Dovie, think nothing of it. Of course you're right."

"You know how Mel knew that it might have been Turtle in that car? The Lexus was still registered to Barbara Dupree. Mel called her and she gave him Turtle's name. I guess he got the address from his driver's license, or maybe Dupree knew it. Did she say anything about Turtle when you talked to her yesterday?"

"She did say some ..." Stopping in mid sentence, Tricia felt a chill. Hadn't Barbara made some type of threatening remark about Turtle having been better off minding his own business? Tricia looked up to find Dovie staring at her with alarm.

"What is it Tricia?"

"Did you tell me that Mel thought someone might have blown up Turtle's car? Is that what he said?"

Dovie looked at her with puzzlement. "I don't think he said that. He asked about explosives. Why?"

Tricia shook her head, determined not to add the uncertainty of possible murder to Dovie's load of tragedy.

"Well, it doesn't seem very likely, anyway, now does it? Okay, sweet Dovie. Let me give you one final hug and kiss. I'll call you tonight ... or should I drop by to check on you?"

Dovie assured her that she'd be fine, a phone call would suffice. Tricia returned to her rented Cadillac, its thermostat regulated air conditioner pumping heavily in a battle against the Texas sun's heat. As Tricia backed out she knocked over the neighbor's trashcan, adding another scar to its battered walls.

She paused long enough to sit it back up before steering the lumbering vehicle down to Shoreline Drive and out to the office.

Burdened with a heavy heart, Tricia settled at her desk. These last couple of days had brought troubles aplenty. Poor Dovie! Certainly Tricia's loss hadn't nearly the impact of Dovie's, but still, poor Tricia as well. The Ferrari had been a love object for her. Not just a means of transportation, the sports car merged with her soul. She reveled in its power. She gloried in the stares of admiration whenever she drove the streets. The sleekest, jazziest, hottest car and driver in the city, everyone knew Tricia in her Ferrari, everyone identified them as a set. The only one who would be pleased at this disaster of Tricia's would be Mel — not in petty revenge, but rather because he had always complained that he could never get his feet extended comfortably in the yellow bombshell.

Tricia picked up the stack of memos. Immediately her eyes narrowed on the challenge of a lawyer. Harry Harper had called, huh? At memories of some previous dealings with this scumbag, Tricia's mouth turned up at the corners, a mean sadistic smile. Harry blustered and connived and cheated. A few years ago he managed to get elected to the state legislature. He was voted by "Texas Monthly" as one of the ten worst legislators, quite an achievement for a freshman.

Harry usually hired out to the rich and ignorant. Tricia wondered who had fallen into his incompetent hands this time? She still laughed when she remembered the time he had described himself as a "Ball Busting Barrister." The challenge of bantering with Harry appealed to Tricia.

There's nothing like a good fight to relieve depression; especially a fight against an idiot. She picked up her phone and placed the call.

Four rings later a female nasal Texas twang answered. "Offices of Harry Harper. May I help you?"

Not even having met the girl, Tricia pitied her. She imagined how subservient the secretary would have to act, saying "Yes sir, Mr. Harper … Oh you're so brilliant Mr. Harper," when in reality she would be thinking "You're such an ass, Mr. Harper."

"Good afternoon," Tricia answered. "This is Patricia Tracy returning Mr. Harper's call. Is he in?"

"Just a moment, I'll check," the girl answered.

That's ridiculous, Tricia thought. *If the boss were out, she'd know right away. Therefore, he's in and she needs to find out if he'll talk with me.*

While she waited, Tricia thumbed through the rest of her "in" box. There were four other memos and three letters. Peter Kriten and Jesus Morales both wanted her to call. The third note said that William Tucker had called, but hadn't left a message. The final message came from Mel Sweeney asking about

Tricia's new lawyer. New lawyer? How peculiar. First her mom, and now Mel were asking about this imaginary new lawyer.

The three letters were about columns from the previous week, one complimentary, one scholarly and mildly disparaging, the third an irate ugly criticism. She wadded up the last one, before placing all three in the trash can. After a moment's thought she fished out the first one and placed it in an inter-office mail envelope, marked to the attention of Bob Randolph. A little self promotion never hurt.

She placed the phone on "speaker" so as not to have to hold the receiver. Seeing that this might take awhile, she started up the word processor, hoping to get an inspiration for her column. She had a paragraph or two pieced together about Metro Ministries where she was going to be working that evening when Harry Harper finally came on the line.

"Howdy, Miss Tracy. Harry Harper here." Harry spoke with a voice so deep it had to hurt. This was one of Harry's ideas of impressing people — a deep royal voice. Tricia supposed that he thought it sounded trustworthy. That worked fine, until in the courtroom when the case started to go against him, as it usually did. Then his voice cracked and traveled in the falsetto range.

Tricia imagined him as she had last seen him, being reprimanded by a judge for some courtroom antic or other. He stood five foot eleven, perhaps sixty years old, though he tried to look younger by keeping his hair dyed jet black. Sagging alcoholic eyes marred an otherwise handsome face.

"Hello, Harry. What is it you want this time? No, wait. Give me a chance to guess. Let's see. I got it. You're representing that armadillo I ran over last week. The widow and children want lifetime compensation. No doubt you have witnesses that will testify to my negligence. Why don't you just contact my lawyer and she'll negotiate for an out-of-court settlement. A buck and a quarter ought to do it, don't you think?"

Harry produced a two syllable chuckle. Tricia considered it a shame that Harry seemed to revel in the excitement of courtroom trials, for he performed so poorly at them. She supposed it had to do with promoting his self image, being in the limelight.

"Very funny, Miss Tracy. You always have had a quick, if inappropriate wit. Such atrocious gaffes in public decency are commonly found in your columns. I can't imagine how you manage to keep your position at the paper with some of the inflammatory and blatantly slanderous accusations you write. In fact, today's call involves a case in point."

Tricia grimaced. So, Harry was calling to pester her with another nuisance suit. She tried to remember how many times he had bothered the newspaper with such nonsense. Four? Five? Some lawyers were ambulance chasers, Harry was a newspaper chaser. He must get his money up front, she was sure, for she had heard that he had only once gotten money from the paper. And that time it was only a pittance.

"Go ahead, Harry. We both know that this phone call has no meaning other than as an ineffectual attempt at harassment. If you had a legitimate legal proceeding in mind, you'd have contacted the paper's lawyer. But, hey, tell me. Who is it that you've managed to get into your incompetent clutches this go round?"

For some reason, an image of Lupè flashed into her mind. Immediately she shook it away. Lupè already had a good lawyer.

Harry's deep voice clucked in admonishment. "How extremely callous to have insulted so many people that you can not guess which one would be hurt enough to summon legal assistance. Perhaps it would be appropriate for me to gather several of your victims into a class action suit."

The barrister paused, causing Tricia to shake her head in wonderment. She realized that he actually thought he had given himself a good idea. If he weren't such a clownish buffoon he might be dangerous. She maintained her silence, letting him stew in his own sour creative juices.

"Actually, Miss Tracy, I represent Mrs. Barbara Dupree. She takes great umbrage at being referred to as a raccoon. Further, the implications of her illegal activity grate heavily against the sterling reputation of this community leader. You have far overstepped the boundaries of human decency, as well as outraged societal morality! One wonders why you newspaper vultures must feast on the successful movers and shakers of our civilization? Does it compensate for your own failings?"

Tricia snorted. "You're nothing but a mealy mouthed mouthpiece, you moth-eaten moldy monster. Save your vapid insults for the jury room, Harry. I'd write a column exposing your lack of legal skills, but everyone already knows that story. Is that all you wanted to say to me? If so, I've got some real work to do. Though I have somewhat enjoyed the little fantasy ride."

"No, no, Miss Tracy. I'm calling to let you know that I intend to obtain a restraining order to prohibit you from making any further slanderous comments about my client. This is an official warning. Do you understand that further writings will cause you to be in contempt of court?"

Tricia laughed hard in his ear, hoping it hurt. "You'll never find a judge to go along with that nonsense, Harry. Though you'd like to ignore it, there is a first amendment to our constitution. Go ahead though. No doubt you're milking Mrs. Dupree for a tidy sum. Go through the motions. But don't bother me any more. You know how to reach the paper's lawyers."

She abruptly hung up on him.

"Verminous parasite," she grumbled. Securing a new dial tone, she punched in the extension for Peter's desk.

"Finance desk, Peter Kriten here."

"Hi Peter. It's Tricia."

"Good to hear from you. When I came looking for you this morning Luke Merino told me that you usually didn't come to work until late afternoon. Not a very conscientious employee I see."

Tricia flushed. "Really, Peter, it's none of your business what hours I choose to take. I get my columns in on time. Unlike some of you who just sit at the desk, I'm out late at important social events." She made a mental note to take Peter off her Christmas card list.

"I'm sure your late night forays are essential to the accomplishments of the modern working girl's career. Never mind, then. In any case, I called to give you a bit of information. I made some inquiries into the recent disruption at the Public Works Department I had mentioned in our meeting Monday. It seems that a supervisor named Bruce McDonald was terminated rather abruptly."

"Bruce McDonald? His name was Bruce, like in the note that said 'Bruce says it's going to cost $50,000 to get this changed'?"

Tricia heard Peter chuckle. "Indeed, Patricia. Not likely to be a coincidence, I would surmise. The department has instituted new safeguard policies. My initial inquiries into perking problems seem to be stirring up the old sleeping dog."

Tricia smiled. "So, you'd say, Peter, that my investigative work has produced a good lead for you."

She heard him hesitate. "You know, Patricia, all you did was hand a note to your boss that someone else had handed you. Next time, if you think you have something important, why not bring the item directly to me?"

"Sure, and give you all the credit? I can follow up my own clues, Peter."

She hung up on Peter and dialed Jesus' extension.

"*Estoy* Jesus," his beautiful harmonic tones answered.

"Hi, Poor K. It's Tricia. You got something?"

"Ah, *mia amiga*, I am glad you have arrived. You at your desk, *¿si?* Then I will be right there."

Tricia replaced the hand piece following Jesus' abrupt closure. He hadn't given her a chance to suggest he just tell her his information over the phone. Jesus preferred face-to-face meetings. His eyes never left your face during conversations, reading your emotions as well as hearing your words. It took an experienced fellow to poker face a lie past Jesus.

"*Buenas tardes*, Tricia. You have lunched?"

"Yes. I could take some coffee and a donut, though."

"*Bien*. We'll walk together to the snack shop."

Jesus, ever the gentleman, pulled out Tricia's chair for her. As they descended in the elevator that would take them to the basement, Tricia stewed about Harper's threats.

"Have you ever noticed that the world is made up of good guys and bad guys?"

"*¿Porqué?* Why do you say that?"

"I've just had a phone call from that nasty shyster, Harry Harper. He has to be one of the vilest reprehensible excuses for an evolutionary throwback Neanderthal that Mother Nature ever burped upon this planet. Surely there's not a redeeming trait in his character. He lies, he threatens, he connives, he cheats.... If he could make any money at it he would surely sue himself."

Tricia, who had been watching the elevator floor numbers blink down toward 'B', turned to Jesus as she and the elevator reached their finish simultaneously. She found him staring at her in rapt attention, his brows knit in careful consideration of her complaints. She wondered how he managed to walk and talk at the same time, fixing his attention on the person instead of looking where he was going. As they left the elevator the coffee shop's glass walls opened right in front of them. Jesus' careful reply came out gently.

"I think that everyone has both good and evil in them, Tricia. No one is entirely bad. True, some people do bad things often, make wrong choices with harmful results. But if you ask yourself *¿porqué?* Why? Why do they do these things? I find that when I can understand why people act the way they do, I no longer can label them good or evil."

Tricia shook her head. Placing a few coins in the necessary slots, she purchased and brought her coffee and donut to the table. Jesus joined her with an apple and a carton of skim milk.

"So how do you explain the <u>really</u> evil people — like rapists, murderers, and child molesters? Your theory is too bleeding-heart liberal, Jesus. Some of these people have sat under the shower too long. Their brains have rotted. Have you heard that someone blew up my beautiful Ferrari last night?"

Jesus' expression broke into compassionate sorrow. He placed his hand on her wrist and expressed his sympathy.

"Thanks, Poor K. I appreciate that. I haven't had a chance to grieve, what with so much going on. I also found out this morning that one of my best friend's housemates died last night; a car accident. Oh, it was the fellow who found that note written by Dupree."

Jesus face and voice reflected his sympathy and concern. "*Una tragedia grandè!* You say an accident?"

Tricia shrugged. She found herself trying to stare at Jesus the whole conversation as he did at her. She found the focus disconcerting, so instead concentrated on her snack as she replied. "Maybe yes, maybe no. Apparently the police aren't sure. Speaking of Dupree, what have you found out about our case?"

Jesus finished off the last two bites of his apple before replying. Carefully he cleaned off the table top with his napkin, wrapping it around the core. He placed the package in the trash can before replying. He looked steadily upon her face, his dark piercing eyes holding her in a magical grip. Yet to Tricia, the gaze seemed diminished. Two days ago she had been attracted to this swarthy fellow reporter. His natural good looks, kind manner, and respectful demeanor caused her pulse to skip a dance. Since meeting Bill, though, Tricia found Jesus plain and naive.

"I have identified Bruce," he replied.

Tricia smiled smugly. "Oh, that's old news. He's Bruce McDonald from the Public Works Department, recently terminated."

"*Mia amiga,* you amaze me. How did you find out?"

Tricia tossed her head. "Oh, I have my sources. But tell me what you know, I'm dying to hear."

"Bruce McDonald was in a supervisory position until he resigned two months ago. *¿Porqué?* I ask many people 'Why did he resign?' Everyone shrugs and turns away. Something *esta malo aqui*,[1] Tricia. I think Bruce McDonald changed more reports than just this one. I have a few leads I'm working on."

"Why would he do that? Was he taking bribes? Where is he now? Did he know Barbara Dupree?"

Jesus shrugged. "*No se, Señorita.* These all are very good questions. His phone has been disconnected. But I'll find out some answers. You wish to help?"

"Of course I want to help! Maybe I can prove to Uncle Bob that I deserve to be an investigative reporter. What do you suggest?"

"Perhaps you might contact Mrs. Dupree? *Gracias, Señorita.* I have still some sources to question. We talk again *por mañana, ¿si?*"

Tricia returned upstairs and settled into her work station. Before placing her call to Dupree she turned on the recorder attached to her phone. As the placed call rang, Tricia wondered if Barbara would be there. She'd reached Harry, Peter, and Jesus, though each had been expecting her call. Barbara, on the other hand, may have been fending off phone calls all day as a result of Tricia's article. In such a circumstance, she might not be answering.

---

1   Very bad here

After the fourth buzz, Barbara's answering machine clicked on.

"You have reached 555-2700, Dupree Development Company. We have just the land you want. Please leave a number and I will return your call. Beep."

An instinct led Tricia to believe Barbara might be using the machine to screen her calls.

"Barbara? It's Tricia ... Patricia Tracy. Please pick up the phone if you're there."

She waited, considering whether to say some other inducement. Just as she was about to hang up, Barbara answered.

"Hello?"

"Thank you for taking my call, Barbara. I received a call from your lawyer just now."

"Oh, Mr. Harper you mean? Well, you know, he called me this morning. He and about twenty other people. It's amazing how many acquaintances come out of the woodwork when you get your fifteen minutes of fame. Can you believe it? I heard from people today who haven't spoken to me in five years! So I want to thank you for the article I guess. I feel like the politician who told the newspaper men; 'Sirs, I don't care what you say about me, as long as you spell my name right.' You know what I mean?

"Anyway, so when Harry called this morning, that's Mr. Harper you know, he seemed so upset about your writing of me. Well, I didn't think it was that bad myself. Raccoons are kind of cute, aren't they? But Harry and I go way back. Frankly, he's not that good, as lawyers go. Still, he wanted to do something for me so I said okay. I hope he didn't get you too upset.

"Though he had a valid point. One must be careful what gets said about one in print. You know what I mean? After all, you really made quite a mountain from a molehill. I explained that the paper you found was an error. That black fellow paid a heavy price for turning it over to you, didn't he?"

A shiver swept through Tricia.

"What do you mean? How did you know something happened?"

"It said so in this morning's paper. It's a real shame. He seemed like such a nice guy. Big, but nice, you know what I mean? But when people start causing trouble, they stir up the fates against them. I mean, after all, accidents happen, now don't they? So, naturally, if you believe in actions and causation, you put together events in your mind.

"But, as I was saying, Harry and I go way back. One time he helped me settle a five month old dispute with one of my concrete contractors. Can you believe it? Ever since then, we've kept in pretty close contact. So, naturally, when he saw my name in the paper he called, asking if he couldn't help out.

He is <u>so</u> persuasive, you know what I mean? He said I can't have my reputation trifled with. I hope you won't take it personally."

Tricia did take an implied lawsuit and a threatened court restraint quite personally. Taking advantage of this opportunity to speak, she asked, "Mrs. Dupree, how well do you know Bruce McDonald?"

Barbara sputtered. "McDonald? Why do you ask?"

"Are you going to deny that you know him?"

"Well, no. I did know him once. But I believe he's left town. I haven't heard from Mr. McDonald in quite awhile."

"Really? I'm trying to track him down. Do you have any idea how I might get hold of him?"

"I don't know." Barbara's voice tones sounded defiant.

"But you did know him. Isn't he the Bruce who you paid $50,000 to change your perking report?"

"I don't like you questioning me like this, Mrs. Tracy. Is it Miss or Mrs.?"

"Miss, but you may call me Tricia."

"Why do you care about my developments? I'm just a working girl trying to make an honest living. I agreed to be in your column because they're usually so fun. I had no idea you were going to stir up so much trouble."

"I don't mean to irritate you, Barbara. I'm just trying to figure this out. Why don't you tell me what happened between you and Bruce?"

"It's just like I told you yesterday. The inspection was wrong. When Bruce … I mean Mr. McDonald, checked into it, he was able to properly certify the property."

"What did the first inspector find wrong? Surely he based his denial on something?"

Barbara hesitated again. Tricia guessed she was trying to decide if Tricia knew anything more. Tricia decided to take a stab, "Did you have the land reperked?"

"No. It was just a mistake, that's all. Look, all the documents are in order. Why don't you just leave me alone? I'm not hurting anyone. Just leave me alone!" She abruptly hung up the phone.

Tricia sat quietly, considering the two issues. Was Barbara involved in Turtle's death? Had McDonald accepted a bribe to change the fact that part of Westchester Acres failed its perking test? Jesus and Peter were working on the answer to the second question. The first might prove much more difficult to unwrap.

Tricia returned to her computer and finished her column. Before shutting down for the day, she gave Dovie a call.

"Hello?"

"It's Tricia, Dovie. How are you?"

"Okay, I guess. I've been meditating. You planning on dropping by after work?"

"I wouldn't be able to come until late, after nine o'clock."

"I think I'll be asleep by then."

"How about I drop by in the morning then?"

"Thank you, Tricia. Can you come about nine?"

Tricia pushed away from her desk, rose from her chair, and turned; right into a huge bouquet of flowers. Stepping back, Tricia saw Bill's smiling face above the yellow and red blossoms.

"Besides being your favorite color, yellow is for our eternal friendship. Red for our love, a magical mesh of mystical lovers brought together by the grace of the gods. Our love goddess must be the gorgeous Aphrodite. I can visualize her now, snubbing the jealousy the other goddesses feel at your beauty by granting us this gift of our intense love. How say you, my lovely Helen of Troy? Come to the bay with me and see if your incomparable magnificence launches a thousand ships!"

"Now how can I be angry with a man who unleashes such flattering prose?" Tricia answered gleefully. Trying to maintain a mock seriousness, she demanded, "But where were you? One moment you were standing next to me at the park, and the next minute you had vanished! What happened?"

"I offer my deepest apologies, My Beauty. I became momentarily indisposed, and then couldn't find you in the crowd. Did you wait long?"

Tricia felt abashed. No doubt he had simply gone to the toilet or some such necessity. Instead of giving him the benefit of a short wait she had immediately assumed that he had abandoned her. How long had she and Dovie scanned the crowds? It couldn't have been but a few minutes.

"Oh, I forgive you, you sweet flatterer. Umm, these flowers smell delightful! However did you gather such a collection of chrysanthemums? And roses? Marigolds, too? What an eclectic mixture!"

The sexuality of Bill's laugh sent goose bumps jolting up both Tricia's arms. Studying his handsome face she felt the warm longing that had filled her yesterday morning at his boat. She felt her heart race, a yearning for this fellow, an illogical compulsion consuming her.

Shaking free of the hypnotic spell, she glanced down at her watch.

"I have less than an hour. Let's grab some coffee across the street."

As they walked through the newsroom, Bill asked, "What's on your agenda for this evening?"

"Someone once accused me of being a spoiled self-centered Narcissus, and I fear that twenty-eight days a month, it's true. But twice a month, on alternate Wednesday evenings, I volunteer my services at the Corpus Christi Metro Ministries. It's an organization that provides free meals and beds for the hungry and homeless. The patrons are from a totally different planet. Have you heard of it?"

"Yes. Some of the boat hands call it their second home."

Tricia smiled and took his hands. "Would you like to come with me? We can always use a helping hand."

"I'd rather prepare for our evening. What time do you get off? I'll treat you to dinner."

"Nine o'clock. That'd be grand. You name the place!"

Bill smiled and cocked his eyebrows. "My choice, huh? Then ... my choice is my boat. I'll make a scrumptious meal!"

Tricia hesitated. "Give me a minute on that one, Bill. I'm not sure I'm ready for an evening alone with you on your boat."

As they rode down alone in the elevator, Tricia held his hands, staring into his face. She cocked her head up, closing her eyes. Their lips met in loving embrace; soft, yielding, exciting connections of personal sharing. Tricia reached around, hugging him close to her in passion. They didn't quite break apart in time, receiving a round of applause from three people in the lobby when the doors opened.

Over coffee, Tricia told Bill about her grand adventures; dinner with Dovie, confronting Lupè, and her Ferrari's death. He grabbed her hands.

"That man is a maniacal stalker. He threatened your life and blew up your car."

Tricia shook her head. "I'm not afraid of him. Don't forget I stared him down last night."

"You ... you were lucky. What did the police say?"

"They didn't seem very impressed."

Bill shook his head gravely. "No, they never are until it's too late. After all, it's not their job to guard you. They specialize in trying to arrest the perpetrators after the crime. What you need is a bodyguard. I just happen to know of one who is available."

She looked at him solemnly. "So which is it you want, to be my bodyguard or to be my lover? Both? Do you intend to possess me like some object? Bill. I'm used to being a very independent woman. I need to know your intentions."

"Do I have to choose? I fear for your life, with Lupè on the prowl. Guarding your safety is paramount. Should something happen to you that I might have prevented I would die a thousand deaths. My intentions for you are honorable, My Beauty. My love for you is growing with every passing moment, and I pray that yours is for me. Hold on a moment and I'll walk you back to your building." He took the tab to the register.

They crossed the street in silence, stopping at the newspaper doors.

"I'd still love to have dinner with you at nine," Tricia said. "But I will not be bodyguarded by the man who also wishes to kiss me. I can't stand being possessed. I'll only be at your boat if you've made your choice. Bodyguard, kisser, or out to a restaurant?"

Bill leaned forward and kissed her lips. She pushed him away quickly. "I'm not ready for public kissing. But, yes, you chose correctly. I'll see you at your boat at nine."

18

Interview: Barbara Dupree
Date: Wednesday, September 14th
Place: Dupree home, 1004 Wesson Drive

Sweeney: Mrs. Dupree, as I just explained, I like
                to tape these interviews. You said that
                was okay, right?

Dupree: I suppose so, Officer. You said you wanted
                to ask about my old car?

Sweeney: Just some routine questions, this won't
                take up much of your time. For the record,
                today is September fourteenth. Present
                here are Mrs. Barbara Dupree, Realtor,
                Mel Sweeney, detective, and Samuel Byrd,
                police sergeant. I'm sorry to bother you,
                Mrs. Dupree.

Dupree: This late in the day I'm winding down any-
                way. It's been a heck of a day, I'll tell
                you that! I've had more phone calls today
                than a week of Mondays. It sure does pay
                to get your name in the paper, that's for
                sure. Did you see it this morning, Officer?
                No? Don't tell me you're not familiar with
                Tracy's Tidbits? It's my favorite column.

Sweeney: Sure, Tricia Tracy is my girl friend. Uh,
                well, she was. I haven't read today's
                paper, though.

Dupree: Trouble in the nest? You'll pardon my say-
                ing, but she can be a bit of a tart. Still …
                if you do get married I'd be happy to take
                you and Tricia out for lunch some time.

Maybe you'd like to discuss your plans for housing? I can get you a great deal on pre-construction prices. I always love reading *Tracy's Tidbits*. She writes such fun, gossipy type things. Of course, when the gossip is turned on you it's not quite as much fun. Not that this one was so bad, you know what I mean? She called me a raccoon. Last week she called a policeman a bulldog. I used to have a dog. It was a nice enough dog, I suppose. It was a toy poodle, you know, one of those little lap dogs. Susie used to hide under the bed whenever there was a thunderstorm. Jasmine, that's my youngest daughter, Jasmine took Susie with her when she went to college. Do you have a dog, officer?

Sweeney: Nope, never did. When I was a kid we had so many mouths to feed, a mongrel would have starved to death. Now I live in an apartment that doesn't allow pets. My oldest sister, Katie Rose, used to keep a goldfish. It wasn't much for sitting on your lap, though it handled car rides just fine. Speaking of cars, I need to ask you a few questions about your Lexus.

Dupree: Yes, that's a tragedy about that poor black fellow. Jones was it?

Sweeney: Sidney Jones. He went by the name of Turtle.

Dupree: A lot of pets in our conversation, huh, Officer? When I was a kid they used to call me bug eyes. I always have had to wear these thick glasses. Contacts just don't fit me well. And they're so much trouble, you know what I mean? Have you ever had to wear them?

Sweeney: No.

Dupree: Well, I tried once or twice. They had to
                put me in the hospital overnight when I
                scratched my eye. My dumb ex-husband kept
                trying to get me to go without my glasses.
                Can you believe it? He's a nincompoop. Who
                cares what you look like? It's what you do
                that counts. Don't you agree, Officer?

Sweeney: Absolutely. What you do is much more impor-
                tant. Like me, last night I was taking care
                of my sweet Mum. She fell and broke her hip
                a couple of weeks ago. Fortunately, there's
                a bunch of us kids around. Last night was
                my turn to stay with her. How about you,
                Mrs. Dupree? What did you do last night?

Dupree: I'm afraid my evenings aren't very excit-
                ing, Officer. After a hard day on the job
                site or trying to sell my properties, I
                like to relax with a book. I'm reading
                one of the Cat books, "The Cat Who Wasn't
                There," by Lillian Braun. You ever read
                any of her books, officer? Great reading.
                Did you ever own a cat? I'd have one, but
                I'm allergic to the dander. I get around
                one of those things and I start hacking.
                You know what I mean? Then you've got to
                put up with the litter box smell.

Sweeney: No, I never had a cat, either. I can't say
                I like their attitudes. Sort of stand off-
                ish. Last week I arrested a cat burglar,
                but that's not the same thing of course.
                He used to drive a black van. Speaking
                of driving, I see you have a new car out
                there, Mrs. Dupree. Before you got that
                one, you drove that brand new Blue Lexus,
                huh? Why did you sell it? Were you having
                problems with it?

Dupree:	Nope, it worked great and drove great. I bought it new from Gateway. They have a pretty good service department, I'll give them that. Not like that Jeep place. I had a Wagoneer before the Lexus. I'd never buy another one. You'd take it into the shop, they'd never have it ready on time, they charged you too much, and it was never fixed. I just felt like getting a new, bigger car, something that would impress people. People see you in a Lexus, they say, "That's nice." But when you're driving around in a fat Lincoln Continental, people know you've made it. It's the "Wow" thing, you know what I mean?
Sweeney:	I wish I could get a new car every year! I'm driving an old Chevy that's so beat up Tricia is embarrassed to be seen with me. Gosh, you dumped a perfectly good car, huh? The brakes were good? The steering felt tight? You kept it well maintained?
Dupree:	Sure. I'm sort of a compulsive type person. When the warranty says, oil change every four thousand miles, I'm there before the odometer hits four thousand and five. You can call Gateway. They have complete records. I tell you, that Jones got a good deal when he bought that one. Too bad he crashed into a retaining wall. That's what the morning paper said, you know. In any case, as far as I know it wasn't the car's fault. It always worked fine for me.
Sweeney:	I remember a case I had last year when a window casing in a home fell down on a lady. The husband swore it had always worked fine for him. It turned out he had greased it just before she had used it. Speaking of homes, how did you know Mr. Jones' address when I called this morning?

Dupree: Well, I am a realtor, Officer. I'm famil-
           iar with most of the neighborhoods in this
           town. When I sold him the car I asked for
           his address on Naples. I pretty much could
           visualize the place. That's not a particu-
           larly nice part of town, though the loca-
           tion is excellent. Of course, the houses
           on the bay side of Santa Fe are worth much
           more. You said you're living in an apart-
           ment, huh? Whenever you're ready to move
           into a real home you should let me show
           you around, Officer. I'm sure you could use
           the tax advantages of a home, rather than
           throwing away your money on apartment rent.
           You know what I mean?

Sweeney: I'd love to have a house someday, Mrs.
           Dupree. This one is huge. You sure could
           raise a family in this one! My Mum and a
           couple of my sisters still live in the home
           I grew up in. There were nine of us kids,
           stuffed into four bedrooms like sardines.
           I see pictures of kids on your walls. Are
           those your children?

Dupree: Oh yes, the joys of my life. The old-
           est, that's Briana, she runs a business in
           Austin. And Jasmine, sweet little Jasmine,
           lives in Seattle. She's the one I told you
           took the dog with her. I sure do miss my
           girls. But baby birds do need to leave the
           nest, you know what I mean? When you've
           had children, you feel like you've done
           something for the world, passed on your
           genes. I'm naming my newest development
           after my youngest … Jasmine Townships. I
           feel sorry for people who never had chil-
           dren. You think you and Miss Tracy?

Sweeney: Hmm. Well … right now we're sort of on the
           outs. Maybe someday. This reminds me of
           a case I'm working on about a couple who

never had children. They got involved with
illegal adoptions.

Dupree: I feel so sorry for people who've never had
children. Did you read *Tracy's Tidbits* on
Monday? That couple, Maria and Lupè Garcia
never had children. Maybe if they had, he
never would have killed her and stuffed her
down the well. I actually knew that couple.
Lupè used to do small jobs for me, and I
got him a job with Bevis, my sub-contrac-
tor. Can you believe it? I supervise a lot
of construction out on these developments.
We use Mexicans for laborers, you know.
They're pretty good workers, usually. Lupè
likes to drink, but he can handle a shovel
okay. His wife, Maria, would come pick up
his paycheck every now and then. I like to
help out people in need like that. Scratch
my back, I'll scratch yours. But I didn't
want bad publicity about my project, you
know, a murderer working on my development? When I read that article I suggested
that Bevis might not want to keep Lupè on
the payroll. You know what I mean?

Sweeney: Lupè isn't Mexican and he hasn't been con-
victed of any crime yet, Mrs. Dupree.

Dupree: Now don't think I didn't hear your "yet,"
Officer. Tricia seemed pretty sure, didn't
she? Does she get her information from
you? Ha! I can see from your face that
she does. You must tell her all sorts of
things in private, don't you? Oh, what a
great source for gossip!

Sweeney: Mrs. Dupree, you mentioned that Maria used
to pick up Lupè's check sometimes. How did
that work?

Dupree: Well, paymaster is in a small shack on the job site. Some of the women like to wait in the payment shack until the checks are ready to be picked up. That way their husbands won't take it out and spend it all on beer the first night. I can sympathize with that. Can you believe it? My ex-husband used to waste all our money, too! Ridiculous little man, that's what he was. The only useful thing I ever got out of him was two beautiful children.

Sweeney: Are the wives ever alone in the shack?

Dupree: Have you ever been on a construction site, Officer? Well, let me tell you. It's not a real formal place. People come and go. They're supposed to keep the shack locked, you understand. But gosh, during the hot summer months it would be cruel to keep those women waiting in the sun. The little shacks are air conditioned so we let them sit around. The money is kept locked up, of course.

Sweeney: Seems like you're out on these construction sites a lot, huh? I mean, you have to do extensive preparations, don't you?

Dupree: Plan and prepare, that's what I'm always doing. This is my fourth project, so I pretty well know what to do and how to do it. My stupid ex-husband could never even do the same thing right twice. It just takes some experience, learn from your mistakes, you know what I mean? Now I know which contractors I can trust. And when I need to get an inspection or a license, I know who to contact in which city office. And money? A lot of money goes out in these things before you start to get anything back, let me tell you that! I've got that grubstake now, but it wasn't always like this. The first time it took me almost two years just to get the money together! Can you believe it? Now I'm two steps ahead all the time.

Sweeney: I know what you mean about following through. When I'm on a case I keep after every little lead. I had a case of arson last year where I spent a week just tracing who had access to the explosives. Speaking of that, when you're preparing the land, you use bulldozers and explosives, huh?

Dupree: Bulldozers and explosives? Heck yes! I love getting my hands dirty. I'll get up on those big machines and feel like I'm on top of the world. Hah. Can't nobody push you around when you're in a bulldozer. Better than driving an SUV. I love the explosives, too, though we don't get them out too often. This is Corpus Christi, after all. Not a bunch of mountains to level. I do love to hear that big boom and watch the dirt fly! Like taking out a big stump or something, you know what I mean?

Sweeney: Boy that does sound like fun. I love watching fireworks on the fourth of July. I suppose it'd be a little bit like that, huh? Could anyone pick up explosive experience on the job site? Like maybe you or Lupè?

Dupree: You're supposed to have a special license for that kind of thing, but Bevis would let me fire it off occasionally. I can't imagine Bevis letting Lupè touch that stuff, you know what I mean? I'd let Lupè carry stuff for me, you know, little things that won't explode. But you have to know what you're doing when you deal with explosives. Lupè drinks too much. Of course, we all have our faults. I guess mine is I talk too much.

Sweeney: What kind of things did Lupè carry for you, Mrs. Dupree?

Dupree: Oh, I was just using that as an example. I mean, like if I needed something delivered somewhere, well, you can't do everything yourself, you know what I mean?

Sweeney: What kind of things did you have Lupè deliver?

Dupree: Just things. Construction site things. Look, Detective, can we talk more another time? I'm sort of tired.

Sweeney: Thank you for your time, Mrs. Dupree. You've been very helpful. That's it, Sam, you can turn off the recorder.

End of recording.
MS/sb

19

Corpus Christi Metro Ministries provided free meals to about sixty people each summer evening and twice that many in the winter months. Besides food, the converted warehouse had cots and lumpy mattresses capable of providing shelter for eighty men and twenty woman. Early each morning all sleepovers found themselves on the curb with the doors locked behind them. The ministry served as a temporary shelter only, though in the winter months some of the homeless slept there every night.

Bundles of belongings kept in plastic grocery store bags rested along a wall, behind the battered piano, or hung onto the line of coat hooks near the entrance. Table top space served as dining areas and as a playing surface for after dinner cards or dominoes.

Tricia helped in the kitchen, chopping carrots, potatoes, and stew meat. A couple of the ministry staff supervised, compensated below minimal wage by community contributions. Most of the Ministry's workforce came from volunteers such as Tricia, taking turns in the kitchen, on the serving line, and supervising the sleepers. Three hours of evening work twice a month gave Tricia a feeling of giving something back to the community.

After clearing the dinner tables, Tricia and two other volunteers washed dishes and scrubbed the stewpots. Returning to the dinning hall, she surveyed the crowd. In one corner a grainy TV picture fluttered with an Astros and Braves game. Some of the diners had left, either standing outside for a smoke or preferring to seek their own sleeping arrangements, thinning the earlier crowd. Tricia spied a man she had seen here several times, a regular named Jack.

Sitting by himself in a corner, Jack thumbed through a magazine with obvious boredom. As Tricia approached, he dropped the journal to the floor, welcoming her with a broken toothed grin. Jack was a ready talker.

"Howdy, Pretty Lady," Jack called out from ten feet distant. At forty-five years old, he looked sixty. Wispy gray strands of dirty hair spewed out below a blue baseball cap. A droopy gray mustache hung over three day beard stubble. His nose veered to the left, pointing away from a long right cheek scar. His eyebrows and forehead and chin held a roadmap of scars. These came from Jack's chronic seizure disorder, a problem which also kept him unemployable and homeless. Jack tried his best to cooperate with the doctors' efforts at controlling his seizures. In a lap belt pouch he kept bottles of Dilantin, Tegretol,

Phenobarbital, and Depakote. Despite this overflowing pharmacopoeia, twice weekly breakthrough seizures tortured his life.

Tricia perched on a rickety chair next to his worn armchair, her hands resting comfortably on her knees.

"Good to see you, Jack. How's life been treating you?"

He shook his head, a boyish smile and a twinkling eye giving him a mischievous look.

"Now, Pretty Lady, what you expect? Poor Jack ain't got home, ain't got job, ain't got woman. Jack struggle every day to get food. Say, you want some pills? Darvocet? Valium?"

Tricia looked at him warily. "Where do you get all those pills, Jack? Do you steal them?"

He shook his head vigorously. "Oh no, Pretty Lady. Jack no thief. These honest pills; hospital stuff. Look, they in package so you know they genuine. The E. R. doctors give 'em to Jack. Ten bucks, your choice. Please, Pretty Lady. Jack need the money."

Tricia watched as Jack carefully removed a prescription bottle from his lap pack. Twisting off the tamper resistant cap, he shook a half dozen pills in package into his left palm. She checked her first impulse to immediately say "no". The last few days had brought such stress, a little Valium would be welcome. She looked around to see if anybody was watching. In fact, two or three heads did immediately turn away as she glanced in their direction.

"I don't know, Jack. I don't want to be caught in something illegal here."

"But ... what?" Jack asked. "Valium or Darvocet? If you was to want them, which?"

Tricia felt embarrassed, even somewhat dirty. "Well. I was just thinking that I wouldn't mind having a little Valium around. I've been going through some hard times lately. Someone destroyed my car last night."

"Ah. Ain't that a shame, Pretty Lady? Jack like seeing you in that hot little banana. Out on the streets the guys see you zip past and make up stories about what you up to. Well, it weren't one of Jack's friends. We all know you and love you, Pretty Lady. Who do you think done it? You got ideas?"

"I have my suspicions, all right. You know Lupè Garcia?"

Jack didn't answer right away. Taking a minute to put his drugs back away he left out three Valiums, palming them in his left hand. Surveying the room, he surreptitiously dropped them into Tricia's right palm.

"Twenty-five dollars for three."

Tricia slipped the pills into her purse.

"Yep. Jack and Lupè Garcia, us am drinking buddies. Lupè okay, 'cept drink too much. Then mean. Seen him hit Maria. Jack say Lupè blow up your car if drunk. What for? You get in his way?"

"I suppose so. I wrote about him in the paper and he says it cost him his job. He's attacked me twice."

Jack whistled, a low toned song of concern. "Lupè pretty dumb, Pretty Lady, but strong. How come miss you twice? You know karate?"

"Hardly. But I can take care of myself. I am thinking of getting a body-guard, though. What do you think?"

"Not Jack, Pretty Lady. Jack not face Lupè. Maybe Jack find someone. You want Jack to look?"

"I didn't mean you. I meant what do you think of the idea? It seems a bother and an invasion of my privacy, but I'm beginning to think it might be worth-while. Actually, I already have someone in mind. You seem to know everybody around here, Jack. Have you ever met William Tucker? He's a sailor that came into town recently."

"Don't ring a bell."

"He's pretty distinctive looking. Bill's not tall, maybe five foot six or seven. He's got dark sandy hair, about my color, with a black eye patch on the left. There's a scar that runs above and below the patch."

"Sure," Jack said with a grin. "Jack know him. That Nate."

"Nate? What do you know about that?"

Jack looked smug. "Nate drink with Jack and Lupè at Coyote. We have grand time. Yuck-yuck." Jack's guffaw interrupted his story as he slapped his knee in remembered merriment.

"Coyote? You mean the Lonesome Coyote? Who was there, Jack?"

"Sure. Weren't they a funny group? Jack and Maria and Lupè and Nate and Fat Bob, quite a funny group. Nate buy drinks all around. Jack don't drink. It make seizures worse. Ain't that the pits? Lupè and Maria sure like those free beers."

"Nate and Lupè are drinking buddies? Have you seen them together more than once?"

"Yep, plenty of times. Nate and me go way back."

"Wait a minute. Bill Tucker's only been in town a month or so I think. You sure this is the same person?"

Jack shrugged. "Got a patch. Which eye?"

"Left."

"Maybe. Don't remember, now. Nate nice to Jack. Buy Coke and wings."

Tricia took a handkerchief from her purse, leaned forward, and wiped some food residual off of Jack's mustache.

"Thank ye, Pretty Lady."

"No problem, Jack. You're telling me that Lupè and Maria and Nate were all drinking together? Was Lupè angry with Maria that night? Did he hit her?"

"Lupè like getting drunk. Sometime he pass out on table. That funny, yukk-yukk. When Maria drunk, she friendly. Kiss Fat Bob. Kiss Nate."

"Maria and Nate kissed? You mean like a little peck of friendship or something more passionate?"

"He like it. When she ask for ring, he gave it. Pretty ring, lots of sparkles."

"Really, now! Did they all leave together?"

"Jack not sure. Jack leave first."

"Thanks for the story, Jack. Here." She took twenty-five dollars from her purse. Trying to hide it in her palm she passed it to him as they shook hands farewell.

Tricia checked in the kitchen one more time. Finding all squared away, she checked out with the staff-in-charge.

"See you in two weeks," she said, as the swinging door swished behind her.

20

Interview: Sally Bellows
Date: Wed. Sept. 14
Location: Lonesome Coyote

Sweeney: Hello again, Mrs. Bellows. Thank you for letting me tape again. You seem to be in a better mood.

Bellows: Apparently you can buy my pleasure. You fellows want drinks again? Yes? Two Mountain Dews, coming right up. Here you go boys. Now what is it you want tonight?

Sweeney: Just thought I'd come in to see if you could point out someone who might be familiar with the Garcias. See anyone here tonight who liked to hang out with them?

Bellows: Let me see. Nah. That's the Friday night crowd, I told you that. Though Lupè was here a couple of times last week.

Sweeney: Really? What was he doing? Who was he with?

Bellows: Some sailor who's been hanging around recently. I mentioned him last time you were here, didn't I?

Sweeney: What does this sailor look like?

Bellows: Pretty distinctive looking. He's got an eye patch and he limps. Why? You know him?

Sweeney: I might. Did Lupè or this sailor hang out with other people?

Bellows: You know what's funny, Detective. Do you read *Tracy's Tidbits* in the paper? That woman that Tracy wrote about this morning, Barbara Dupree, she knows Lupè. Barbara's always talking to me about buying a house, as if I could afford it on my income! Hah. That's a good one.

Sweeney: Barbara Dupree comes to this bar? She told me she stayed home and read books in the evening. Does she and Lupè hang out together in this bar?

Bellows: Yeah, they've known each other for years. I get the feeling that he does things for her. Errands and things.

Sweeney: Did you ever see the three of them together? The sailor, Dupree, and Lupè I mean.

Bellows: Yeah, one night. They huddled in that corner booth for about a half hour. Maybe a month ago.

Sweeney: Tell me what you remember. Did Lupè seem to know the sailor or did Barbara?

Bellows: I don't think either one of them knew him. You know how it is when you're new in town, Detective? You find a local bar and see if you can make a friend.

Sweeney: Or a contact. Has Dupree done that before?

Bellows: Done what?

Sweeney: Picked up sailors in a bar.

Bellows: Har har! That's funny, Detective. You know what Dupree looks like? I don't think your average sailor is THAT desperate for a piece of ass. Well, then again, I've known some who were.

Sweeney: Seriously, does Dupree hang out in this bar frequently to meet new sailors?

Bellows: Now that you mention it, I'd say yes. That does seem a little strange. You think she's a pervert?

Sweeney: No, I suspect she has other reasons. You mentioned Fat Bob last time, from the newspaper?

Bellows: Yeah, he's a typical Friday nighter. He drinks Scotch by the way.

Sweeney: You said he was a regular with Lupè and Maria?

Bellows: Yeah, he's friendly with them. He drinks with them and anyone else who'll have him. He's a talker, that one. Likes the hot wings too. Say, you boys want some wings?

Sweeney: No thanks, Miss Bellows. We'll be going soon. Do you remember seeing Bob with that sailor with the patch?

Bellows: Sorry, Detective.

Sweeney: Well, thanks again, Miss Bellows. Let's go Sam.

Bellows: Twenty dollars again? Hey, Detective, feel free to drop by tomorrow night.

End of Recording
MS/sb

21

The drive from the Ministry to the L-head took only five minutes down Ayers Street. The white Cadillac glided heavily down the road, taking forever to pick up speed and almost as long to stop. At the 'L' head all but two of the parking spaces were full. Either of those two would have fit the Ferrari, but never the Cady. Tricia circled back out to the street and parked in a business lot across Shoreline Drive. Recrossing the street she made her way down the L-head pier to Bill's boat.

"Ahoy?" she called out. "Anyone on board?"

Bill stuck his head up from the galley and hoisted himself on deck.

"Ah, my shining beacon of iridescence has arrived! Welcome aboard, oh Aphrodite, goddess of beauty and purity. To thee I give homage. May Poseidon, the God of the waters, provide gentle sailing for your visit upon his home."

Tricia accepted his proffered hand. He lifted her easily across the lapping waters, holding tightly until he was sure she had her footing.

"You speak of Greek deities often, Bill," she said. "Do you really believe in that mumbo jumbo?"

He fixed on her face, his expression quiet and serious.

"A sailor respects the forces beyond his control, My Beauty. I have seen too many people die young to not respect and honor the supernatural. I remember one winter off the coast of *Côte d'Ivoire*. I was second mate on a 36-tonner, a rusty leaky tub flying a Liberian flag called *The King Joseph*. We had off loaded our American soybeans and picked up a full cargo of mahogany logs. Let me tell you, those mahogany logs are three times heavier than any log should be. *Joseph* sat so low in the water, three foot waves washed onto the deck. Well, when that squall hit us the old bucket hadn't a chance.

About an hour into the storm the cacophony of creaks and groans culminated with an ear shattering boom as the hull cracked right down the middle. The aft half sunk like a baby's bronzed shoe, a fast track rocket to the bottom. With all those logs, though, the wreckage to which I hung stayed high atop the surface. As the storm raged, twelve of us hung desperately to the gunwales. One by one the fellows lost strength, sometimes washing away with a scream. More commonly they were there one minute, covered by a huge wave, and gone when it cleared.

"After three hours only four of us still clung to our tenuous perch. Just as suddenly as the storm had come, it dissipated. A rescue ship responding to the ship's earlier SOS picked us up. Why had only four sailors survived from a crew of thirty-two? Why me?

"Sure, some of it was luck. And some of it was youth and endurance. But I believe in the fortune of the Gods. Yes I do. The Greek Gods especially appeal to me. Zeus and Hera rewarded those who were bold and decisive. Their heroes didn't have to be particularly good people, not like with modern Christian mythology."

"I hardly consider Christian beliefs mythology," Tricia stated.

Bill gazed upon her in silence for a moment. "I didn't mean to offend you. Here, let's talk of pleasanter subjects. I have some fresh shrimp and chilled champagne. Let's have an appetizer before we take the boat out for a late night supper under the moon. Are you hungry?"

"Starved!"

Over the shrimp and wine Tricia asked Bill about his background.

"We only met two days ago," Tricia said. "I hardly know you at all."

Bill peeled the shell from the last shrimp, dipped it into the cocktail sauce, and popped it into his mouth. He washed down the bite with the last swig of his wine before answering.

"Let's go up on deck and hoist anchor. I'll spin my yarn as I guide the *Adventure* out of port. There's a bit of a storm in the Gulf tonight, so I was planning just a cruise into the bay. Sound okay?"

"Sounds good to me. And what about dinner? These shrimp were good, but they won't hold me through the night."

"Just wait and see. I'll be preparing a special gourmet feast I learned in Rio de Janeiro. It's sort of a fresh fish fajita."

The two climbed up to the deck and cast off the lines. Under Bill's experienced hands the boat forged a path out of the protective breakers and into the middle of the bay. The early moon's glow glittered golden upon the bay's light ripples. As they sailed Bill told his story.

"Born in Seattle, Washington, I started life as the youngest of four children in a middle class family. My mom was a very sweet lady who always seemed to be distracted. Whenever I picture her I visualize an image of a head of gray and black ringlets framing a face that is staring off into the distance.

"In contrast, my Dad was the down to earth type. Down to earth, but never home. His profession was his life, his patients his family. As a family physician, he prided himself that he would always make time for a patient's needs. I doubt that he had dinner with us twice a month. Seeing the kind of chains he wore, I swore I'd never be a doctor!

"Not so my siblings. Two of my three siblings, my oldest brother and my sister, followed in my father's footsteps, both physicians in Seattle. Envenomed by the money bug, my other brother went into business. The last I heard of him he had a huge house overlooking the ocean in Santa Monica and a cabin nestled in the hills of Washington State on two hundred acres. I haven't seen any of them in twelve years.

"I'm afraid I've always been the black sheep of the family. I don't know if I was too smart for school or too dumb. In any case, I dropped out of the tenth grade. Too young to get a job and too short to lie about my age, I stowed away on a boat. Only a day out of port they found me. You can't imagine the anger of that captain! He threatened to set me adrift in the lifeboat, though what he really wanted to do was have the Coast Guard pick me up and take me home. I promised him that if he just kept me until the next port my father would wire the money.

"I earned my passage that trip as a deckhand. Despite the hard work, I loved it! The independence of the sailor's life satisfied me like nectar from the gods. By the time we reached Honolulu I had made friends with the captain and crew. Subsequently I was off on my world adventure. I dropped my parents a letter and never looked back.

"Within a year I had circled the globe twice. Exciting and romantic ports opened doorways of adventure and opportunity. In the Orient I learned hand-to-hand combat skills. I became an excellent marksman with all types of weapons. I hired myself out as a bodyguard, a service in great demand in this dangerous world. It's an easy occupation. Usually just the presence of a body-guard is enough to dissuade any monkey business."

"So that's how I came to my current spot in life. I work when I have to, otherwise I spend my days traveling the world, looking for answers. And now, I find one of my greatest questions has been answered. The question; 'When will I find my true love?'"

The crying of a seagull and the distant ringing of a buoy added musical tones to the nautical sounds of the waves and the whiffing sails. "Coming about!" he called, as he pulled the boom across in a new tack.

Tricia ducked below the boom, then came up again as the boat leaned in its new direction. Bill tied off the lines, setting the automatic rudder in place. A cool breeze teased her hair, causing Tricia to scrunch a little further below the gunwale. "Say, could I have a blanket?" she asked.

"Certainly, My Beauty." He reached into a cabinet and handed her a soft cotton tweed. She cuddled into it, feeling warm and secure.

"See that platform?" he asked as he pointed ahead of them. "We'll pass just to starboard then go on a mile or so and anchor. That's another half hour or so of sailing. After that I'll prepare dinner. Meanwhile, it's your turn for a tale. Tell me about your family."

Tricia settled against the cabin. "I envy your larger family, for I always felt the loneliness of being an only child. In fact, I'm the only child of two only.... Oh. I'm so used to saying that I'm the only child of two only children that it comes out automatically. This is the funniest thing, but I just found out that I may have an aunt!"

Bill looked at her with puzzlement. "You just found out? You didn't know your father had a sister?"

Now it was Tricia's turn to stare. "How in the world could you know it was my father's sister?"

Bill smiled broadly, his face lighting up delightfully. "I suppose I should take credit for having E.S.P. Actually, when you said you had an aunt it could only have been your mother or your father who had the sister. I guessed your father."

Tricia nodded. "I've never met anyone as intuitive as you, Bill.

"I suppose my Mom knows about her, though I don't feel any urgency in tracking down my aunt. I certainly haven't heard from her in all these years. To use your own term, I suppose she must have been the black sheep of the family for no one to have mentioned her. Though, now that I'm thinking about it, I am a little curious. I wonder if she's still alive? Gosh, I may have some cousins somewhere. Wouldn't that be strange?"

Bill shrugged. "I have cousins I've never met. Some families are close knit, others go their separate ways. Tell me about your parents."

A dreamy smile of contentment formed across Tricia's face. "Oh, you would have loved my Dad. Everybody did! He was short, but extremely good looking, with penetrating brown eyes. He wore a sharp manicured mustache and fine black tuxedos. He would take me everywhere, bragging about his beautiful little girl. Everyone in town knew him, from the mayor to the trash collectors. People loved his quick humor and sweet disposition. I loved my father like only a fourteen year old girl can. When he died suddenly of a heart attack I cried for weeks. He was only fifty-two! And he never smoked. I guess bad genes run in my family, though. My grandfather died about the same age of a heart attack, too.

"My great-grandfather made a fortune in stocks in the early twenties, bailing out of the market before the big crash. Just like now, in those days if you had money you could make money, and the Tracys have always had the knack. My grandfather, Herbert, brought his stake to Corpus Christi and started the H.E.B. grocery chain. Eventually his fortune passed to my father, Richard.

My father continued that family tradition of successful investments, eventually making a rather substantial nest egg. Someday soon it'll be mine.

"Dad was wonderful, making wise choices in everything but marriage. Meredith, my mother, must have seemed like the ideal wife I suppose. She was beautiful and rich, the daughter of one of Corpus Christi's established families, the Randolphs. She turned cold and vindictive. It seemed to me that she resented the love my Dad gave me. Maybe she was incapable of loving anyone, I don't know. Listen. My nickname for her was 'the Iron Maiden'."

"You're using the past tense. Your Mom's dead too?" Bill asked. "I thought you said you were going to ask your Mom about your aunt?"

"No, not dead. Estranged. We have very little contact, usually letting our lawyers handle our business needs. When we call each other it's always for specific reasons, never to chat. We haven't seen each other in months. Alma told you that she lives here in town, in a big mansion on Ocean Drive."

"Lots of servants?"

"No. She tried several over the years. People come and clean for her some mornings, but she prefers to live alone. She's not that old, after all. Last May she turned fifty, though you wouldn't know it to look at her. She keeps her hair dyed. My hair color comes from my father, this lovely auburn color … like yours."

They were nearing the oil rig now. Bill took hold of the rudder to guide their boat away from the pilings. As they swung out he asked her "Why do you hate her so? Did she abuse you?"

Tricia considered the question. "Not physically, no. But yes, I'd have to say she abused me. When I was ten or eleven she became paranoid and depressed. She used to blame me for everything, screaming at me and being so hateful. When my father tried to stick up for me she would turn on him with inhuman viciousness. She tried to keep us apart. She tried to keep me from everything I loved. The day after my dad died I moved into the boathouse, a small apartment separate from the mansion. I've never set foot in that house since.

"After I finished high school, I enrolled in the University of Texas at Austin. May of last year I graduated with my degree in journalism and I've been working at the paper ever since. Not an exciting history, I suppose. Soon, though, this may all change. In January I turn twenty-five and gain control of my inheritance. Then it's see the world time!

"Speaking of seeing the world, let's have another story. I love hearing your tales. You're better than a dozen travel agents!"

Bill laughed with her. "Well, I don't think you'd want to see the world the way I have. Sleeping under bridges, eating out of trash cans, drifting from port to port like flotsam may sound like fun, but actually wears a body out.

Although I have enjoyed my body-guarding profession, it hasn't always been a safe haven. Witness the scars I sport."

Tricia reached over and gently touched the gouge across his left cheek. She dropped her hand to his muscular shoulder, giving it a loving squeeze.

"Tell me how you lost your eye? Would you mind?"

Bill gave her a gentle smile. A chill ran through Tricia. She felt that a part of her life that had always been locked away was finally being let loose.

"Of course, My Beauty," Bill answered. "This story began in Indochina about 1971."

Tricia cocked her head in puzzlement. "Indochina? I thought you told Mel it was Nairobi."

Bill let out a short laugh. "Nairobi! Yes, that's where this happened. I was going to tell you a little introductory tale first. But Kenya is where we should start. Right you are.

"It was 1978, I was only twenty-seven at the time but well on my way in my bodyguarding career. Kenya was a wild place then; full of beauty yet pulsing with fear. Have you ever been to Kenya?"

"No," Tricia said, already enthralled by the story.

"Well it's a magnificent country, let me tell you. Americans tend to think of the wild animals, zebras and such. And, truly, it's a naturalist paradise. But this story involves the politics. Kenya's politics have been corrupt and violent for thousands of years.

"My job was to guard Daniel arap Moi, the candidate of Kenya's only legal political party. It was like guarding a piece of cheese in a cave full of hungry rats! Nine out of ten people in that country wanted him dead.

"I wasn't in charge of security, thank Heavens. The police force handled that job, and did it well. I stood as the last line of defense. The goalie. If all else failed I was there to jump in front of the tomahawks.

"We stayed in a suite on the upper floor of the Nairobi Hilton. Through the open windows I could hear the bongo drums echoing across the plains and see the fires dancing in villages a dozen kilometers away. One Saturday evening, for reasons known only to Dionysus, God of madness, Daniel decided to take a walk. The weekend market buzzed with entertainers; jugglers, singers, and musicians. Families carried bags full of their weekend shopping. Merchants strolled through the crowds, hawking their wares. In his double-breasted cream-colored suit Daniel blended in like a lion at a watering hole.

"The hordes, recognizing him from his ubiquitous campaign posters, melted away as we approached. When Daniel stopped to look at a bauble the merchant would agree to any offer just to get him out of his shop.

"All we passed stood quietly, their eyes glued to Daniel. My head swiveled in constant motion, watching these statues. Not even their mouths moved, the betel juice dribbling down their chins. Ahead, the warning of our approach spread forth, Swahili sing-song filtering to my ears like a radio station just out of tune.

"We walked a couple of kilometers down the street before circling back on the other side. I urged him to hurry; the street lights struggled awake with a good twenty blocks remaining to our hotel.

"Only two blocks remained when trouble sprang upon us. Out of the shadows came a tribal attack scream, followed by four leaping assassins. Their jagged daggers glinted in the moonlight. Their screeches echoed off the walls.

"I kicked out Daniel's legs, causing him to crash to the ground with an 'OOF'. My vision beheld a dancing shadow of knives and cutlasses. Spinning in a classic Tai Chi swing, my leg swept them like a broom. Three fell down, pushed off to the right. The fourth jumped nimbly away, retreating to reconnoiter.

"As the three struggled to regain their feet I pulled out my revolver, pumping two shots into each. Even if I didn't kill them I knew it would slow them down enough to give up the idea of the attack.

"I twirled just as the remaining attacker leaped, his knife slicing into my face. Flashing lights exploded in the last view this left eye ever had. I emitted a howl of agony. My knees crumbled. I fell, blood pouring through my hands held against my face.

"I managed to look up through the crack between my fingers with my right eye, expecting to see the thug ready to give me the finishing blow. Instead he stood with raised saber over Daniel, incanting a prayer.

"That two second prayer gave me the time I needed. From my strong crouched position I juggernauted into his side, knocking him flat on the ground, like a rotten totem pole. Grabbing his head in a full Nelson grip, I broke his neck. A reflexive jerk ran down his legs.

"Holding both hands over my left eye I nudged Daniel with my foot. He peeked out from under his arms, his eyes wide in terror.

"'You ... you killed them all?' he managed to ask.

"Despite my pain I had to laugh. 'Sure,' I told him. 'Come on. Let's get out of here.' He ran all the way back to the hotel."

Bill sat quietly for a moment, the sea breezes gently rifting the sails. He brought the boat about, resetting the automatic rudder. He looked across the bay, seeming to head toward a church steeple, shining from floodlights.

Tricia held the blanket tightly around her. *Shivering from the sea breeze*, she told herself.

Quietly, echoing across the boat, she heard Bill murmur.

"Only two blocks further and I'd still have this eye today."

They sailed in silence until Bill dropped the anchor. Tricia stayed on deck as Bill went down to the galley to prepare their meal. She listened dreamily to the serenading night sounds and the distant call of the city. When the sweet smells of dinner reached her, she climbed down to be with Bill.

The gentle lapping of the waves against the *Adventure*'s hull provided a pleasant background to the classical music coming from the tape player. On a small portable stove Bill stir-fried some fresh fish, onions, peppers, and other chopped vegetables. Tricia lounged comfortably on the cabin's cushions as he worked. She inhaled deeply, enjoying the flavor filled sea air spiced by the Brazilian aromas.

"Here." Bill brought the skillet to the table. He filled four tortillas with the sizzling food, two for each plate. Dropping the pan into the sink, he sat down next to her behind the table.

"Eat up. I picked up some baklava for dessert."

After finishing the first one too quickly Tricia decided to nibble at the other one, savoring its many flavors and textures.

"Bill?"

"Yes, My Beauty?"

"You haven't been in town long, have you? I mean, you seem to know your way around so well. You've met so many people. I've lived here all my life, yet you've been in places I've never seen."

Bill smiled, the shifting shadows thrown up by the ship's kerosene lantern dancing against his white teeth. "No doubt what you say is true. Yet many of the places I've been to in this town are places you don't ever want to see. Not that I frequent the brothels, but a sailor does get a different perspective on a town than a socialite. Smoky bars and backroom poolrooms are no place for a lady. Most of the people I've met have never attended any of your parties. Though I have met some lovely people too, like your friend Alma Trevino."

"And Lupè? Where did you meet Lupè? At a bar?"

"A poker game, actually. There's a little tavern off of Laredo Street, so rank it doesn't even have a name on the door. A couple of weeks ago I joined Lupè and a half dozen other fellows there in an all night poker game. Lupè drank too much and lost too much. Afterwards I gave him a few bucks for a taxi ride home. I guess that's why he thought I was his pal. Some people are like that. You do a small kindness for them out of pity and they think you're their friend."

"And that's it? You two met that once?"

"Why?" Bill's voice didn't sound suspicious, just curious. "Is there something special about Lupè you want me to find out for you?"

"No. But he did seem awfully familiar with you. What was it he called you? Nate?"

Bill took longer to answer this time. He cut another bite off of his fajita, gathering a hunk of fish, a slice of red pepper, and a mushroom together on his fork. He chewed slowly and thoughtfully. Then he took a sip of his wine to wash down the food before answering.

"Yeah. Nate. Look, I'm not out of line in insulting Lupè, right? The man is an uncouth lout, a viscous menace of the worst type. I've met some wonderful people in my world travels. You, My Beauty, are in a class by yourself. However, some of the people I've met have not been so nice. When I'm with a new group of people I don't trust, I keep my defenses alert. I keep my back to the wall and my knife unlatched. At that poker game I used a pseudonym; just being careful, you understand."

Tricia felt uneasy, trying not to let it show on her face. "How do I know that William Tucker really is your name? Why should you be telling me the truth?"

Bill started to laugh, but then saw how worried Tricia looked. He reached over to her, carefully holding her face in both his hands. He looked deeply into her eyes, his one brown orb glowing intensely. Tricia felt his touch pulse through her cheeks. Once again, his magic penetrated to her soul, melting her with inexplicable sensations. She wanted to believe him. She needed to believe in him.

"First off, I have no reason to lie to you, My Beauty. I protect my identity with dangerous men, true. But with you, my heart is open, my soul is bare. More important, you know I'm using my real name. We met through your friend Alma Trevino. Remember? She helped me get my insurance and title information together. I couldn't possibly be using an alias and get all that stuff done, now could I?"

For a moment longer she hesitated. Then she closed her eyes, parted her lips and leaned forward. His lips joined hers, sending electric sparks jolting through her body. She reached forward and held him tightly, pulling them together passionately. She became aware of his hands unbuttoning her blouse. The realization shattered the spell. She pushed away from him violently, knocking him against the cabinet above.

"Ouch!" Bill exclaimed. "What happened? I'm sorry, I thought ..."

Tricia shook her head, confused and unhappy.

"Oh, Bill. I'm so sorry. I wish I could make love with you. I want to. Oh, how I want to. But you don't understand."

Bill smiled kindly and took her hands in his. "I can feel your desire in your kiss. Talk to me, My Beauty. What is going on in that beautiful head of yours that is interfering with your heart?"

Tricia bit her lip. She worried that he would reject her. "Bill. You've been with many women before, right?"

He looked at her gravely. "They have no meaning in this conversation. They don't relate to us."

"No. That's not my point. No doubt some of them have been … what is the term? Frisky?"

Bill grinned. "Frisky might be the word all right. What are you trying to say?"

Tricia took her time. She needed to lead into her problem gently so as not to hurt Bill's feelings or her own.

"Well, some were not so frisky, right? I mean, you had to woo some women for quite some time. And even then, perhaps, there were some women who you desired but could never … have. Isn't that right?"

He looked deeply into her eyes, melting her heart, jumbling her mind. "I don't need to have you, Tricia. You're not some sort of conquest for me. I don't have a black book or a score card I keep. I was kissing you because I love you. You are an intelligent, beautiful, loving, lovely woman whom I adore. I think you feel the same way toward me."

Tricia quickly reached out to hug him. "Oh. Oh, Bill. I do! I do! I love you more than you'll ever know. When I see you, when I touch you, when I'm with you, there's magic. My knees grow weak and my mind spins. I want you. I want to make love with you so much that my body aches. I just … I just can't."

Bill continued to hold her, and then gently pushed her back and gazed into her face.

"I do want to understand, Tricia. Please tell me why you can't."

"I … I'm frigid. I'm sorry, Bill. I don't want to be. But I can't have sex. It scares me to death whenever I try. My boyfriend Mel and I have tried it a few times. We've used lots of lubricants and junk. Well, we do have sex, I guess. But it's not fun. It's not what I want between us."

Bill pulled her to him, hugging her lovingly.

"I know more about this than you think, Tricia, My Beauty. It's okay. Don't be frightened. The time will come when you no longer will be troubled. We don't have to make love. I won't leave you or reject you for this. Tonight we'll sleep together in each other's arms. And that's it. We'll just sleep."

Tricia felt tears running down her cheeks, unable to speak. When she did, it came out cracked in tone.

"Thank you, Bill. I feared you wouldn't understand."

They held each other in silence, listening to the sea sounds, rocking with the gentle rhythm of the boat.

"I would like to ask you to do something," Bill said in a quiet, soothing voice. "Something small, but perhaps very important for your problem."

"Anything, Darling. What?"

"No. Maybe I shouldn't ask. Never mind."

Bill held her in silence until she pushed him away to look in his face.

"What is it, Bill? What do you mean, something that could help me?"

Bill turned away from her, gazing out the porthole at the bay waves beyond. When he turned back he seemed to have made up his mind.

"I'd like to get a blood sample from you."

"What?" Tricia found the request not distasteful or frightening, but somewhat bizarre. "A blood sample? Whatever for?"

"This may sound strange, but I know a little about medicine. I spent a year in an Arabic medical school in the Sudan. There are certain tests that can be run; thyroid, electrolyte, hormonal levels."

Tricia shook her head. "You continue to astound me, my fabulous Bill. Do you really think that you can help me?"

He smiled reassuringly. "Maybe. Couldn't hurt, now could it? Would you mind?"

She smiled broadly and shook her head. "Of course not, silly. I'll make an appointment with my gynecologist and see if she can run those tests. She's a good doctor, though, and she's never found anything wrong with me."

"I meant now. I was hoping you'd let me take a sample of your blood now."

"You mean right now? Right here and now? On this boat? You have the equipment for taking a blood sample? Whatever for?"

Bill shrugged. "A good sailor needs to have all sorts of things. Would you mind? We won't do it if you don't want to."

Tricia considered it for a moment and then shrugged. "Sure. Go ahead if you'd like."

She watched with fascination as Bill took out a small box from one of the boat's drawers. He unpacked a rubber tourniquet, some alcohol packets, and a blood drawing needle. Laying three tubes on the table, he wrapped the tourniquet around her left upper arm. After cleaning in the inner elbow, he drew out the first, then the second, and finally the third tube full of blood. He had her sign three labels and attached them to the tubes. Then he placed them in the ship's icebox.

He kissed her again, this time a gentle kiss, a kind touch of trust and faith. She hesitated when he again reached to unbutton her blouse, and then acquiesced. They lay together, each dressed only in underpants, snuggling under a blanket. Tricia felt his warm breath on her neck as she fell asleep, inner spoon.

Tracy's Tidbits
by Patricia Tracy

Corpus Christi Caller Times
Thursday, September 15, 1994

Metro Ministries Serves the Needs

Champaign brunches, spring jaunts to Paris, tux and tail dinners fill the schedules of the privileged. On fine September nights I raced through the empty Texas country, the top down on my Ferrari, the wind rushing through my hair. Last night these fun jaunts came to an explosive end, as my car burnt, sitting in the parking lot.

Though I grieve its loss, I am lucky. I can get another car. For hundreds of Corpus Christians, the loss of their vehicle would be the disaster that sends them over the edge. How can one get to work without a car? How can one pay the rent without working? How can one find another job with no home and no car? Once on the slide, one can spiral down to poverty faster than one can race a Ferrari.

There are those who end up destitute due to their faults, such as over extending in debt, or from alcohol or cocaine. There are those who fall from good fortune by a blow of bad luck, such as losing their job, the death of a spouse, or through illness. Whatever the cause, when one is homeless and destitute, how can one eat? Where does one sleep?

Our society has few safety nets. We have the Rainbow House for battered women. We have the Salvation Army. We have Metro Ministries, a soup kitchen and overnight shelter. When I volunteer at Metro Ministries I see the people who come through; the mentally ill, the drug addicts, the socially incompetent. I used to wonder why they don't just get a job. They can't. They have no clean clothes to wear to apply. They can't even get to the interview.

We, the privileged, can make the difference. Look through your closets and donate your extra clothing. Look in your pocketbook and donate your extra money. Look in your schedule and donate your extra time. Look in your hearts and donate your good wishes.

Saving a life isn't done only by doctors in the E.R. Do you know a cocaine addict? Direct her to the Carter Clinic. See a homeless panhandler? Help him find the Metro Ministries. Your friend wears her dark glasses inside? Bring her to the Rainbow House. The simple actions that you and I take can lead people on the road to recovery.

22

Dovie arranged the bouquet of flowers Tricia had brought her.

"Daisies are my favorite, you know," Dovie remarked. "More than the flowers, I appreciate your company. Turtle was such a presence. He didn't talk a lot, and I suppose when I rambled on I was talking as much to myself as to him. But with Turtle around I never felt lonely. Last night was miserable. The night before, Tuesday night, when he didn't come home, I was worried. Last night, knowing that I'd never see the big fellow again, I tossed and turned and cried all night. Oh, I'm so sad, Tricia. Absolutely devastated."

Tricia hugged her friend securely. They held each other, tears flowing quietly down Dovie's cheeks.

"Have you eaten?" Tricia asked her. "I'll scramble up some eggs and vegetables for some taquitos."

Dovie shook her head. "I don't feel much like eating, Tricia. You can go ahead if you'd like."

"You need to eat. I'm happy to cook for you. Maybe once you smell the food you'll find your appetite."

Tricia was right. Over the delicious aromas and tastes of the Tex-Mex breakfast they talked of Dovie's plans.

"It's very difficult for me, Tricia. Yesterday evening I was looking through some of Turtle's things, trying to decide what to do with them. What do you do with personal treasures? Throw them out because to look at them calls up such painful memories? Leave them in place, trying to hold on to the phantom? Store them in the vain hope that someday you'll know better how to deal with them?"

They sat in companionable silence, drinking freshly squeezed orange juice. Tricia loved living here in Corpus Christi with its balmy weather, fresh citrus fruits, and snow white beach. It was like a tourist spot without all the tourists.

"What are you going to do now?" Tricia asked.

"I don't have any plans. I feel like a washcloth that's been wrung out and left drying crumpled on the washstand. I can't seem to make any decisions. Maybe I'll try to find something to do. I have my dancing and my substitute teaching. There's a Montessori school in town that had offered me a position. Now that the school year's started they've probably already filled it, but I might give them a call. Oh, I can't think about tomorrow right now."

Tricia asked if Dovie wanted to hear about Tricia's day.

"I've gotten involved with a new man. I mentioned Tuesday that Mel and I have sort of broken up. Well, I met this new guy named William Tucker. There's something magical about him; every time I see him I get shivers up and down my spine."

Dovie seemed interested, glad to have something positive to talk about. "Yes, you mentioned Bill Tuesday night. You said you'd just met him?"

"Yes, only three days ago. He's a sailor, just came into town last month."

"Patricia Tracy, I can't believe it! This sounds so unlike you! What are you doing, being swept off your feet by some strange sailor? He must be extraordinarily handsome and glib!"

"Oh, he is. He's been all over the world and has had wonderful adventures. When I hear him talk I'm tempted to chuck everything and sail away with him into the sunset. Doesn't that sound exciting?"

"The sunset is in the west, Tricia. If you sail away from Corpus you'll be going east."

"Okay, don't be so technical. I'm talking about love, here."

"You're talking about adolescent cupidity. But, hey, I shouldn't be the one to pop your bubble. Just don't give him all your money. That's usually what these con men are after."

Tricia smiled. "He's not like that, I promise you."

Dovie began sobbing. "At least you have your man," she said through her tears.

"I'm so sorry for you," Tricia said, getting up to give her friend a hug.

"Oh, poor Turtle. He was so sweet. He deserved so much better out of life. Poor, poor Turtle."

The silence that ensued was shattered by a pounding at the door. They looked at each other in surprise, startled by the intensity of the noise as much as by the unexpected intrusion. Tricia volunteered to answer the knock.

Looking through the peephole Tricia was astounded to find Barbara Dupree standing beyond. She turned to Dovie and whispered her discovery.

"Barbara Dupree?" Dovie seemed totally mystified. "The woman who sold Turtle that car? I've never met her. Well, let her in. Let's find out what she wants."

Barbara appeared just as surprised to see Tricia as Tricia had been to see her. She hesitated at the doorstep.

"This … this is Anna Dove's home, isn't it?" she asked.

"Yes. Mrs. Dove is a good friend of mine," Tricia told her. Dovie came up beside Tricia and extended her hand.

"I'm Anna Marie Dove."

Barbara broke into a smile and took Dovie's hand in a firm shake. "Howdy. It's a pleasure to meet you. I mean, I'm sorry. I mean, I came to express my condolences. Here."

Releasing her hand, she offered Dovie a small bouquet of drooping flowers. Dovie took the offering and invited Barbara into the house. Tricia closed the door behind, shutting out the furnace blast of the morning.

"It's kind of you to come, Mrs. Dupree," Dovie told her. "Would you like something to drink? I have some freshly squeezed orange juice."

Tricia sat on the loveseat across from the big arm chair Barbara had taken. She glared at Barbara suspiciously.

"That would be very nice," Barbara answered. "Though ... you wouldn't happen to have any iced tea, would you?"

"Of course. I'll put the kettle on."

When Dovie disappeared back into the kitchen, Tricia asked, "What are you doing here, Barbara? You hardly knew Turtle."

Barbara brought out a compact case and a box of tissues from her huge reed purse. Squinting through her thick glasses into the tiny mirror, she used the tissues to wipe off her face and clean off her old lipstick.

"Well, I got the address from him when he bought the car. You need that sort of information when you make a business transaction, you know what I mean? After all, the law requires you to register these title transfers. And I don't want to have to pay any taxes that aren't necessary. Who does? It turned out to be useful when the police called me yesterday morning after the crash. He never registered the car. I mean, it's not that you're trying to keep this a secret, are you? I just came by to offer my condolences. I certainly didn't expect to find you here.

"Though your *Tracy's Tidbits* did inspire me this morning. I had no idea you volunteered at that soup kitchen. That's very giving of you. I figured I could give of myself, too. Can you believe it? It's not like I don't have a million other things I could be doing. But just like you, one has to be kind to make the world work."

Dovie came back from the kitchen, sitting next to Tricia on the love seat. "The water will be ready in a minute or two. It's kind of you to stop by."

"Oh, you're welcome. Of course, I hardly knew Mr. Jones, but he did seem like such a nice gentleman. Quiet. Very quiet. But nice. And Big. That's with a capital B. When the two of you went out together you must have attracted a stare or two. What are you, five foot even? Of course, with an escort like that you wouldn't have to worry about being pestered, now would you? Today you just can't be too careful. I don't know what the world's coming to. I read in the paper yesterday that Corpus Christi is on a pace to set a new record for murders this year. Can you believe it? One of my workers was killed in February. And of course, there was Mrs. Garcia, Lupè's wife. Oh. Not that I mean that Mr. Jones was murdered. We don't think <u>that</u>, now do we?"

Dovie put her hand to her chest. "What do you mean, Mrs. Dupree? That seems like a strange thing to say."

Barbara was fidgeting with her purse again. She brought out the same small packet of tissues, taking out another to wipe her glasses. She squinted through them from the opposite direction and placed them back on her peaked nose.

"Well, actually, that's one of the things I've come here about. I mean, really, I came to offer my condolences, just as I said. But after that detective came by to ask me about this fellow's death I figured I should come over and reassure you. Really. The car I sold Mr. Jones worked just fine. There wasn't anything wrong with the brakes. I know there wasn't. You can tell the police that. I told them that. And you," she said as she turned toward Tricia. "And you can tell your boyfriend that too. I honestly don't know anything about Mr. Jones. I never met him before and I surely wouldn't want to kill him. What I want is to be left alone. That's what I really wanted to ask you. I mean, I'm just a hard working woman, an honest business woman who never meant anybody any harm. How could it be my fault that Mr. Jones fell asleep at the wheel and crashed into a retaining wall? It must have been a freak accident. Accidents happen, don't they? I'm real sorry for you, and all." She turned again toward Dovie who was staring at her in horror.

"What are you looking at me like that for?" Barbara asked. "What's wrong with you people?" She looked from one to the other. In the ensuing silence, the sound of the kettle's whistle blew its insistent beckoning. No one moved to get it.

Barbara stood up. "Well, I must have said something wrong. Sorry. Look, forget the tea. I really am sorry about your friend. Or was he your husband? Anyway. Sorry. I've got to be going, anyway. I've got an appointment I'm supposed to be at. Um. Let me know if there's anything I can do. I'm in the book. Under Realtors. Oh, if you want to sell the house, now that Mr. Jones is gone, I mean, here's my card. Don't get up. I'll just see myself out."

Dovie and Tricia stood too, watching Barbara until she reached the door. She turned, seeming to want to say something, changed her mind, and slammed the door behind her.

Dovie stood staring at the closed door. "That woman killed my Turtle," she said, her voice deep and firm.

Tricia turned to her in surprise. "What? What did you say?"

Dovie shook her head, as if breaking away from a trance. "Let me turn off the kettle, I'll be right back."

She returned carrying two mugs of herbal tea. "No sense in letting that hot water go to waste. Here, Tricia, drink this. It'll relax you. Heaven knows I need it after that."

Tricia took the mug from her, taking a moment to smell the delicious aromas. Sipping gently, she savored the delicate flavor on her tongue, the warm spices billowing up into her nose and head.

"Just now, when Barbara left, what did you say?" Tricia asked.

Dovie thought a moment, sipping from her cup and staring at the table. When she spoke her voice seemed dream like, it's deep based tones musical.

"I had an image. Do you believe in E.S.P.?" Dovie shook herself from her reverie to turn to Tricia, searching her face for an answer.

"It's not as simple a question as it might seem," Tricia said. "Most of that stuff like U.F.O.s and past lives seems like hocus pocus. And yet, I can't completely scoff at the supernatural. Some people do seem to have abilities and experiences that go beyond simple scientific explanations. I'm willing to suspend disbelief in your case, Dovie. If anyone has magical powers it surely should be you. And if mind reading were to occur anywhere, this room would surely be the place. I know when you did that Tarot card reading for me here, its accuracy was astonishing."

Dovie paused to take another drink from her mug.

"Okay then. Suspend disbelief. When Mrs. Dupree was sitting there, just a few minutes ago, I suddenly had this image of Turtle being murdered. It was an image like from a dream, yet as real as if it were a photograph. I visualized a sharp knife slicing his throat from ear to ear. Next I saw him in that blue car as it was run into a retaining wall. Someone blew it up, a huge explosion designed to destroy the evidence of his murder. Oh, it was horrible!"

She sat there hugging herself with crossed arms, shaking with tremors. Tricia reached over to hug her, but Dovie shook her off.

"I can't stand it, Tricia," Dovie said. "I could accept Turtle's death by accident. It's a horrible thing, but God gives to us and takes his gifts away. But now that I'm convinced that Turtle was murdered … Oh, I just can't stand it Tricia. It's too horrible for words."

She broke into a wail, a mourner's song such as Tricia had never heard. The columnist watched Dovie rock back in forth, her chant rising and falling in a dark eerie cadence. She got up and began dancing through the house, her eyes half shut, her arms sweeping in strange slow gyrations. Tricia stood and watched, confused and sad.

After several minutes she asked, "Would you like me to stay?"

Dovie didn't interrupt her dance or song, but shook her head no. Tricia slipped out the door quietly, the pervasive chant echoing through her mind.

23

Interview:	Marvin Bevis
Place:	Bevis Construction Co., 2100 Staples Rd.
Date:	Thursday, September 15

Sweeney: As I just explained, I'll be taping this interview. You understand that, right?

Bevis: Yeah, sure. Could we get on with this, Detective? I've got to get back to the job site.

Sweeney: I hope I'm not inconveniencing you too much, Mr. Bevis.

Bevis: Well, the quicker the better. I've got a good crew out there, but its better when I'm there. You never know when something might go wrong. Get it?

Sweeney: I remember one case I had last winter. I was down with the flu and couldn't follow up on a certain clue. I let Sam, here, handle it. Though you did a great job, Sam, I felt antsy that I couldn't do it myself.

Let me just take a moment to mention that this interview is taking place on Thursday, September fifteenth, at Marvin Bevis' construction office. Present today are Marvin Bevis, construction contractor, his secretary, Carol Dorset, Mel Sweeney, detective, and Sam Byrd, police sergeant.

Now, let's get to the point. I'm investigating two car explosions that occurred the night before last. According to the Bureau of Firearms, you reported the theft of two sticks of dynamite recently?

Bevis: Yeah. Like I told the feds, it was some-
                time during the week of August 29th through
                September 3rd. I've had a lot of stuff
                ripped off before, but this is the first
                time they've taken dynamite. Mrs. Dorset
                had to fill in forms out the kazoo.

Sweeney: I bet you got a charge out of that. Get
                it? Explosives? Charge? Well, never mind.
                How'd it happen?

Bevis: Like I told the agents, we followed all the
                rules. The explosives are kept in a locked
                box in a locked shed. The keys to both were
                in a locked desk drawer in the office. Me
                and Mrs. Dorset are the only ones with the
                desk keys. Someone broke into the desk and
                stole the keys.

Sweeney: The office where the desk was, is that the
                paymaster shed, where the wives would wait
                sometimes?

Bevis: Yeah. How'd you know that? People are in
                and out of that office all the time, though
                most of the time it's empty. It's more
                important to be at the job site, you see.
                I gave the feds a list of the people who
                were in and out of the place that week. It
                was a pretty complete list I think. Do you
                want a copy too?

Sweeney: Yes, I sure would.

Bevis: Mrs. Dorset?

Dorset: Give me a minute, Boss. I've got to pull it
                up on the computer here.

Sounds of a printer.

Dorset: Here you go Boss.

Bevis:	Here. See? There're about sixty names on it.
Sweeney:	Heck. It looks like it could have been anyone and his brother. Even the postman made your list. Let me see if I recognize any of these names. Here's Dupree. She's basically your boss, huh?
Bevis:	I suppose you could say that, since I'm her main contractor. I've been with her from the beginning. She can be a real bitch to work with, but she's prompt with her payments. Oops. I forgot you were taping this. Could you edit out that part about me calling her a bitch, please?
Sweeney:	Don't worry. She'll never hear it from me. You've worked with her on all her projects, huh? She told me that she had a hard time coming up with the money at first.
Bevis:	Yeah. Well, I'm not sure I should talk to you about that. Anyway, that was ten years ago. What difference could it make now?
Sweeney:	I worked on a case a couple of months ago about a blackmailer. When he was down and out he found out a dark secret about someone rich. Said he only planned to do a little until he got on his feet. But then, he liked having money so much he kept milking it for all he could get. Now, you tell me that Dupree got a bunch of money illegally ten years ago, and I see her living in a huge mansion, it makes me wonder if maybe she's still getting money illegally.
Bevis:	I didn't <u>say</u> she got the money illegally, Detective, now did I?
Sweeney:	You didn't deny it either.

Bevis: Look, what's past is past. As far as I can tell she runs a legitimate business. That's all I'm going to tell you. I thought you wanted to ask about the explosives?

Sweeney: Okay, that's fair. Let's see who else is on this list. Lupè Garcia. Does he know anything about explosives?

Bevis: Garcia? Nah. I don't think so. He's just a laborer. A good pick and shovel guy, Garcia. If he wasn't too drunk he'd give you a decent day's work. I was real sorry to let him go.

Sweeney: Why did you fire him? Was he dishonest or insubordinate?

Bevis: Sure. Always. But that's not why. Dupree told me that she didn't want him on the job site. She said that if people found out about him being there it might give her development a bad reputation.

Sweeney: Does that explanation make sense to you?

Bevis: Who knows? She's peculiar enough. It's real easy for her to say "fire him", when she doesn't have to find someone to replace him. Once you start firing people it begins to get harder to find good people. You get a reputation, get it?

Sweeney: Mrs. Dupree said that Lupè would make deliveries for her. Any idea what that was about?

Bevis: She recommended I hire him, and then she told me to fire him. I guess he's her boy.

Sweeney: What about his wife, Maria Garcia. She's on this list. Could she have taken the key?

Bevis: Yeah, well, I suppose she <u>could</u> have sto-
                  len the key. Doesn't seem very likely. I
                  hardly knew her, probably couldn't have
                  picked her out of a crowd.

Sweeney: There sure are a lot of names on this list.
                  Let's try a different tack. Can you give
                  me a list of people who were on payroll on
                  August 31st but aren't on payroll anymore?

Dorset: Hold on. That's asking a lot of my com-
                  puter skills. Well, maybe. Okay. Only
                  three. Frank Bernard, Nathan Cohen, and
                  Lupè Garcia.

Bevis: Bernard's okay. He's worked off and on with
                  me for years. Cohen doesn't ring a bell,
                  though. Mrs. Dorset, you remember Cohen?

Dorset: I could pull up his folder in the files.
                  Give me a minute.

Sounds of file drawers and shuffling papers.

Dorset: Not much here, boss. Worked here only four
                  days, Tuesday August 30th through Friday
                  September 2nd. Took his pay on Friday and
                  didn't come back. Wasn't he the fellow with
                  the eye patch?

Bevis: Yeah, you're right. He was a good worker.
                  Bit of a limp.

Sweeney: You have a picture, or references?

Bevis: You don't often get references for jobs
                  like this, Detective. Get it? He came,
                  worked for a few days, and left. It's a
                  common story. I bet Mrs. Dorset's got a
                  dozen files on guys that worked here less
                  than a week this year, huh, Mrs. Dorset?

Sweeney: Mrs. Dorset, do you have a forwarding
                address or Social Security number for
                Cohen?

Dorset: No forwarding address. Here's his SSN.
                I've got his W4 here too. You want a copy
                of his signature?

Sweeney: Please. Say, this number was issued in the
                Northwest, Oregon or Washington State.
                Maybe I can track down Cohen through birth
                records or a relative.

Sound of copier

Bevis: Anything else, Detective? I'd really like
                to get back to the job site.

Sweeney: Be frank with me, Mr. Bevis. I've got two
                sticks of dynamite stolen from your con-
                struction site. I've got two cars blown
                up, one probably involving a murder. Can't
                you help me out a little more than this?

Bevis: Hmm. I don't know if this has any rele-
                vance of not. But when the desk was broken
                into, it looked like someone messed with
                Mrs. Dorset's notary equipment.

Sweeney: Messed with it? You mean someone took her
                notary stamp out of the drawer and used it
                and then placed it back?

Bevis: Well, someone messed with it. They might
                have used it, or just moved it around.
                Mrs. Dorset noticed it wasn't put back just
                right.

Sweeney: Thank you, Mr. Bevis. You never know when
                a clue is going to be helpful. I remember
                a case I had last year when …

Bevis: Excuse me, Detective? Would you mind if we
                  skip the old cases and let me get back to
                  work?

Sweeney: Sure. Okay, Sam. Shut it off.

End of recording.
MS/sb

24

Traveling along Shoreline Drive to the newspaper office always refreshed Tricia. Even when it only took her a mile or so, as with today's trip, the sight of the shimmering bay renewed within her the connection with the seas. A score of sailing ships skipped in the sea. Tricia decided to swing into the boat dock, hoping to find Bill. She parked in the lot and walked out on the dock, but his berth was empty, along with all his lines and accessories. Disappointed, she returned to her car and drove on to the office.

As she neared her desk, she found Jesus standing there, writing her a note. When he saw her, he put it away.

"*Buenas dias, Señorita bonita.*"

"Hi, Poor K. What's up?"

"I have made an important discovery. I have found *Señor* McDonald."

For just a moment Tricia couldn't place the name. "McDonald? Oh yeah! The Bruce from Mrs. Dupree's note. Yesterday you told me that he resigned two months ago and no one knew where he was. How'd you track him down?

"We owe it to you, *Señorita,* your *Tidbits* in today's paper. A contact of mine who had claimed to have no knowledge earlier, read your column and felt he might help *Señor* McDonald. Apparently Mr. McDonald is, as one says, 'down and out.'"

"Where is he?"

"I have an address in Kingsville. You wish to come with me to see if we can find him, *Señorita?*"

"You bet, Jesus. Let me make a quick pit stop to freshen up and I'm ready to go! When did you want to leave?"

"*Ahorita. Vamos.*"[1]

The drive to Kingsville took just under an hour. South of Corpus Christi, the straight two lane highway bisected the flat land, its monotony broken by mesquite and non-pumping oil rigs. Forty years earlier Kingsville had been a booming county seat, capital of the famous King ranch made wealthy first by cattle and then by oil money. The King ranch still had money. Its yearly horse auction brought participants from around the world. With the severe

---

1   Now. Let's go.

depression in the oil market, most of the good oil rigging jobs had disappeared. Kingsville's economy suffered from a ten year slump.

On the way Tricia asked Jesus how his contact had obtained the address.

"I have a few *amigos* who are struggling with their own *diablos. Señor* McDonald is known to one or two of them. It seems that he is a source for snow. *¿Comprendes?*"

Tricia pushed the accelerator to the floor as she tried to pull the rented Cadillac around a cotton loaded truck. What would have been a three second maneuver in her Ferrari brought protesting honks from a semi-tractor approaching them from the other lane as Tricia passed the truck just in time.

"Snow? You mean cocaine?"

"*Si, Señorita.* It seems *Señor* McDonald had a use for the drug of the angels for several years. According to *mi amigo,* the man has been a part of the distribution system for some time. One must ask *¿porqué?* Is this why *Señor* McDonald participated in illegal activities? *¿Para el dinero?²* Is this how he lost his job?"

They discussed what type of approach they should take. Tricia suggested that they act like cocaine buyers that had been sent by Jesus' informant. Jesus didn't like the idea. First off, he pointed out, it would finger the informant. Secondly, he didn't believe in subterfuge.

"I find when I tell people that I am a reporter, most of the time they understand why I ask so many questions. They are more willing to try to answer them. Though, of course, not always *a la verdad.³* Do you wish to lead the interview?"

"Yes, thanks. I know his ex-wife, Marion. She came from old money."

Tricia followed the directions Jesus had written down to the "La Conquistador" apartments, six squalid doors labeled "A" through "F." Three of the ten parking spaces held cars, one with four flat tires and another sat on blocks. A dented pick-up truck guarded the door in front of apartment B. Tricia followed Jesus' suggestion and parked in front of the first apartment. Black smudges from an old fire lined the window frame of apartment "A," a few shards of broken glass offering a shark smile opening. The windows of the other five apartments each sported a window box air conditioner.

Jesus asked Tricia to wait in the car a moment. She watched him disappear around the building. When he returned he politely held the door open for her and took her hand to help her out. He slung his camera case over his arm.

---

2   For the money?

3   With the truth

Jesus' informant had directed them to Apartment E. Second from the far end, it and apartment B were the only ones with air conditioners running. The two reporters knocked on the paint peeled door, the solid thuds bouncing back at them. For several minutes they stood waiting. Tricia turned her back to the door and looked across the street at a strip shopping area. Of four available slots, three were for lease. The one still in use, a Laundromat, had only two patrons.

"I guess no one's home," Tricia said with a sigh. "A long drive for nothing."

Jesus shook his head. "*No, Señorita.* I saw him peek around the curtains. We wait. He'll answer soon."

Jesus knocked on the door again. Just like the first one, his knock came in three strong steady sounds, no increased force or signs of impatience. Eventually he knocked a third time.

"Maybe he got out the back door?" Tricia suggested.

Jesus shook his head. "No back door and the *baño* window is too small. He'll answer."

Sure enough, a male voice finally called from the other side of the portal. "What do you want?"

"Mr. Bruce McDonald? My name is Patricia Tracy. Could you open the door please?"

"What do you want?" the voice repeated. "I'm not interested in buying anything. I don't have time for surveys. I don't want to register to vote."

"We're with the newspaper, Mr. McDonald," Tricia told him. "We'd like to talk to you."

After a long stretch of silence the voice called back. "So you finally tracked me down, huh? Well, it won't do you any good. Go away. I'm not interested in talking to any reporters."

"We're not the police, Mr. McDonald," Tricia called out. "What harm can it do to talk to us?"

Again there was a pause. Tricia saw a face peek out from around the curtains and study them. It searched the parking lot, straining to reach the corners of the window's view. The curtains fell back into place. Tricia heard the chain lock being lifted and then the dead bolt lock being turned. The door opened inward, letting out a blast of highly air conditioned apartment air.

"All right. I guess I have no choice. Come on in then."

It took a few moments for Tricia's eyes to adjust to the gloom. The efficiency apartment came furnished, if you were generous enough to call the decrepit pieces furniture. An unmade bed held a mattress deeply indented as if it had seen years of use by a hunchback. A plastic coated particle board table lay hidden under a landscape of fast-food take out bags. A small kitchenette had dirty dishes overflowing the sink and the miniature counter top. The refrigerator door lay open, empty except for a half full bottle of beer and two open cans of soft drink. Besides a slight glow coming in from the closed curtain, the ice box's bare light bulb provided the only illumination. Cigarette butts lay everywhere, having polka-dotted the carpet with their burn marks.

The room reeked of mold, stale tobacco, and rotten food. From the window the air conditioner roared, accompanied by an occasional slight rattle. Tricia shivered in the fifty degree temperature. She suppressed a quick wave of nausea as she saw a dozen cockroaches scramble off the counter, disturbed by the light from the door. They returned at their leisure, accompanied by a score of their comrades.

Composing herself, she held out her hand. "Good afternoon, Mr. McDonald. I'm Patricia Tracy with the Caller Times, and this is my comrade, Jesus Morales."

Bruce McDonald looked uncertain for a moment. Without answering he took her hand in a weak handshake, followed by Jesus'. Bruce indicated that Tricia could take a chair as he plopped down on the edge of the bed. She pulled out the wobbly one tucked under the table, and taking a paper napkin from a spilled Burger King bag, wiped the crumbs and slime off the chair. She settled into it, bringing out a small pad of paper and a pencil. Jesus stood quietly near the door, his arms crossed.

Tricia studied Bruce before beginning. He certainly didn't have the appearance of a man who recently held a responsible position in the Public Works Department. Uncombed graying hair added a circle effect to unruly beard. God had forgotten to paint his face, sporting pale lips, indeterminate eyebrows, and light gray eyes. Perhaps Bruce had used up all the color just like he used up all the rest of his life. Below his sagging face, flabbed a saggy body. The bed creaked in protest as it shifted under his weight.

"Mr. McDonald, we understand that you recently resigned from the Public Works Department."

"Resigned? Is that what they told you? Yeah, I suppose so. I was advised to get out of town quickly and to keep my mouth shut. So I did. Now that you've found me I suppose I'll have to move again. Not that I'm too sure that jail would be any worse than this life. Yeah. I suppose it would."

"What is it that you're supposed to keep your mouth shut about, Mr. McDonald?" Tricia asked.

Bruce looked at her with cocked head, and turned to look at Jesus, who remained immobile. "What do you already know?" Bruce asked

Tricia turned to Jesus, indicating he should answer.

"Many problems are showing up with your past work, *¿no?* Were you making *muchos* mistakes or just slack on your standards?"

Bruce laughed, a low rumble that indicated that he really didn't think there was anything funny involved.

"*Muchos* mistakes, huh? Yeah. That's it. *Muchos* mistakes. That's the story of my life. I married a rich bitch. Yeah, that was my first mistake. She turned me on, then divorced me when I couldn't get turned off. Yeah, *muchos* mistakes. The story of my life."

"Your wife turned you on to cocaine, *Señor?*"

Bruce stared at him, then lowered his head and nodded dejectedly. "Yeah. Cocaine. That's my curse all right."

"How long have you been divorced?" Tricia asked.

Without looking up, Bruce said "One year. It was easy when Marion paid the bills. We had champagne with breakfast, lunch, and dinner. At her parties cocaine came out like canapés. At first I didn't touch the stuff. Then I took a little just to be social. Soon it was morning, noon and night. Marion started complaining about the expenses. Yeah. Even the rich bitch couldn't afford a thousand bucks a day for my habit.

"I tried to make ends meet by dealing the stuff, but I was snorting up more than my profits could support. My work suffered, sure. It was a mess."

Jesus asked, "You say your work suffered? *¿Porqué? Es possible* you did more than sloppy work, *¿Si?*"

"What do you mean?"

Tricia answered with a question. "Tell us about Barbara Dupree, Mr. McDonald."

Bruce stared at her, his pale face drooping in despair. "So. You know about her, huh? Well, that was the big one, all right."

Jesus prompted, "But not the only one, *¿Si?*"

Bruce nodded. "No, there were others. But Dupree was the big one. She had a lot of money sunk into that property. When she failed the watershed test that land suddenly became useless. I let her know that maybe I could fix her problem."

"*¿Porqué* the land failed?"

"The drain-off will inevitably get into the city's water supply. They're overbuilding along the Nueces River. The perking there hasn't the flow necessary to decontaminate the sewage. And the elevation is too low to compensate with accessory fields. Once that place gets built it's going to be a big mess to fix it right."

"So you altered the report for her and charged her $50,000 for that change?"

"You already know about that, huh?"

"I imagine your salary doesn't provide that much take home pay in a year."

Bruce rubbed his fingers across his palm, looking like he could still feel the money in his hand. "You're so right I deserved it. Besides, what's fifty thousand dollars to Barbara Dupree? Have you seen her house? She must be loaded!"

"Why didn't you get help?" Tricia asked. "There are several good rehabilitation programs. Your insurance would have paid for a full course at Charter Hospital or the Carter Clinic."

"Ha! Yeah, right. Sure, they'd pay for my rehabilitation. They'd pay by firing me. I suppose it would have been better in the long run. You just don't see that when you're getting high on the snow. Now look at me. Cold turkey. Living in hiding on the dregs of my savings. No future. Nowhere to go. Nothing to do."

The three were silent. Bruce's head had drooped, his face covered by his hands. After a couple of minutes he shook himself and got up. He walked over to the table and shifted through some crumbled packs, trying to find one that might still have half a cigarette in it.

"Either of you smoke?" he asked. Both reporters shook their heads.

"Damn," he said. "Well I've got to have a smoke. What time is it anyway?"

Tricia looked at her watch. "Two thirty."

"I haven't eaten today. Could you loan me a fifty and maybe take me over to Whataburger? I guess you'll be turning me over to the police, huh?"

Tricia looked at Jesus whose expression remained calm and non-committal.

"I think when we publish this story the police will come looking for you. Perhaps it is a good time for you to think about your future. *¿Si?* If you choose to go to the police on your own, perhaps they may be more considerate."

Tricia added, "You can't live like this much longer, Mr. McDonald."

He looked around. "Yeah. You're right about that. I'm too chicken for suicide. And I'm too old and too tired to run. Yeah. Do you think they'll throw me in jail?"

"I doubt it," Tricia answered. "You didn't kill anybody. But you will need a good lawyer."

Bruce stood in silence for a moment, staring at the floor.

"You want us to drive you to Corpus Christi?" Jesus offered.

Tricia felt like smacking him. If Bruce accepted the offer she could hardly refuse. She didn't cherish the thought of transporting this fat, stinking, cigarette smoking slime ball on an hour's trip in a closed up Cadillac. She held her breath as Bruce considered the offer.

He said, "Nah. I'll need to think about it. I could use some money, though. You got a twenty you can lend me?"

Jesus shook his head. "No."

Bruce turned to Tricia. "You? Please. Look, I gave you some information. How about helping me out?"

She considered a moment. Charity was one thing, but handing out money to this cokehead seemed ridiculous. Still.

With a sigh she took a twenty dollar bill out of her purse and handed it to Bruce.

"Thanks," he said with a smile.

The acknowledgment lit up his face. She saw some vestige of what once might have been a handsome, ambitious, intelligent man. Bruce's features fell back to their same pale blandness.

"Forget the ride," he said. "I'd just hold you up. Why don't you guys head back to Corpus? Yeah. Go back to your young happy lives. I was once like you. I remember being young and happy. Yeah. Go on. Get out of here. You got what you wanted."

Tricia rose as Jesus held the door for her. The bright Texas sun reflecting off the concrete added to the oppressive heat, hitting the two of them like a tropical wave slamming onto the beach. They opened the four car doors, and Tricia leaned in just to start the motor and turn the air conditioner on full. The two reporters waited until they could sit on the over-heated seat cushions without getting burnt before heading back home.

25

Interview: Jack
Date: Thursday, September fifteenth
Location: Lonesome Coyote Tavern

Sweeney: Thank you for allowing me to tape this
                 interview Jack. Present for this inter-
                 view are Jack, no other name, no occupa-
                 tion, Sam Byrd, police sergeant, and Mel
                 Sweeney, police detective. How are you,
                 Jack?

Jack: Jack cause nobody no problem. No need
                 bother Jack.

Sweeney: We're not here to bother you, Jack. I just
                 need to ask you some questions. Sally told
                 us that you used to hang out with Lupè
                 Garcia.

Jack: Lupè okay if not drunk. Lupè hit people.
                 Jack no hurt nobody.

Sweeney: Sally told me that you and he hung out
                 together a lot. She said you and Lupè and
                 Maria were good friends.

Jack: Maria nice to Jack. Maria buy Jack a
                 Coke.

Sweeney: Do you remember the last time you saw Maria
                 here?

Jack: Jack thirsty. You buy Jack a Coke?

Sweeney: Miss Bellows, please bring Jack a Coke.
                 Thanks. Now, Jack, do you remember Maria?

Jack:	Sure, Jack remembers. Maria nice to Jack. Buy Jack Cokes and sometimes wings. Even rode with Jack to hospital once when Jack have seizure.
Sweeney:	Tell me about the last time you saw Maria.
Jack:	Not sure which were last time. We drink together, Maria and Lupè and Fat Bob and Nate.
Sweeney:	Nate? Could that be short for Nathan?
Jack:	Jack don't know.
Sweeney:	Does this Nate have an eye patch and a limp?
Jack:	Yep, that's Nate.
Sweeney:	Tell me about that time, Jack. What do you remember?
Jack:	We drinking together and Maria poke him in ribs and say "Ain't you Bert?" Something like that. Nate get mad, then happy, and buy everybody drinks.
Sweeney:	Bert? Who's Bert?
Jack:	Maybe Benji? Jack not sure.
Sweeney:	Jack, you're on medicines for your seizures, huh?
Jack:	Jack take pills good. You wanta see? Here.
Sweeney:	That's a big selection, Jack. How do you keep them straight?
Jack:	Jack know his pills. Take three with orange stripes every day.

Sweeney:	Let me see. Dilantin. And this one's Depakote. And this one's Valium. You take Valium for your seizures, Jack?
Jack:	Valium stop seizures. Jack feel jittery, Jack take Valium. Not everyday.
Sweeney:	What else do you do with the Valium? Ever sell one or give one away?
Jack:	Jack shouldn't say. You trying to trap Jack?
Sweeney:	You're right, Jack. That would be illegal. But, you know, I really need to know. I promise I mean you no harm. Maria was nice to you, and we're trying to find her.
Jack:	Jack like Maria. Would like to help.
Sweeney:	Did you give or sell any of your pills to Nate?
Jack:	Yep. Jack sell three Valium to Nate.
Sweeney:	What else can you tell me about Nate, Jack?
Jack:	Nate love yaky-yaky. Tell stories. He fight in war. Green Beret. He guard people. He kill people. Many stories. Jack like listen Nate.
Sweeney:	Jack, you were saying Fat Bob was there too. Are Bob and Maria good friends?
Jack:	When Maria drunk, she good friends with everyone. Yukk-yukk. She kiss boys.
Sweeney:	I had an interesting case last summer where a couple was running an adultery scam. She'd be picking up rich men and taking them home for sex. The husband would bust in on them and then the two would black-

mail the poor rube. So, you've seen Bob and Maria kissing?

Jack: Lupè pass out. Maria play.

Sweeney: Did you ever see Bob give Maria money?

Jack: Yep. He like Maria. Kissy. Give money.

Sweeney: I understand that Fat Bob comes here often. He makes a lot of friends?

Jack: Yep. Bob and Jack go way back. Bob buy Jack Coke and wings. Jack tell Bob all about people Jack meets.

Sweeney: Are Fat Bob and Nate good friends?

Jack: Yep. They yaky-yaky.

Sweeney: Do you know what Fat Bob and Nate talk about?

Jack: No, Jack not hear. Jack see money though.

Sweeney: You saw money, Jack? Who was paying who?

Jack: Jack not know. You buy Jack some wings?

Sweeney: Okay. Miss Bellows, please bring Jack an order of wings. Jack, do you know who Barbara Dupree is?

Jack: No.

Sweeney: Big glasses, big bottom, gray ponytail. Talks a lot.

Jack: Oh, yeah. Jack know her. She not friendly to Jack, never buy Jack a Coke.

Sweeney: What have you noticed about her?

Jack: Jack not notice.

Sweeney: You haven't noticed her talking to Nate or other sailors in here.

Jack: Maybe. Lots of people here yaky-yaky. Some buy Jack a Coke.

Sweeney: I guess we'd better be going. Enjoy your wings, Jack. You've been a big help.

Jack: You find Maria?

Sweeney: We're trying Jack. Here Miss Bellows, keep the change.

Bellows: Hey, thanks. Don't forget tomorrow is Friday night. Maybe Fat Bob or that sailor will be back.

End of recording.
MS/sb

26

During the ride back to town Tricia and Jesus discussed the interview. Jesus took notes and together they developed copy for a preliminary article. Back at the news building, Jesus and Tricia put the report together. Jesus left to run it past Bob, and Tricia went to work on her *Tidbits*. Excited about her evening plans to be out with her friends, Tricia put together a column about the social scene.

She fought rush-hour traffic all the way back to her townhouse. She became so aggravated with the Cadillac's inability to weave through the traffic she began honking and getting dirty looks. Once home, she lolled in a long hot shower, washing off the aggravation of the drive, as well as the sweat and smells of McDonald's apartment.

Tricia threw a dozen outfits on her bed in search of the right one for the night's activities. Choosing a black pants suit, she finished her make-up and left her home a little after seven.

Though Tricia arrived almost an hour after the appointed time, Becky hadn't finished dressing. Martha offered to bring Tricia a cocktail as the younger woman climbed the stairs to Becky's bedroom.

"Jack Daniel's Old Fashioned," she requested.

"And no forget crush fruit," Martha added, before Tricia could say it. Tricia smiled and nodded.

Tricia found Becky primping in the boudoir, sipping a colorless refreshment. A green olive bounced happily as she set the glass firmly on the make-up tabletop.

"Oh. Hi, Tricia. Here already?"

"It's seven thirty," Tricia said. "We were supposed to be meeting Pam and Alma at the Cannery a half hour ago."

Tricia watched Becky's reflection line its eyes in the mirror.

"Well," the blonde said. "We'll be there eventually. Why don't you have a drink? I'm sure they're having one."

"Martha's bringing me one."

Tricia watched in fascination as Becky continued her preparations. As a model, Becky had once told her, she would sometimes change her make-up seven times for a single shooting. Each time the application had to be perfect.

"Your boyfriend was here this afternoon," Becky said, touching the underside of her cheeks with a darkening hue.

Tricia's eyebrows lifted in surprise. "Bill was here?"

Becky turned to look at Tricia, curiosity broadcast on her face. "Bill? Who's Bill?"

Tricia blushed. Now why would Bill have come to visit the Smyths? Becky had meant Mel of course.

"Oh, nobody. So Mel was here, huh?"

Becky turned back to the mirror, putting on a few more touches. Martha arrived with drinks for each of them. Tricia took a small sip of hers, savoring the rich flavors. Becky drained hers, putting both this empty glass and the one from her prior drink on Martha's tray. Becky waited for the chubby maid to leave.

"Yeah, Mel. Remember him? Tall police detective you used to love. How long ago was that, anyway? Tuesday?"

Tricia smiled at Becky's sarcasm. "So what did Mel want? Is he going to charge you with sexual crimes against the state?"

Becky gave her a raspberry. "You're so silly. He brought a box of old letters to Martha. Okay. Now 'fess up. Who's Bill?"

Tricia hesitated. She hadn't really planned on telling Becky about Bill. After all, she had only known him these few days. But especially after last night, he filled her every thought.

Tricia shrugged, trying to appear nonchalant. "Just a guy."

Becky didn't reply right away as she carefully applied the lip liner, completing her make-up. She led Tricia back to the bedroom where she had laid out her clothes for the evening. A green pencil-strap dress with a low-cut back lay stretched out across the bed. Holding it up, she asked, "Like?"

Tricia whistled in appreciation. "On anyone it would look hot. It'll make you absolutely stunning."

Becky blew her a kiss of appreciation. Lifting the dress over her head it slipped on easily. At Becky's request, Tricia fixed the back.

"If he's 'just a guy', how come you thought I was talking about him when I said your boyfriend had come by? Tell me the truth now, Tricia. Who's Bill?"

"He's Mr. Wonderful, that's who. He lives on a boat at the dock. Last night we went out sailing. I had the most enchanting evening of my life."

Becky looked up from the high heels she was working with to give Tricia a smile. "That's great! I'm so happy for you. You've been doing a lot of sailing recently, huh? Monday night you were out on the bay, too."

"That was the same boat. Did I already tell you about him? It was his boat that I swam to shore from."

Becky looked at her quizzically. "Yeah? I thought you said he was screwing Alma. What's this about? Are you stealing Alma's man?"

"He and Alma aren't still.... I mean. That was never serious. But with me, he's really committed!"

For a moment it looked like Becky was going to comment. Instead she shrugged. "Ready to go?" She asked. "We'll talk in the car on the way over."

She led them downstairs. "We'll take your car, okay?"

At the bottom of the steps Martha was waiting. In one hand she held a tray with another set of drinks. Draped over the other arm lay Becky's coat.

"Thanks, Martha," Becky said, picking up her drink and carefully sipping through the small swizzle straw. She finished it quickly, leaving the empty glass on the tray. Tricia picked hers up, noticing that Martha had conveniently made it in a plastic take-along glass. She took a sip, finding it as delicious as the first drink. She returned it to the tray.

"You have quite a talent with this," she told the maid.

"*Gracias.*"

"But since I'm driving I'd better leave it here. Say, Martha, Becky told me that Mel was here. When was that?"

"*Hace tres horas.*"

"Three hours ago? What did he want? Was he asking about me?"

Martha shook her head, regret showing on the ponderous features.

"*No, Señora.* He brought letters."

"Oh. Doesn't sound like there's anything of interest to me there, huh?"

"Maria, she have big box, letters from my sister, Juanita. She have letters and pictures from *su tia,* Beverly."

"My aunt? You have letters written by my aunt? And maybe a photograph of her? Can I see them?"

Becky interrupted. "Come on, Tricia. Let's get going. You can look at old family letters later. Surely you've read letters from your aunt before."

Tricia turned on her. "I only found out two days ago that I even <u>had</u> an aunt. I've never seen any letters from her."

Becky stepped back, holding her palms up in defense. "Okay, okay. Sorry. I suppose if a girl can't keep track of her relatives one has to make allowances."

"*Si Señora.* When you want? *Ahora?*"[1]

Tricia looked at her watch and sighed. "No, we're running so late already. I'll come back soon, though. Okay, Becky. Let's go."

As they stepped out the door Becky stopped short.

"You're driving that Cadillac? Oh my God, I just remembered! I read in this morning's *Tidbits* that your Ferrari blew up!" She looked over and saw the grief on Tricia's face.

---

1   Now?

"Oh, I'm so sorry, Tricia. What happened?"

"It burnt up," she said sadly. "I think it was arson. There's this nut named Lupè Garcia who's been harassing me. I've told the police, but I don't think they can do anything about it."

They climbed into her car and Tricia headed toward the nightclub.

"So tell me about Bill," Becky prompted.

"It's going to sound silly to you, Becky. But, okay. Do you believe in love at first sight?"

"Sure. The first time I saw a picture of Fabio I went ga-ga."

They both laughed. "No," Tricia insisted. "I mean really! Have you ever seen someone from across the room and felt like you two were destined for each other? Was it that way for you and Larry?"

Becky laughed, a soprano trill of pleasure.

"No, Tricia. We had to work hard at it. Sure, we had that unexplainable romantic attraction. But I think there was a lot of reasoning involved, too. Here I was, an eighteen year old high school graduate in search of a rich husband. And here he was, a forty year old recent divorcee in search of a trophy bride. We fit each other's expectations and needs. I suppose there's some of that in any successful marriage.

"Which is not to say we didn't love each other. But I don't think it qualified as love at first sight. As I remember it, we had lots of lust at first sight, if that counts for anything."

"But you're avoiding the subject again," Becky said. "Tell me about Bill. I'm not going to say another word until you answer."

"We met Monday afternoon. You remember the Mayor's fund raiser? I don't think I saw you there."

"I was there for a little while. Arthur and Larry were friends."

Tricia continued. "In any case, Bill was there as Alma's date. Apparently she had helped him with some legal question or other. When I saw him from across the room I felt a chill pass straight through me. I don't know why. But every time I see him I have the same effect. It's as if we were lovers in a past life."

"So then what happened? You went out with Alma and him on his boat that night?"

"Yes. We went for a midnight sail. Well, I told you already about waking up and jumping off the boat. I guess I was already in love with him. Maybe that's why I left the boat, struck with jealousy. In any case, I met with him the next day. Next thing I knew, we spent last night together on his boat."

"Really! Why Tricia, I didn't know you were such a fast girl!"

"Oh, nothing hap ..."

"Go on," Becky urged. "Did something happen or didn't it?"

Tricia looked confused. "I'm not sure. I mean, a girl should know, shouldn't she? But when I woke up this morning … Well, never mind."

"So tell me, what's he like, this mysterious Bill? He owns a boat you say? He must be fairly well off."

Tricia snorted. "Hardly. I think the boat is all that he owns. Bill's a sailor. Yet, oh, so much more than a mere sailor. He's a free spirit who travels the world. The stories he tells of adventures in exotic places make me catch my breath. It really makes me want to drop everything and run off with him.

"Based on his stories, I guess he's a bit over forty. You should meet him, Becky! He's terribly good looking, with rippling muscles and a patch over one eye. Though he's every bit the gentleman, he's been in some nasty scrapes, even has to walk with a cane. You know, he saved my life with that cane! It's true! That first night, Monday night after the party, Lupè Garcia attacked me with a knife! Bill knocked the knife out of his hand with a swing of his cane. I think he broke Lupè's arm."

"Wow! A knight in shining armor to the rescue, huh? No wonder you're infatuated with this guy. I'm not so sure I can call him an improvement, though. First you go for a cop and now for a sailor. Didn't your mama ever teach you the value of education and status?"

"Oh, she tried, Becky. She tried. Now don't get too excited. I didn't say I was going to marry this guy. Though … I do miss him. I haven't seen him all day since he left me off at the dock this morning. Maybe I'll drop by his boat later tonight and see what he's up to."

They found The Cannery humming. Almost two hundred people squeezed into a restaurant and bar that should have held half that number, with closely packed tables and booths creating an obstacle course. In the lounge, a long wooden bar stretched along one wall. People rested on each bar stool and stuffed themselves in between. The pint sized tables hardly left room for a bowl of popcorn and a couple of drinks. The patrons carried on boisterous conversations, nearly shouting so the person next to them could hear.

They found Alma and Pam stationed at a back table. Alma's long black dress stretched suggestively over her body as she and Pam watched the young men watching them. Turquoise earrings and matching necklace complimented Alma's green eye shadow and shoes.

Alma had met Pam, a new addition to their circle of friends, a few months ago. Pam worked as a legal secretary for a real estate attorney. Since then the two women had been bar hopping several times. Pam finalized her divorce two months ago. She now described her interests as finding the most screwable men in town, and then screwing them.

"Hi!" Becky shouted to them, as she and Tricia pushed their way to their table.

"Hello yourself," Alma answered. "Let's see...." She paused to consult her watch. "Only ninenty-three minutes late. Not bad for you, Becky. You're two drinks behind though."

"No we aren't," Becky said. "We had ours before we left home. So how are the pickings? Any new prospects?"

Becky signaled the waitress who waved, indicating that she had seen them and would get over to them whenever humanly possible.

"Hello Alma, Pam," Tricia said. She set her purse on the floor, and leaned on the table, with no available seat. "How have you been?"

Pam smiled. Her lids were heavy, the make-up pretending to hide the effects of too many late nights laden with too much alcohol. "I've been fine, thanks. You?"

Tricia nodded. "Okay. And how's Peter?"

Alma laughed. "Peter is passé, Tricia. That was last month's man. Besides, he was too nice to Pam. You know she only likes them when they're mean and thoughtless."

Pam smiled and shrugged. "So who's looking to get hitched to a nice boy? The self centered ones are easier to drop."

Tricia looked over the three women. Alma winked at her, smiling in return of her greeting. In contrast, Becky and Pam had their attentions shifting around the room, scanning the males.

The waitress came to their table, bringing a beer for Pam and a Bloody Mary for Alma. Becky ordered a gin and tonic, Tricia requested Jack Daniels Old Fashioned.

"And make sure they crush the fruit," she told the waitress.

As the waitress left Tricia recognized someone standing at the bar.

"Look! There's Barbara Dupree!"

Becky and Pam looked in the direction Tricia pointed. Alma continued to look at her drink.

"Let's not all look at once," Alma muttered.

"Oh, no one will notice us in this crowd," Tricia said. "Do any of you know Barbara?"

Alma and Becky shook their heads. Pam said, "I do. She's a pretty aggressive realtor here in town. My firm does a lot of closings with her properties. Frankly, she's a bitch. I'd rather not attract her attention."

"Look," Becky said. "Some man has just come up to her. Oh, what an awful looking suit. It must be twenty years old."

"Oh my God," Alma said. "That's Harry Harper, a scumbag attorney if there ever was one. Do you suppose Harry and Barbara are having an affair?"

"Ooh," Pam whined. "That's disgusting! I know those two people and they're both disgusting!"

"Well at least they have that in common," Becky said. "Some couples don't even have that."

Pam giggled.

Barbara stood up suddenly and began scanning the room. Tricia turned her head and said, "Somebody watch her and see if she's looking for me."

"Oh God, I hope she's not coming over here," Pam said. "I couldn't stand listening to her voice. Please, God. Don't let her see us. Please God. Please. Please."

"Too late," Becky said. "She's seen us. She's getting up. She's coming over."

"Damn." Pam said.

Becky said, "No. I'm wrong. She's going toward the restrooms I guess. Another crisis avoided."

Pam sighed. "Ha! Praying does work! Oh, look. That guy looks interesting."

Having made eye contact, a young fellow in dude cowboy attire ambled over to their table. He looked Pam in the eye, placing his beer on their crowded little table. Tricia examined his hand as he did this. She approved at finding it to have been scrubbed so clean it shone pink. The hand was attached to a thick muscular arm, and that to a broad bulging chest. The top three pearl snaps of the fancy shirt hung open, the collar pushed apart by chest hair. All in all he looked as macho as a Marlboro billboard.

"Howdy ma'am. Can I buy you a drink?" His Texas drawl stretched out the words, making the invitation sound musical with his deep tones. He looked expectantly into Pam's eyes, who returned his gaze happily.

"Sure, cowboy," she said, as she stood. "Let's head for the bar." Tricia took her seat.

"Well, one down," Alma said, watching Pam disappear into the crowd. Turning back to the group she asked Becky, "How have you been? Had any good modeling contracts lately?"

"I went to four interviews this week, but I didn't get any assignments. It's incredibly competitive. You can't imagine. I'm only twenty-five years old, in the prime of life, yet these eighteen year olds are already beating me out. Well, there's always next week."

The waitress came with their drinks. Becky downed hers quickly, Alma and Tricia sipping on theirs. The women discussed their lives, single women in a world that bubbled with opportunities. Their talk turned to dating.

"Pam certainly had no trouble finding a man for the evening," Alma said. "How about you, Becky? You've already been here thirty minutes. Have you picked out your prey for the evening?"

"Umm. Now that you mention it...."

Becky's reply got no further as a distinguished gray-haired fellow in a business suit came up to their table.

"Why, Rebecca Smyth! For God's sake! How have you been, you tigress?"

He leaned down to share a peck on the lips with the blonde model. She turned and directed his attention to her tablemates.

"Fred Scouras, let me introduce you to two good friends of mine. This is Alma Trevino, an attorney."

"*Mucho gusto por conocerlo usted, Señora bonita,*"[2] Fred said in perfect Spanish, leaning forward and applying a kiss to the back of Alma's hand.

"*Igualamente, Señor,*" Alma replied.

"And this," Becky said, indicating Tricia, "is my friend Patricia Tracy. Perhaps you've read some of her writing in the paper."

"Of course I know Miss Tracy," Fred said. In answer to her somewhat puzzled look he explained. "Your father used to bring you into my gallery."

"Oh! Frederick Scouras. You're an art dealer, aren't you?"

Fred smiled in deprecation. "I do make a feeble attempt at dabbling in the arts. Your father was always very kind to me. Perhaps you have some of the pictures that he purchased from my gallery? A Picasso? A Hopper?"

Tricia shook her head. "Nope. All the art work resides in my Mom's home. You still have your gallery over on Doddridge?"

"Retired. I'm a little in-between businesses right now. I maintain a small inventory if you're interested?"

Tricia laughed. "My art collection days will have to wait until I get my inheritance. Meanwhile I'm concentrating my resources on replacing my car. Still, give me your card. I'd love to keep in touch."

With a flourish he brought out a gold calling card case from an inner vest pocket. From it he extracted a bright purple card which he held out for Tricia. When she reached to take it, he took her hand in both of his and kissed it, sending a chill down her spine.

---

2   A great pleasure to meet you, beautiful lady.

Fred turned his attention back to Becky. "I was so sorry to read about Larry's death. What a tragedy. And he was so young, too. I must chastise myself for not calling to offer my condolences on a timelier basis."

Becky nodded slightly. "Thank you, Fred."

"You seem to be doing pretty well."

"Life goes on."

"Have you eaten? Perhaps you could join me for dinner?"

With a wink at her friends, she said "That sounds great! Let's go! Bye, girls."

As she walked off Tricia shook her head. "Wow! That didn't take long, did it? What about you, now? Will you be running off with some guy in the next five minutes?"

Alma shrugged. "That seldom turns out to be my fate, Tricia. Our two companions have the looks to attract them. And by 'the looks', I mean more than just beauty. Haven't you noticed the men who look your way?"

Tricia looked around in surprise. "Me? Who? I haven't noticed anyone."

"And that's why they haven't been able to get through to you. Your antennas are down. In contrast, Pam and Becky keep their reception open. Never mind. At least we have each other to talk with this way."

"You're not always unsuccessful with the men," Tricia noted. "You and Bill seemed to get along well."

"Yeah, he was a fine one. But Bill's a transient. Here today, gone tomorrow. Or, in his case, here yesterday, gone today."

"What do you mean?"

Alma looked at her in surprise. "Hmm? I didn't know you cared about him. Say, have you been holding out on me? Did you two get together this week?"

Tricia blushed. "Well, actually, yes. We've seen each other a couple of times. I didn't mean to step in on your act."

"Oh, think nothing of it. Just a one night stand, though we did have a good time. That was pretty dangerous, taking a swim in the middle of the night. Couldn't you at least have left a note?"

"I'm sorry, Alma. You're right. At least I called you the next day."

"Okay. But, you were saying that you and Bill ...?"

"I really like him, Alma. Isn't he special? I only last saw him this morning and yet I can hardly wait to see him again."

Alma looked at her strangely.

"What's wrong, Alma?"

"Tricia, didn't you know?"

"What? Know what?"

Alma shook her head. She reached out and placed her hands on Tricia's across the table.

"I'm sorry, Tricia. Some guys just aren't going to be up front with you."

Tricia took Alma's hands, squeezing them in anxiety. "What, Alma? What are you trying to say?"

"Bill left the country this morning."

"WHAT?"

Alma nodded. "He only had a month's lease at the boat dock and it ran out today. He consulted with me about helping to arrange his travel visa. He's headed south to Belize."

Tricia remained silent, dumbfounded.

"Tricia. Tricia, are you okay?"

She shook her head. "I … I just can't believe it," Tricia finally managed to say. "He's left town? You mean, like gone forever?"

"Who knows about forever? He left a forwarding post office box with me. Somewhere along the West Coast, Seattle I think. Tricia! You really look green. Maybe I should take you outside."

Tricia pushed away from the table and elbowed her way through the crowd to the restroom. There she kneeled down over the bowl and vomited.

She hung onto the porcelain rim, swaying, sweaty and sick. After what seemed like an hour but was most likely only five minutes she heard Alma behind her.

"Tricia? Can I do anything? I've brought you a cup of ice water. How about a damp cloth?"

"Thank you Alma. Both would be great." She flushed the toilet and turned around to sit on it. She took the cloth from Alma, wiping off her face and lips. Gratefully she took the ice water, swishing away the foul taste.

"So, you really fell hard for this guy, huh?" Alma observed. "That's rough."

"I just can't believe it, Alma. He told me he loved me. I just can't believe that I could have been such a fool."

"Well, it's happened to all of us. Look at me. I have a three year old *chico* to show for my error. You still look terrible. Are you going to be okay?"

"Yeah, Alma. It just shook me, that's all. That, and not having any dinner. And then downing Jack Daniels on an empty stomach. Just give me a few minutes. I'll be okay."

Alma nodded, waiting patiently by the stall door. "Well, you don't look okay. How about I drive you home?"

"Thanks. I think I'd feel better if I could get something to eat. Not here, though. It's much too crowded. Give me a few minutes to freshen up and we'll go somewhere for a sandwich. Any suggestions?"

"Denny's is down the street."

"Great. I'll meet you out at the bar in ten minutes."

At the bar, Alma again offered to drive, but Tricia insisted she felt well enough to drive herself. They pulled out of The Cannery's parking lot in caravan, Alma in front.

Alma promised to keep them on the service road. Tricia pulled in behind her at the first red light. As they picked up speed between the two sections, Tricia noticed a pick-up truck pulling up beside her. Suddenly it accelerated sharply and slammed into her driver's side.

The big white Cadillac screeched as the metals scraped. Tricia held up her hand to fend off the shattering glass from the driver's side window. Though it broke, the pieces stayed in place. Her car bounced hard to the right, the wheels jumping up onto the curb. Tricia pulled the car back onto the road and stopped. Using her purse she knocked the broken glass pieces out into the street.

Looking out the front, Tricia saw that Alma had stopped up ahead of her. The pick-up truck pulled ahead, accelerating up the entrance ramp of the highway. Tricia gunned the engine, urging the rented car to its maximum effort. She merged into the heavy freeway traffic.

She spotted the off-white pick-up as it climbed the overpass ahead. She pushed the Cadillac's accelerator to the floor, weaving through traffic at eighty miles an hour. The wind rushing in the empty driver's window buffeted her hair.

She slowed as she pulled even on the driver's side. She nodded as her guess that the driver would be Lupè proved correct. He turned to look at her, his mouth dropping open in surprise.

Stomping hard on the accelerator, she swung her automobile hard against Lupè's truck. The impact sent his truck careening toward the highway's shoulder. With a squeal of tires, Lupè pulled his truck back into his lane. Tricia heard his engine roar and he slammed his truck back into her car. The Cadillac's metal squealed in protest, glass pieces tingling on their way to the road. Tricia struggled to keep control of her clumsy machine, the bent frame trying to pull the car in two different directions at once. Keeping her foot hard on the gas pedal, she raced to catch up and pass Lupè's truck. Once she had her bumper two feet in front of his, she turned the steering wheel abruptly to the right, slamming into Lupè's truck, dragging it onto the shoulder. The wheels of both vehicles squealed as she forced Lupè's truck further and further off the road. With an explosive crunch Lupè's right fender caught the guard rail, wrenching it off of Tricia's side. Once relieved of the heavy truck, the Cadillac lurched forward, limping down the highway.

All around her drivers who had swerved to get out of the battlers' way honked and glared at Tricia. She smiled and waved back at them, proud of her victory. She nursed the car off the highway at the next exit ramp.

She found herself at the Oso turn around. With a final shake and jolt, the car stopped in the middle of the underpass loop. Tricia sat and looked out over the quiet Oso, peaceful and dark. The driver door squealed in protest as she pushed hard in opening it.

Tricia made a slow inspection tour around the car. Both sides of the Cadillac were crushed, the right rear passenger door hung on by one hinge. All windows on both sides of the vehicle yawned broken, both side view mirrors were gone, and the right front headlight hung across the grill by its wires. Shards of colored glass marked where the right rear turn signal once sat. Both right side tires collapsed in flat rubber puddles, like tar washed up on the Padre Island beach.

Looking around her, Tricia realized the nearest convenience store with a public phone was a mile away. Seldom did cars come this way, and even if they did, she wouldn't want to hitchhike. Her whole body ached, especially her neck and left leg. A long walk seemed the only option. Sighing, she placed the car keys in her purse and began to trudge along the road in the direction of town.

As she walked she heard sirens going by on the road above her. She smiled in satisfaction, fantasizing about Lupè. She wondered how badly he was hurt. "At least as much as me, I hope."

Once she reached the nearest convenience store, she called a cab. As she waited she sat on the store's curb, enjoying a cup of coffee and a Hostess Ding-Dong.

From the back seat of the cab on the way back to her home, passing on the other side of the freeway, she saw blue lights spinning at the site of Lupè's truck.

"Lots of police, huh?" the cab driver commented.

Tricia remained silent the whole trip.

Wearily, she unlocked her townhouse door, dropping her purse and shoes inside the entryway. She picked up the phone to quiet its incessant ringing.

"Hello?"

"Tricia? It's Mel. Thank God you answered. Are you okay?"

"Mel, I can't talk to you now. I'm fine. Just give me a night's sleep."

"They just brought Lupè in. Alma called and said he purposely hit you. Can't you tell me what happened?"

"Sweetheart, please. Come by tomorrow. I'm absolutely exhausted. Please?"

"Okay. I'll come by tomorrow morning then."

"Not too early, I hope."

Her answering machine was blinking with messages, but she felt too exhausted to listen. Upstairs, she stripped off the rest of her clothes in the bathroom and emptied her complaining bladder. She noticed the three Valiums sitting by the sink. Remembering that Valium helped muscle aches, she popped one in her mouth, downing it with a gulp of water. Back in her room, she dropped naked onto her bed and fell asleep immediately.

27

Interview: Lupè Garcia
Place: Police Station, Precinct 2
Date: Thursday, September 15

Sweeney: Here we are again, eh Lupè? You, me, your
                lawyer, David Hopsteader, and Sam Byrd.
                All sitting around this tape recorder.

Hopsteader: On tape, I repeat my objections to this
                near midnight interview. I don't see why
                you couldn't wait until the morning for
                this, Mel.

Sweeney: Attempted murder doesn't wait, David.

Garcia: Attempted murder? *No hizo nada!* You should
                be arresting that reporter girl. She ran
                me off the road. I'm hurt! I'm gonna press
                charges, cop-man. That's what I'm gonna do.

Sweeney: Today's date is September fifteenth. As
                before, we have your permission to tape
                this interview, right?

Garcia: Hopscotch says yes, cop-man. All I want is
                to go lay down. Can they make me sit up when
                I'm all beat up like this, Hopscotch?

Sweeney: We ran you past the doc in the E.R. He
                okayed you.

Garcia: He didn't give me no pills. I'm hurting.

Sweeney: Lupè, tell us what happened.

Garcia: I was driving down the road, minding my
                own business, cop-man. This crazy reporter

181

slams into my car. Jesus! I'm lucky I wasn't killed. *Muerto!* She's loco, cop-man. Why you arrest me?

Sweeney: It's a funny thing about that, Lupè. I have a witness who says you slammed into her car first.

Garcia: A witness? Who saw me, cop-man? You're setting me up.

Hopsteader: We have the right to know the witness' name, Mel.

Sweeney: If it becomes necessary for you to know, I'll tell you. This very reliable witness told me that you purposely hit Tracy's car on the Padre Island Drive service road. That's assault with a deadly weapon, Lupè.

Garcia: So slap my hand. She got her revenge. Where is loco-Tracy now? Asleep in the next cell? Ha! No jail time for white girls, is there, cop-man? Hey, Hopscotch, can you get them to arrest that *puta*?

Sweeney: As I said, Lupè, it's a matter of who went first. How did you know where to wait for Miss Tracy tonight?

Garcia: Just lucky, cop-man. Yeah. I've always been real lucky.

Sweeney: Someone told you that Miss Tracy was in that bar. Someone told you what kind of car she was driving. Someone hired you to wait outside the bar and then try to kill her when she came out. Isn't that right, Lupè? That's attempted murder, Lupè. You're going back to prison for this one, Lupè.

Garcia: *Ca-ca!* I ain't taking the fall. Make that bitch Dupree go to jail, not me. She's the

one who's setting me up. I'm always get-
tin' set up.

Sweeney: Dupree? Barbara Dupree? Tell me about it,
Lupè.

Garcia: I hate that *puta*.

Sweeney: Dupree?

Garcia: No, she's the bitch. I meant the *puta*,
Tracy. Tracy calls me a murderer so Bevis
got to fire me. I go to Dupree to complain
and she say she can keep me on the payroll,
but not on the job. "So what's this?" I
ask. She say she'll call me to do things.

Tonight I'm sitting at home drinking *cerveza* and watching TV. What the hell? I'm
getting *mi dinero.* Dupree calls me. She
tells me that the *puta* is at The Cannery
and driving a white Cadillac. She tells me
to go give her a good scare.

I ain't there but a few minutes and out
she comes. She and that other *puerca*[1]. So
when she drive off I come up beside her
and give her a little bump. It's just a
little bump, cop-man. She ain't hurt. But
I guess she got pissed. Next thing I know
she's slamming my truck into the guard-
rail. *¡Hola!* And me driving with this broken arm, too.

Sweeney: What other things has Barbara Dupree asked
you to do for her?

Garcia: I been doing things for her for years.
Painted her house once. Doing errands.

Sweeney: Did she ask you to get some of the explosives from the construction site for her?

---

1   Sow

Garcia: *¿Que?* Get *mi mano* blown off? *Eres muy loco.*[2]

Sweeney: So what does she ask you to do?

Garcia: I deliver boxes.

Sweeney: What's in the boxes?

Hopsteader: Don't answer that, Mr. Garcia. Mel, I should have a talk with my client before further discussion of these boxes.

Sweeney: It's late, David. We've already established Garcia's a carrier. I won't ask what's in the boxes if you'll let me discuss what he does with them, okay?

Hopsteader: Okay. Go ahead.

Sweeney: Big boxes or small?

Garcia: Baby shoe boxes.

Sweeney: When was the last time you transported a box for her?

Garcia: Yesterday about noon. I go to Nate's boat and picked up his last couple of boxes. I took them to the bitch.

Sweeney: Nate? The sailor with the eye patch? Do you remember the name of the boat?

Garcia: *Adventurer*. It's been at the L-Head.

Sweeney: How many boxes do you think you got from Nate in all?

Garcia: *No se.* Maybe thirty. Usually six or seven at a time. I gave Nate the envelope and

---

2   You're quite crazy

got the boxes. Nate's okay … except when he broke my arm. We've been drinking together.

Sweeney: When was the first time you met Nate?

Garcia: At the Lonesome Coyote, about a month ago. Dupree introduced him to me. We arranged for me to pick up the boxes at his boat. Since then I seen him there and he's come over *por cervesas.*

Sweeney: I worked on a larceny case a couple of months ago. Turned out the bank clerk was being manipulated by this gang who would get him drunk and then get him to promise to do things for his old "buddies." Do you have any idea where Nate is now? I went by his slip at noon but it was empty.

Garcia: (laughs). He gone, *tonto.* He sail to South America.

Sweeney: What? When did that happen?

Garcia: He left this morning, at least, that's what he told me he was doing. Ha! Cop man ain't so smart after all.

Sweeney: I … I can't believe that he's gone. Man, I really wanted to question him, too. Well, I guess I'll just have to ask you. Was Nate with you at the Lonesome Coyote the night Maria disappeared?

Garcia: *Por supestro.*

Sweeney: Can you remember everyone who was drinking with you that night? Was Dupree there?

Garcia: Nah, not the bitch. Me and Maria, and Nate. Let's see. Jack's always hanging around on

Friday nights. And, I think Fat Bob was there too. I'm not sure.

Sweeney: Fat Bob? You mean Bob Randolph from the newspaper, right?

Garcia: Yeah, that Fat Bob.

Sweeney: Bob and Maria have been friends for a long time, huh Lupè? Have you ever felt that Maria was too friendly with some of your drinking buddies?

Garcia: Maria shouldn't drink so much. *No puede[3]* handle her liquor. *Mucho problemas.*

Sweeney: Is that what happened that night, Lupè? Did you get mad at her and hit her?

Garcia: I told you, cop-man, I remember *nada.*

Sweeney: Let me help you remember. You were there with Maria and Nate and Jack and maybe Bob. Maria says something to Nate, something about Bert or Benji. Does that sound familiar?

Garcia: Hey, yeah, cop man. How'd you know that? Maria said something about recognizing Nate from a picture or something. Nate seemed mad, then laughed and started buy-ing drinks. *No recuerdo mas.[4]*

Sweeney: A picture?

Garcia: Yeah. And something about how he got hurt. Speaking of being hurt, I'm hurtin' all over. Hopscotch, tell this *vaca tonto[5]* to let me go home.

---

3   She can't

4   I don't remember anything more

5   Stupid cow

Hopsteader:	Mel, is this going to go on much longer? You're strayed far from the subject of tonight's accident.
Sweeney:	Just one more subject, please. Lupè, Maria handled the money in your family, right? She picked up your paycheck and paid the bills, hmm?
Garcia:	*Si*. So what?
Sweeney:	Did it ever seem to you that maybe she had more money than you expected? Was she able to buy a new stove or splurge at times?
Garcia:	Maria was good with money. She pay the bills. We always have *bastante*[6].
Hopsteader:	Please, Mel. You're just wasting time now.
Sweeney:	Okay, I'm done. I suppose a high priced lawyer like you is very busy. How is Garcia paying you?
Hopsteader:	That's privileged information, Mel.
Sweeney:	Could be a clue, David. I'd appreciate the help.
Hopsteader:	Sorry, I can't tell you. Are you going to be holding Mr. Garcia again?
Sweeney:	Absolutely. He's a dangerous man. We'll book him on assault charges.
Hopsteader:	Okay. Then I'll see you at the bail hearing in the morning.

End of recording.
MS/sb

---

6 enough

Tracy's Tidbits
by Patricia Tracy

Corpus Christi Caller Times
Friday, September 16, 1994

The Name Game

The friends you make in youth can last your whole life. In high school I met my best friends Becky Hoyt and Alma Sosa. Becky was our school's prime cheerleader, casing the men and dreaming of a secure future. She married Lawrence Smyth, a successful manufacturer. Alma Sosa and I teamed up as co-captains of our debate team. Her analytical mind kept the opposing forces on the run. Today she practices law as Alma Trevino. These names are honorable, long standing Corpus Christi names that experience drapes with trust.

Our private high school, the Omega School for Girls, brought together young women of quality. Becky's father, Bruce Hoyt, worked construction. His modest home glowed with love and encouragement. Alma's dad, Noe Sosa, represented our district in the State Senate for eighteen years, an honorable and clear thinking man. My pop, Richard Tracy, made his fortune with investments. He practiced charity and appreciation of life in the home and throughout the city. Honorable fathers bring honor upon their children.

When someone tells you their name, they're asking you to trust that name. They proclaim "This name brings honor unto me." Our names are synonymous with our credit. Who would invest with Benedict Arnold Insurance? Would Judas Iscariot win election? What might be on the menu of Adolph Hitler's Bar and Grill? We bank with experience, we vote for integrity, we dine at quality.

Yet, there are places we go seeking the unknown. Sometimes I join my friends at one of the local pick-up places, The Cannery, the Western Palms, or the Lonesome Coyote. We gossip about those we see, and sometimes delight in meeting strangers. There I've found a stand-up dozen John Smiths, a double handful of Jim Browns, and a score of Joe Blows. They all want to dance, to drink, and to take me home. Before we go anywhere, John, tell me how long have you been in town? What does your father do? Do you bring honor on his house? Or disgrace? I'm asking, "How do I know I can trust you?" I want to know, "What's your real name?"

Corpus Christi Caller Times
Friday, September 16, 1994

Westchester Acres Developer Bribed City Official

Jesus Morales and Patricia Tracy, Staff Writers

BRUCE McDONALD, recently of the Public Works Department, has admitted to accepting bribes in exchange for altering water studies. Over the past two years, according to Mr. McDonald, he has taken monetary presents in exchange for water restriction leniency several times.

According to two sources in the Department, Mr. McDonald was asked to resign two months ago over these improprieties. Prior to this he held a supervisory position, making it possible for him to overrule other agents' findings.

The most serious example of these bribes came last year with a reportedly $50,000.00 payment by Barbara Dupree, of Dupree Development Company, developer of Westchester Acres. According to the first inspector, Gary Miles, Westchester Acres was denied a building permit because of the danger of contamination to the Nueces River. The Nueces is the primary source of the city's water supply.

Mr. Miles, who now works as a consultant for the private chemical company Water Checks, reports that he has run tests confirming that contamination from some of the existing structures has already leached into the river. Not only pesticide and fertilizer contamination, but certain bacteria associated with septic systems exceed the upstream levels. Mr. Miles recommends an immediate moratorium on all building in Westchester Acres, as well as reinspection of those lots already permitted. Mrs. Dupree has refused to answer any of our questions, directing all inquires to her attorney.

In another series of problems with Mr. McDonald's inspections, the Southhampton subdivision has had to be entirely reinspected. Several building sites have had their building permits withdrawn. Other lots are being cited with requirements to place special effusion pumps.

Mr. McDonald graduated Cum Laude in mechanical engineering from Texas A&M in 1964. The next year he began working in the Public Works Department, rising to the supervisory position in 1988. He married Marion Bartlett in 1968.

Over the past two years, though, Mr. McDonald's fortunes have been troubled. The McDonalds divorced a year ago August. According to police records, Mr. McDonald was charged with possession of illegal substances in May of this year. A plea bargain resulted in a suspended sentence. Since leaving the Public Works Department, Mr. McDonald has moved out of the city.

28

Interview: Bryan Matthews
Date: Friday, Sept. 16
Location: Carothers & Matthews office, 301 Shoreline

Sweeney: As you see I have now turned on my recorder.
                You said that was acceptable?

Matthews: Yes, of course.

Sweeney: For the record, today is September six-
                teenth. Present here are Bryan Matthews,
                attorney, Shirley Davis, his secretary,
                Mel Sweeney, detective, and Samuel Byrd,
                police sergeant. Thanks for coming in so
                early this morning to talk with me, Mr.
                Matthews. Say, these sure are nifty offices.
                What a view! Look, you can see one of those
                huge tankers coming in!

Matthews: Thank you, Mr. Sweeney. I should take
                advantage of the view more often. I've
                become so involved with my daily activi-
                ties I rarely notice. Of course, I'm sel-
                dom in the office this early. Look at all
                the boats out today. Do you sail?

Sweeney: Hmm? No. Not me. I tried it once but got
                terribly seasick. How about you? I bet
                you've got a nice size yacht, huh?

Matthews: Actually, the firm owns a small boat,
                strictly for business purposes you under-
                stand. When I was younger I loved to sail.
                I used to have my own boat. But after my
                heart attack I decided to give it up. They

say the second happiest day of your life is the day you purchase your own boat.

Sweeney: Okay, I'll bite. What's the happiest?

Matthews: The day you sell it.

Sound of laughter.

Matthews: We contacted Mrs. Tracy yesterday morning as you requested and she authorized our cooperation in regard to the material requested by Patricia Tracy's attorney. So, what can I do for you today, Detective? Or should I call you Mr. Sweeney?

Sweeney: You can call me Mel, if you'd like.

Matthews: First name basis is fine with me. Please call me Bryan.

Sweeney: I'm working on the disappearance of Maria Garcia. Did you ever know her or her mother, Juanita Gonzalez? In the 1940s and early 50s Juanita worked for Herbert Tracy as a nanny. Here's a picture of her, the one on the left.

Matthews: Herbert? You're talking about a long time ago, Mel. I'm sixty-three years old, been a lawyer here since I was twenty five in 1955. I joined Newton Carothers fresh out of law school. Herbert was a client of Carothers already, though he died shortly after I joined the firm. I don't ever remember meeting Juanita Gonzalez. Would you like me to have Shirley check the files?

Sweeney: Yes, but later if you don't mind. Here's Juanita with a young woman. Do you recognize the girl?

Matthews: No. But I know who she was. That's Beverly
            Tracy isn't it?

Sweeney: Yes. You seem hesitant, Bryan.

Matthews: Well, it's a rather unfortunate story. What
            do you need to know?

Sweeney: Whatever you can tell me.

Matthews: Okay. I suppose this late after the events
            the scandal could hardly matter. If the
            same thing happened in today's morality
            the outcome would be much different. I
            never met Beverly Tracy, though I've kept
            track of her.

Sweeney: Today's morality? What happened?

Matthews: Beverly became pregnant at age fifteen. That
            was the early fifties, maybe 1950. Abortion
            was out of the question. I suppose the
            family would have encouraged adoption. But
            that was before my time. In any case, she
            had a boy; Benjamin. That was her only
            child, for she never did marry. She took
            an alias in Norfolk, living under the name
            of Lewis. She died last year.

Sweeney: How come you remember this so well? Some
            people say I remember my cases too well,
            but I'm not sure I'd remember things that
            long ago. How come you kept such careful
            track of Beverly?

Matthews: For two reasons. Under the terms of the
            Tracy trust I've been sending Beverly a
            thousand dollar check every month. At first
            she didn't cash them, but the last twenty
            years they've been deposited. In addition,

for inheritance purposes, I keep track of the first degree relatives of each family.

Sweeney: Why's that?

Matthews: I'm the attorney for both trusts; the Randolph estate and the Tracy estate. Meredith and Patricia are nearly the last members of both fortunes, now that Beverly's dead. Only if both should die would I need to contact distant relatives. Of course, once Patricia turns twenty-five, next January, she comes into her inheritance and the Tracy trust dissolves.

Sweeney: Who are these other distant relatives?

Matthews: Meredith has one other living relative, Robert Randolph. He's an editor at the paper.

Sweeney: Are you telling me that Bob Randolph will inherit both fortunes if Meredith and Patricia die before Patricia turns twenty-five?

Matthews: I haven't carefully reviewed the documents lately, but I suppose that's right. It's not very likely, now is it? Robert is over sixty, Meredith turned fifty this year, and, of course, Patricia is quite young. Robert is overweight as well.

Sweeney: All right, let me change the subject. Do you remember receiving a letter from some-one representing themselves as attorney for Patricia Tracy? Meredith Tracy thought his name might have been Nathan Kahn.

Matthews: Shirley? Do you have that file?

Davis: Yes sir, Mr. Matthews. Right here.

Matthews: Thank you. Let's see now. There are two requests from the law office of Nathan Cohen. One came directly from the attorney, bearing Patricia's signature, asking for a copy of the Trust papers. The other was forwarded from Meredith, requesting copies of the Randolph estate foundation papers and Mrs. Tracy's will. Everything was sent out last week.

Sweeney: I know Tricia's signature. This one's been forged.

Matthews: Oh? Let me see. Well, both forms are properly notarized, Mel.

Sweeney: Here, look at Nathan's signature I picked up at a construction office. It seems to be the same one as on your requests.

Matthews: Yes. I agree. They look …

Sound of a phone ringing

Davis: Hello? Just a moment, please. Mr. Sweeney? There's a call for you.

Sweeney: Hello? What? Don't let anyone touch anything. I'll be right there. Bryan, this is terrible news. Apparently when Meredith Tracy's maid came in to do the cleaning this morning, she found Meredith dead.

Matthews: Oh my God! How awful!

Sweeney: Come on, Sam. Let's go.

End of Recording
MS/sb

29

After her doorbell rang for the second time, Tricia opened her eyes to check her clock. It showed 9:43 in the morning. Reluctantly she sat up on the edge of the bed, holding her head with her hands. She was about to fall back onto the bed when the chime rang again. Struggling out of bed, she grabbed her soft terrycloth robe on her way downstairs. Mel's face stared back at her though the peephole.

"What's up, Mel?" she called through the door. "I'm not presentable."

"Let me in. I need to talk to you," he told her. "Even at your worst you're still the most beautiful woman in the world."

She smiled at his gallantry. "Thanks! But I still need to freshen up. You can use your keys, but wait a half minute before coming in. Why don't you invite Sam in too? Make us some coffee while I get ready."

From upstairs she heard the door open and the sound of Mel's voice. Sam was always so quiet she couldn't be sure whether he had also come in, or if Mel was just talking to himself. She hurried through her morning ablutions.

As she again descended the steps the sweet coffee aroma reached her. She found Mel sitting at the table looking over some notes and Sam Byrd in her little kitchenette rattling the pans. Mel placed his notes down on the table and greeted her.

"Hi, Sweetheart. Are we friends again?"

She walked around the table to give him a kiss. It began as a small peck, the type passed between good friends or siblings. But Mel reached up to draw her in, extending the kiss in passion.

"Umm," Tricia said as their lips finally parted. "I missed that."

"Me too!"

She walked back around the table to sit in the chair facing the kitchen. "Have you got enough coffee for me, Sam? I like mine with a touch of cream and two teaspoons of sugar."

"Yeah. Minute."

She turned her attention back to the detective. "Thanks for giving me a break last night, Mel. You can't believe how exhausted I was! And sore! Not that the soreness is any better this morning. I can't move my neck to the right at all, it's so sore. And look...."

She pulled up the hem of the print skirt she had donned. "Look at the bruise on my left thigh! That's where the car door hit me when that assassin tried to kill me! I hope you have enough to keep him in jail <u>this</u> time! Did you come to take a statement? I'm ready, that's for sure! Get out your recorder."

Sam brought Tricia's coffee along with three plates and forks. He returned with a skillet full of scrambled eggs which he distributed among the plates.

"Umm!" Tricia said as she inhaled deeply, enjoying the egg aroma. "Sam, you're a marvel. Can you bring some hot sauce from the refrigerator, please?"

"Tricia, I've got something important I have to talk to you about."

"Oh hush. Let's not spoil this delicious meal. I promise to give you a complete confession after breakfast."

Mel was about to object when Sam returned with the hot sauce in a bowl. Mel shrugged and held his tongue.

The three dug into their steaming plates of breakfast with vigor, putting aside conversation in favor of their appetites. Sam picked up the empty plates to return them to the kitchen.

"Boy, that was just what I needed," Tricia announced. "You've set me up, coppers. Now I'm ready to make my confession."

"Though I do need to get a statement from you, that can wait. There's something more important we need to talk about. I … I don't know how to tell you this."

"Don't worry, I already know that William Tucker left town. Alma told me last night. You were right all along. Like some foolish school girl I fell head over heels for his charms. I hate to admit it. But that's all over now.

"I really don't know what got into me," she continued, shaking her head. "When Alma told me I became sick as a dog. It was like telling a child that there really isn't a Santa Claus. I didn't want to believe it, though I knew it was true. He was no good, just like you said. So now, you've come out for the 'I told you so,' huh? Well, go ahead. I deserve it. And, I tell you what, I am very appreciative that you are who you are Mel. Here you sit, willing to take me back, forgive me and love me as if I hadn't been the prodigal girl. And I love you all the more for it.

"So tell me, what did you find out about this charlatan? Isn't that what you called him? Charlatan?"

"That's what I called him all right. And, yes, that's what he is. But he's much more than that, I fear. I've yet to put it all together, but I believe that he's an evil sociopath."

"What? I can't believe it," Tricia said. "Admittedly, he ran off without even saying good-bye, but the fellow's no ax murderer. He saved my life when Lupè

Garcia attacked me. He's cultured and well traveled. You'll pardon me, I hope, but I think your jealousy may have clouded your judgment this time, Mel."

Sam brought the coffee pot from the kitchenette and refilled the three cups. After returning the pot to the burner, he settled into an empty chair at the table. He sat quietly, sipping his coffee.

Mel watched her in silence. He raised his cup to his lips, sipping the steaming black drink slowly, then lowering it carefully again to the table.

"Tricia," he began, carefully. "When did you talk to your mother last?"

A bit startled at the change in subject, Tricia had to think for several moments.

"As you well know, Mel, we're not very close. It's been at least a couple of months, I think. I got a note from her at work on Monday. Does this have anything to do with Bill?"

"Maybe. Your mother is the main reason I'm here."

He sat quietly for a minute, staring into his coffee. When he looked up again Tricia saw that he wore the saddest expression she'd ever seen on him.

"Tricia, I've been a police officer for twelve years. There's a lot about this job I like. There are some things about this job I love. But there are also some bad parts to this job. There's one duty that I find extremely difficult, an assignment that all officers hate to have to perform. Yet it's a job that has to be done."

He fell into silence again. Tricia watched a tear leak down his cheek. She saw his hands pale as he grasped his cup tightly.

"Mel! What is it? What are you trying to say?"

"I'm terribly sorry, dear Tricia. You cannot know how much it hurts me to have to tell you this. But, Sweetheart, I have some terrible news."

Tricia felt her heart race. She had no idea what could be so awful as to affect steady Mel this way. In a shrill voice she demanded, "What? For God's sake, Mel, tell me!"

Tears flowed steadily down both Mel's cheeks now. With a cracking voice he continued. "Tricia, your mother is dead."

Tricia felt numb, frozen in her chair. This gave way to a heated wave of terror. She began trembling, going from a slight tremor of her hands to a full body rattle. A volcanic explosion formed deep within her gut, rising slowly at first, erupting as a terrifying wail of despair.

She saw Mel shudder as her scream reverberated through the kitchen. Shaking her head, her eyes opened wide in horror. She stared at Mel, unseeing, unbelieving.

Mel stood and walked around the table to her. With his help, she rose, and collapsed into his hug. Immediately she began sobbing, shaking with her grief. He held her tightly, stroking her back and talking softly. They hugged as Tricia's crying slowly subsided.

When she looked up she found Sam standing next to her. He held out a box of tissues. "Tough break."

Tricia had to smile, despite her grief. Sam's sparse verbiage gave reassurance.

"Thanks, Sam." She took a tissue to dry her tears. "I'm sorry guys. I never would have thought her death would affect me like this. I mean, we were as estranged as a mother and daughter could be. Yet still, she was my mother. Tell me what happened?"

Mel still held on to her. He looked her in the eyes, a scant foot away.

"Her maid found her at the bottom of her staircase. It looks like she slipped on a top step, tumbling all the way. At the scene, the medical examiner thought her neck was broken. I suppose his report will be ready tomorrow. I feel terrible for you, Darling. When my dad passed away from cancer it wasn't this kind of shock. I lost a sister to drowning and know how that grief turns you inside-out like a heart attack. Come. Let me hug you again."

Tricia relaxed into his arms, enjoying the comfort of his strong embrace. She closed her eyes and gave herself over to the warmth and security of his love. When ready, she gently pushed away. She walked into the living room and collapsed into the recliner. Sam brought her a cup of fresh coffee.

"It's all so hard to believe," Tricia said after a sip. "I wonder how this will change my life? I'll have to call Mother's lawyer and find out what it all means. Will I need to go down to the police station and identify her?"

"No. Just let us know which funeral home you want to use."

Sam leaned against the wall with his arms folded against his chest. Mel perched on the edge of the love seat and cleared his throat. Instead of speaking, he paused in thought.

"Is there something else, Mel?"

"Listen, Tricia. I knew a fellow who won the lottery. Before winning, he was your average Joe. He was a county deputy, traveled around in squad cars, worried about mortgage payments, volunteered for overtime every now and then, decent marriage. When he won he swore it wouldn't change his life. But when that first quarter million check came in, and he realized he'd be getting another one every year for the next twenty, he had to ask himself, 'why work?' Natural enough question.

"He quit his job. He bought a big house. He bought cars for himself and his family. He took vacations. He went through all the money in three months. He had to borrow from the bank just to buy food. In another three months he went bankrupt. His wife left him, getting a lawyer to put a lien on the house and the upcoming lottery payments. Every year he'd get the payment, run through it in a few months, and live in misery for the next nine. Huge amounts of money are incredibly life changing.

"How do you feel about suddenly being rich? How do you think it will affect your life?"

Tricia smiled. "I'm no fool, Mel. I'm not going to quit my job. I love what I do. But, hmm … I'd like to travel. Maybe I'll buy a boat. You needn't worry about me running through the fortune. There's a big difference between having a measly couple of hundred thousand a year versus a nest egg of tens of millions."

"You've always lived within your means. But some people acquire expensive tastes. Let's talk about your Uncle Bob."

"Mel, what are you talking about? Why are you bringing up Bob Randolph?"

"Tricia, I know this is going to sound far fetched, but I believe Bob Randolph is responsible for your mother's death."

"Far fetched? I think you've lost your mind! Surely you're not trying to say he killed her? That's funny, imagining my fat second cousin pushing my mother down the stairs. You can't be serious."

"Unfortunately, I'm perfectly serious. Robert Randolph has accumulated some expensive habits I'm afraid, and the Randolph fortune was staring him in the face. He's been buying outlandish gifts for his paramours. Once one gets the taste for expensive habits, it can get into your blood."

"His paramours? Who are you talking about?"

"I suspect there have been others, but specifically, Maria Garcia. I'm pretty sure Bob was having an affair with her. When she began demanding more money from him, he contracted to have her killed. He felt guilty about Lupè being accused so he hired David Hopsteader to defend him. It's the only thing that makes sense. When I interview him, Bob keeps changing his story."

"He's just a forgetful old man with an active imagination," Tricia said.

"Now comes the worst part. Bob realized that if he had your mother killed, he'd inherit the bulk of the Randolph fortune, at least the part that didn't go to you. He felt comfortable with this plan, because the assassin he hired was planning to leave the country soon anyway."

"Wow! This is beyond far fetched, Mel. You're living in a fantasy world! Who is this supposed assassin?"

Mel walked over and took Tricia by both arms, looking into her eyes, pleading with his gaze to take him seriously. "William Tucker."

"Bill?"

"Absolutely. Did you know that he's an ex-Green Beret, a specialist in murder and intrigue? Also I think he's a smuggler. His nefarious crimes stretch the whole spectrum of lawlessness."

Tricia shook loose from Mel's hold and went into the kitchen, shaking her head the whole way. She spilled her coffee down the drain and rinsed out the cup. She thought about her three days with the fabulous William Tucker. She knew that he loved to tell stories, some of which clearly had been a little out of the range of truthfulness. But he couldn't be a murderer. He had always treated her with respect and honor. And Bob, a contractor for murder? She tried to imagine her fat old cousin having sex with Maria Garcia, a young spry woman. It seemed absolutely ludicrous.

She shook her head again. Drying and putting away the dishes that Sam had left rinsed on the drain board, she spoke to Mel without looking at him.

"I just can't believe it, Mel. What kind of evidence do you have for these outlandish accusations?"

Mel leaned on his elbows, watching her from the dining room side of the kitchen pass-through counter.

"I know there's not much. I found some very valuable jewelry in Maria Garcia's dresser that Bob admitted giving to her. Why would he do that unless she was his lover? Or his blackmailer? I have a witness who saw Bob give money to both Maria and Bill Tucker. They all met frequently at the Lonesome Coyote. It all fits."

"So you're saying Bob hired Bill to kill Maria and my mother? What else are you accusing Bill of doing, this fellow whose nefarious crimes stretch the whole spectrum of lawlessness?"

"I think Bill stole dynamite and killed Sidney Jones and blew up his car, as well as trying to murder you by blowing up your car. I think he misfired on that one, though, and it blew up before you were in it."

"Me? You think Bill wanted to kill me? He certainly had plenty of chances that he ignored, now didn't he? Why would he want to kill me? And Sidney Jones? What possible motive do you have for that, Mel?"

"I don't know yet. Maybe killing you was supposed to be part of the inheritance for Bob? As far as Sidney Jones, I don't have a clue yet. But I suspect Bill of drug smuggling, too. His real name is Nathan Cohen, by the way. He's also guilty of counterfeiting legal documents, and maybe conspiracy to avoid taxes."

Tricia turned on him angrily. "Maybe this. Could be that. Suspicions of this and that. Mel Sweeney, do you have any hard solid evidence of anything? No? No! These two people are my cousin and a fellow I loved!"

She turned away from him, struggling for a moment to control her emotions.

When she turned back she kept her voice quiet and steady.

"Mel, I love you. I love you more than I could ever love anyone in the world. I love you with a strong steady devotion and trust. But there, for a day or two, I loved William Tucker too! I loved him differently than you. I loved him with a fire that consumed me. I just can't accept that he's as evil as you're trying to make him out. And gentle, funny, Bob Randolph? I've known Bob all my life. He wouldn't hurt a fly.

"Mel, you're completely off your nut. A week ago you swore to me that Lupè Garcia had killed his wife. I got in big trouble when I wrote that in the paper. Maria Garcia may have simply run away. All you know about Sidney Jones is that he died in a car accident. My mother fell down the stairs and broke her neck. And now you've got this crazy idea that Bill might have tried to kill me by blowing up my car? Why is it that you're so eager to make my cousin and Bill into Mafia style killers?

"Smuggling? What? A little marijuana? Some gold? Avoiding tariffs on alcohol? What are you accusing him of smuggling?"

Mel shrugged. "I don't know yet, Tricia."

Tricia's laugh was high-pitched and nervous. "Yeah. You don't know yet. But you'll build up something, won't you? I know you, Mel Sweeney. You get your teeth into it and you won't let go until you've torn it to pieces. Let it go, Darling. I know you're angry with Bill. You have every right to be, the way he played with my heart and then ran off. But you're creating a huge fantasy case based on circumstantial evidence and your emotional preconceived misconceptions. The dirt you're slinging is splattering all over my wounded heart."

Mel started to say something, but with a shake of his head he remained silent.

"Thank you for coming by, Mel. I truly appreciate your personal involvement. I think I'd like to be alone for a little while though. I have a pounding headache and I'm sore all over. I've got so much to do. I need to call my lawyer and my Mom's lawyer. Who do I need to call about the funeral home for my Mom?"

"The medical examiner's office. I understand how overwhelmed you feel, Tricia. But listen, Darling. I love you! I'm concerned about you."

Tricia smiled weakly. "Thank you. Just … Just now I need to be alone."

Mel smiled back. He leaned forward to meet Tricia's kiss across the bar. "Sure, Sweetheart. You do that. Come on, Sam. We've got other things we need to do."

Turning back to Tricia he asked, "Call me later?"

She nodded.

"Dinner?"

She shook her head. "No. Give me a day please, Mel. It's all been too much. If you want, you can call me tonight. Say, what's the name of the funeral home that has that large space on Ocean Drive at Airline? That's where Dad's buried."

"Lancasters."

"Thanks."

Tricia stayed in the kitchenette, staring at the closed door after Mel and Sam had walked out. Though she had just told Mel she wanted to be alone, she felt a need to call someone, share her misery with a friend. Immediately Dovie came to mind. *She would understand.*

"Hello?"

"Dovie, it's Tricia. My mother fell down the stairs last night."

"Oh, how awful. Is she hurt?"

"She's ... she's dead."

"Your mother's dead? What a tragic accident. How old was she?"

Tricia felt the warmth return to her heart on hearing the voice of her friend Dovie. "Fifty, this May. I still can't believe she's gone. I worry about in later years all the regret I'll have for our lost love. I feel like I hardly knew her at all!"

"In today's mobile society, most people live so far away from their parents they have precious few shared memories. The key is to treasure the ones you have. Look, Tricia dear, we're both in mourning. Let's put on some fancy jewelry and go get some lunch."

Tricia turned to check the kitchen clock. "It's only half past ten, and I've just eaten. Also, I need to call my mother's lawyer. How about one thirty? Or would that be too late?"

"No, that would be fine. You want to pick me up?"

"How about you pick me up here about one, instead? I'll need a ride."

"Why? What's happened to your rental car?" Dovie asked.

"I'll tell you all about it over lunch."

"Okay, I'm dying to hear about it. How about afterwards we do something you enjoy? What usually cheers you up? Going to a movie? A walk along the beach?"

"Well, I love to shop. Hey, how about shopping for a new car? Although at the rate I'm going through them I wouldn't be surprised if they cancel my insurance."

"Sounds great! After lunch we can hit the car lots. Turtle used to tell me about the local dealers. Are you interested in a new or a used car?"

"New. I'd like something really hot!" Tricia said.

"I'll bring along a stack of Turtle's car magazines."

Tricia had hardly hung up the phone when it rang again.

"Ms. Patricia Tracy?" a sophisticated female voice inquired. "Please hold for Mr. Bryan Matthews."

At first Tricia didn't recognize the name.

"Patricia? This is Bryan. I was just devastated when I heard the news this morning. You have my sincerest condolences. It there anything at all I can do for you?"

The image of her mother's lawyer flashed into Tricia's mind. Although Tricia had a natural inclination to call him Mr. Matthews, she tried to honor his preference for a first name relationship.

"Thank you, Bryan. Mel said she fell down the stairs."

"How awful. I suppose her troubled ankle must have given out on her."

Tricia hadn't heard that her mother had a bad ankle. She wondered how much else she would never know about her mother.

"Who do you advise for a funeral home?"

"I've taken care of that already, Patricia. I called Lancasters, if that's all right with you."

"Yes, of course. Thank you, Bryan. What about her estate and all that?"

"I've just been going over her will. There are a couple of million dollars designated to various charities, and another to Robert Randolph. Except for a few other minor bequests, the bulk of her fortune went to you upon her death."

Tricia's eyebrows rose. "You mean I'm rich?"

Bryan chuckled. "Well, you will be in four months. Technically, it all goes to the Tracy trust fund until you turn twenty-five. However, I'm sure I can get your banker to arrange virtually unlimited access now in the form of temporary loans. The trust has been sending your monthly allowance to Corpus Christi National bank. Who's your banker over there?"

"Banker? I don't have a banker."

"Dallas Foster is a good friend of mine and vice president of premium services. I'll give him a call and make the arrangements."

"Dallas? He's really named Dallas?"

"Certainly. You may not have thought about it, but are you considering moving into the home or selling it?"

Images of her many years living in the Tracy Mansion flashed through her mind. She saw herself riding piggyback on her daddy through the halls. She remembered the huge dining table, set with lace and crystal. She visualized the parties and people that used to make the house so wonderfully exciting. But that had been ten years ago. She wondered how much her mother had changed everything.

"I'll have to think about it. Meanwhile, is there anyone else I need to call?"

"You might call the out-of-town friends. How does a Tuesday morning funeral sound? I'll make all the arrangements. Can you come by my office Wednesday and sign some papers?"

"Thank you, Bryan. Tuesday and Wednesday are both fine. I'll mark them down on my calendar. I appreciate all you're doing, but, you know, I have my own lawyer."

"Of course. I don't believe I've ever heard of him, though. Nathan Cohen, isn't it?"

Tricia took the phone from her ear and gave it a puzzled look, as if it was the phone's fault that Bryan had said such a foolish thing. She vaguely remembered Mel mentioning that name.

"Cohen? I don't know any Cohens. Alma Trevino is my attorney. Where did you ever get the idea that I had a new lawyer?"

Tricia noted a pause of several seconds. When the lawyer's voice returned to the phone he sounded a little chagrined.

"I'm terribly sorry, Patricia. Perhaps I made a mistake."

"Oh, something else just occurred to me. I was in a car accident last night."

"An accident? Were you hurt? Was anybody else hurt? Have you spoken to the police?"

"Just shaken up. I was driving a rental car and left it pretty badly damaged by the side of the road. And, yes, I've talked to the police. Well, I haven't made my official statement yet."

"Have you called the rental company?"

"No. It was Avis at the airport. Could you call for me?"

Bryan hesitated a moment. "Of course. They probably will want to talk to you personally, though. Still, tell me where the car is and I'll see if I can handle it for you. Are you sure you're not hurt? Did you see a doctor?"

"I'll be okay. Thanks. Thanks for everything, Bryan. I suppose a small note in the paper would be appropriate?"

"I'll take care of that, too," he assured her.

"No, please don't. I think I'd rather write it up in my column."

After describing where to find the car, Tricia hung up with a sigh. *It's funny how life can be so unpredictable,* she thought. *One day everything's smooth sailing. A week later I've lost my car, I've broken up with my boyfriend and fallen in love with a sailor, who then immediately leaves the country. And now my mother's dead. Well, I think next on the agenda should be a couple of aspirins and a warm bath. Maybe I'll lie down for a few minutes.*

As soon as Tricia lay down, the phone rang again. She turned off the ringer in the bedroom, letting the downstairs machine pick up this one and all the following calls.

30

Tricia napped for just under an hour, giving her time to write and e-mail her *Tidbits* before getting ready. By the time she bathed and dressed, one o'clock had come and gone. She was still applying make-up when Dovie rang the doorbell. Tricia hurried the last bit, ran downstairs, and joined Dovie in her Volkswagon.

"Your car is as old as Mel's," Tricia said, "But it runs smoothly and looks pretty."

"I believe in taking care of my things," Dovie said. "Turtle used to change the oil regularly ... oh, poor Turtle." She began to sob. "I'm sorry. You never know what's going to bring back those sad memories."

Tricia patted her on the hand. "I know what you mean. Just now, when I picked out these pearls, I saw a broach my mother gave me. I choked up immediately."

Dovie pulled up to Christof's and they were seated immediately. Tricia ordered two dozen Oysters Rockefeller and a bottle of champagne. Tricia told Dovie about the car battle with Lupè from the night before. Dovie told of communing with Turtle the previous night by going into a trance.

"What did he say?" Tricia asked.

Dovie chewed slowly on an oyster as she thought. "It's not as if one can really carry on a conversation with someone who's dead, you know. One just gets more of a sense of the spirit. He's not at peace, of that I'm certain. He won't be able to rest until his murderer is brought to justice."

Tricia clicked her tongue in sympathy. "That's pretty serious stuff, Dovie. Were you able to get clues as to who killed him?"

Dovie nodded slowly. "There's something wrong with their eyes, glasses maybe. I felt a strong tie between Turtle's death and your fortunes."

"Barbara Dupree wears glasses. I don't see how she could be related to my fortune, though."

"Perhaps we should pay her a visit?" Dovie suggested. "If I got near her again I might be able to pick up more images."

Tricia shook her head. "I'm not in the mood for her. Let's see some of those magazines you brought."

They thumbed through the car journals, tearing out the pages of those that interested them and piling the rest on an empty chair. The waiter toted away the empty shells and brought a second bottle of champagne. In the first survey they had eight contenders, eliminated five, and finally settled on their choice for Tricia's car.

"It looks like the Toyota Supra Dual Turbo is the fastest thing on the road," Tricia said. "Three of these car magazines rate it number one."

"Yes," Dovie agreed. "But it lists at $50,000."

"Well, what the hell. It's time to start spending Mom's money! I've always wanted to walk into a car shop and say 'Just wrap it up. I'll pay in cash.'"

The two women giggled in their mild intoxication. Tricia had the bill added to her tab and the women piled into Dovie's car.

Heat waves shimmered off the cars crowded around the Toyota sales lot. Burgundy Camrys, teal Corollas, blue Previa vans all waited in patient rows, their fresh morning baths yielding to the city grime and ocean spray spots. On this hot Friday afternoon not a soul roamed through this mechanical desert.

The cool air inside the dealership showroom felt like a welcome plunge into the Gulf as Tricia and Dovie pushed through the glass doors. Five show vehicles sat scattered around the large parquet floor. Behind them a row of offices lined the back wall. A goofy looking fellow with an overly large smile and a bright orange checked sports jacket came up to them.

"Howdy, Ladies," he said, extending a long bony hand. "My name is Hank. One of you ladies interested in a new car?"

His advance caused the two women to step back a pace. Hank stood six foot five, a fresh peach stubble showed across his chin. He looked like a cowboy just off the range, thrown into a hot shower, and dropped quickly into outlandish salesman clothes. As he walked a sandy brown cowlick bounced happily on the back of his head.

Tricia extended two fingers of her right hand, afraid of what the oversized man might do should he get her whole hand in his grip. In response, Hank brought his other hand up to get a better hold for a vigorous handshake.

"Nice to meet you, Hank. My name is Tricia."

"Great! And you?" he asked, turning to Dovie. His smile stretched his lips so far Tricia imagined she could count all thirty-two teeth.

Dovie fixed him with an icy stare. "We'd like to speak with Scott Birchman, please."

Hank grinned. "He's in the back office. You've worked with him before, huh?"

"I know of him. A friend of mine recommended him."

"Okay, ladies. But I could show you a car. I can get you a quick two hundred off the list of that cute little Corolla right there."

Dovie shook her head. "Birchman, please."

Tricia watched Hank retreat to the row of offices. Through the glass windows she watched him talking to a well dressed man who had been sitting at a desk doing paperwork. Scott Birchman looked at them and then shook his head slightly. Tricia watched him shelf the ledger he'd been using and slip on his jacket. Scott affected a leisurely pace, a quiet distinguished air hanging over him.

"Good afternoon," he said with a deep baritone. "I'm Scott Birchman."

Tricia shook his hand, appreciating his warm firm grip.

"Patricia Tracy."

Scott's eyebrows rose just a little. "You write the *Tidbits* column, don't you? I particularly enjoyed this morning's, about the value of a name. You're Meredith's daughter then?"

"Yes. She was my mother."

"I'm terribly sorry. I hadn't heard of her passing."

"She just died." Tricia raised her hand to her chest as she felt her heart spasm.

"My deepest sympathy. I met your mother on several occasions; flower shows and charity functions. Where might I send flowers?"

"Lancasters. Her funeral will be Tuesday." Tricia felt immediate comfort and trust in Mr. Birchman. She recognized that this was his profession, putting people at ease. He did it well.

Scott turned toward Dovie.

"Mr. Messer mentioned that you had been referred to me."

Dovie received his outstretched hand and slight bow with a light curtsy of her own. "Anna Marie Dove, Mr. Birchman. Sidney Jones referred me to you."

Scott nodded solemnly. "I read about Mr. Jones' tragic accident. He had a fine eye for cars."

"Thank you."

Tricia noted a catch in Dovie's voice. Glancing over at her, Tricia saw her eyes pool.

"Would you like to come into my office?" Scott offered. "What can I bring you to drink? Coke? Iced tea?"

The two followed him into his office, a walk-in closet cubicle plastered with Toyota superlatives. They settled into the comfortably worn easy chairs.

"Lovely earrings," Scott said to Dovie. "Do you have an interest in astrology?"

Dovie reached up and twirled the moon and star earrings. "Indeed I do. Are you a Libra?"

"Pisces."

Tricia realized that Scott was waiting on them. "I'm interested in looking at a new car, Scott."

"Of course. Which features are most important to you?"

"Power!" Tricia and Dovie said simultaneously.

Scott laughed with them. "Two minds with one thought, eh?"

"Yes," Tricia said. "We were looking at some magazines earlier and the Supra caught our eye. That new one with the dual turbo injection has the best ratings."

Scott nodded appreciatively. "It's the fastest commercial car on the road. Anti-lock brakes, removable sun roof, all leather seats, six-speaker surround CD system; it's truly a lovely vehicle. We have two on the lot, one red and the other black. Which would you like to test drive?"

"Red! Definitely the red one!"

They followed him out of the office and across the showroom floor.

"Would you ladies like to take it for a test drive? I'm supposed to go with you, but I feel comfortable waving the rules this time. All I'll need is a copy of your driver's license."

After making the copy he walked them toward the lot. "Would you like me to call your banker while you're out?"

"Do you know Dallas at Corpus Christi National Bank?"

"Certainly. Dallas Foster is a good friend of mine. Here." He removed a silver case from an inside coat pocket, extracting a card that he handed her. "It's three-thirty now. Call me in about an hour. In the meantime I'll talk to Dallas and have the paperwork ready for you when you get back to the showroom."

Tricia fell in love on first sight. The Supra's fast curves and low slung structure reminded her of a panther, muscle and beauty eager to pounce.

As the two pulled out of the parking lot Dovie said, "Pretty sure of himself, wasn't he? Hasn't he heard of people negotiating for their best dee....?"

Dovie caught her breath in mid-word as the car leaped forward, throwing the two occupants deep into their cushioned seatbacks.

"Good God, Tricia. You're going eighty miles an hour on the service road!"

Tricia grinned ear to ear as she slowed down behind a car entering the freeway in front of her. She whipped around it, zooming down the freeway and west toward the farmlands.

"You are not going to buy this car, Patricia Tracy," Dovie said. "The police would jerk your license in three days. How fast are you going now?"

Tricia glanced down at the speedometer for a moment. "One hundred and fifteen! Isn't it fabulous? Watch this! I'm going to take this corner at eighty-five! Whoosh! Hot damn! This is the car for me. Here we go!"

31

<table>
<tr><td>Interview:</td><td>Robert Randolph</td></tr>
<tr><td>Date:</td><td>Friday, September 16th</td></tr>
<tr><td>Location:</td><td>Police Station</td></tr>
</table>

Sweeney: You've just agreed to me taping this interview, correct, Mr. Randolph?

Randolph: Yes, as I said. What is this all about, Sweeney?

Sweeney: For the record, today's date is September the sixteenth. Present for this interview are Robert Randolph, newspaper editor, his attorney Gail Downs, Sam Byrd, police sergeant, and myself, Mel Sweeney, police detective.

Downs: What exactly is going on here, Detective Sweeney? I'm here at Mr. Matthews' request to represent Mr. Randolph, but I have no idea what, if any, charges you are considering.

Sweeney: I'm not certain there will be charges, Mrs. Downs. But when I'm investigating murder, I feel possible suspects deserve legal representation.

Randolph: Murder suspect? Me? Young fellow, I thought you had better insight than this. When I was a reporter younger than you I could read a man's personality like a book. Let me give you some advice there, Sweeney. Look into the eyes. The guilty ones have shifty eyes. They can't keep their focus on you. Look at the hands. They can't keep their hands still, always fidgeting. You

210

could learn a lot from an old newspaper man, Sweeney.

Downs: Just whom are you accusing Mr. Randolph of murdering?

Sweeney: I'm not accusing anyone of murder just now, Mrs. Downs. I said that I felt more comfortable that Mr. Randolph had legal representation. Let's talk about Maria Garcia. You said, Mr. Randolph, that she worked for you briefly.

Randolph: Yes, that's right. About nine or ten years ago. Her mother, Juanita, had been my house cleaner. When she died Maria said she needed the money and asked if I'd let her have the job. I tried her for a few months, but she wasn't that good a housekeeper and wasn't reliable. So I let her go.

Sweeney: During that time, or later, did you ever have sexual relations with Maria?

Downs: You don't have to answer that, Mr. Randolph.

Randolph: Ha! I don't mind answering that, Downs. Sweeney, look at me. I'm an old fat toad. I haven't gotten a woody in twenty years. If you're looking for a sexual motive, you're off your rocker.

Sweeney: Then why did you give Maria all that jewelry?

Downs: You don't have to answer that, Mr. Randolph.

Randolph: Oh, be quiet, Downs. Now that I see where this is going, I'm not worried about this demented detective. Besides that broach you showed me a few days ago, I didn't give Maria any jewelry, Sweeney. I think she stole a necklace that I had bought as a gift. The fact that she stole things from me is one of the reasons I fired her. I think I told you that.

Sweeney: Is this the necklace?

Randolph: Let me see that. Why yes, I believe it was. Can't be sure, after all these years, but it does have that look to it.

Sweeney: Why didn't you ever report it stolen?

Randolph: That's a good question, Sweeney. I wasn't sure that Maria had taken it, for one thing. And I felt sorry for the girl, having just lost her mom. Probably should have reported it, but never got around to it. It wasn't insured, anyway, so I wasn't going to get any money back.

Sweeney: What about this ring? Do you recognize it?

Randolph: Hmm. Nope, can't say that I do. It's a pretty ring, but not very distinguished.

Sweeney: Fred Scouras told me that you've bought several pieces of jewelry from him over the years.

Randolph: Right as rain, Sweeney. Scouras and I have been lifelong friends. I trust his judgment and taste. When I'm looking for a gift or a personal item, he's my man. This necklace was supposed to be a gift for the governor's wife after she arranged for a personal interview with the governor ten years ago.

Sweeney: Which governor?

Randolph:	Umm. That'd be about 1985. Mark White maybe? Not sure now, Sweeney. Been a few years.
Sweeney:	You claim you never had any relationships with Maria, yet I have witnesses who say you kissed her at the bar and gave her money.
Downs:	You don't have to answer that, Mr. Randolph.
Randolph:	I hear you, Downs. But innocent men have nothing to fear from the law, eh Sweeney? I'm an old man. At my age a little kiss from a young girl is good for the ego. We both knew there was nothing to it. I'd give her a few bucks sometimes, pay for the drinks, etc. You read *Tracy's Tidbits* yesterday? Tracy talked about the value of helping out the poor. Those few dollars made a big difference to the Garcias, Sweeney.
Sweeney:	You certainly have an answer for everything, don't you, Mr. Randolph? Tell me about your relationship with the sailor known as Nathan Cohen.
Randolph:	Cohen? You mean the one-eyed sailor?
Sweeney:	Yes, that's the one. You drink with him at the Lonesome Coyote?
Randolph:	Well, I did. Like most sailors, he's here and gone. I think he's left town already. As I told you, Sweeney, I like to talk with people at bars. Get a few drinks in a fellow and he'll open right up. Cohen's a good example. Loves to tell sagas. Get a drink or two in that fellow and you can't get him to shut up. 'Course, I never believed half of what he said. Seemed like

	a nice enough guy. Often enough he bought drinks for everybody. Hung around with the Garcias.

Sweeney: I'm always suspicious of people who are too generous with their money. I worked on a case a few months ago about a fellow who claimed he just liked to give money away because it made people happy. Turned out he was bribing officials. You ever give money to Nate Cohen, Mr. Randolph?

Downs: You don't have to answer that, Mr. Randolph.

Randolph: Will you please be quiet, Downs? Give Cohen money? No need for that. Cohen seemed to have plenty of money. I did buy some jade from him. He had quite a collection of small jade statues he had brought back from China. Kept them in little boxes. Fine quality. I bought three of them. Speaking of Cohen, let me see that ring you showed me a moment ago Sweeney.

Sweeney: Here.

Randolph: I'm not sure, but I think I saw Cohen wearing a ring like this the first time I met him at the Coyote. I don't remember seeing it again, though. Does that help you?

Sweeney: Maybe. Let me offer my regrets about the death of your cousin, Meredith.

Randolph: Shame about that accident. I'll always remember Meredith as a child, how happy she was. Ah, those were the days. Seemed like an ideal marriage, her and Tracy. Made all the papers. John Connally, the Governor of Texas, attended their wedding. You remember him? He was with Kennedy when he was shot.

Sweeney:	What happened to that happiness? Was her marriage bad?
Randolph:	Can't say for sure, Sweeney. I always wondered if Richard Tracy had an affair or some such. Her attitude toward her husband and her child seemed to change abruptly. Ever since, Meredith's been bitter. Well, that's water under the bridge now.
Sweeney:	What will happen to the Randolph fortune? Do you get most of it?
Randolph:	No, I don't think so. You'll have to talk to Matthews about that one, Sweeney. I think I'm mentioned in her will. I have my own money, Sweeney. I presume most of her money goes to Tracy, that is, Patricia.
Sweeney:	Do you remember the night that Maria disappeared? On our last interview you said you were talking with someone else during that time. Yet several people said you were with the Garcias.
Randolph:	I think I said I spent most of the time with other people. I may have been with the Garcias for some of the evening. Newspaper men need to make the rounds, keep up the contacts. I try to have a handshake and maybe a drink with everyone I know.
Sweeney:	Do you remember Maria calling Mr. Cohen some other name? It might have been Bert or Benji?
Randolph:	Does ring a bell, Sweeney. She said something about having a picture of him from her mom, I think.
Sweeney:	She had a picture of him from her mom? That means.... Sam, I just realized who Nate Cohen really is! Come on, we've got to

find Tricia. Thank you for your time, Mr. Randolph, and yours, Mrs. Downs.

Downs: Then Mr. Randolph is no longer a murder suspect in your eyes, Detective?

Sweeney: Not at this time, Mrs. Downs.

End of Recording.
MS/sb

32

They made it to Kingsville in thirty-eight minutes, pulling in at a Quick Stop to use their phone.

"Scott? This is Tricia. I'm calling you from Kingsville! I'm thinking I might head on out to Laredo. I shouldn't have any trouble getting there before dinner! Did you reach Dallas?"

Scott laughed. "The papers will be ready for you when you get back. Dallas negotiated a great price for you. I'll stay here as late as it takes — even until midnight if you decide you want to make that little detour you mentioned. Just give me the name of your insurance agent and we'll get that ready to go too."

As Tricia returned to the car a cowboy gave a long hard whistle.

"Is that car as hot as the magazines all say?" he asked.

"Nope," she said, settling into her seat. "Hotter."

"Where to now?" Dovie asked. "Did you want to go to San Antonio and see if Bergstrom Air Force Base will let you try to lift off from one of their runways?"

"Since we're here, you know anyone in Kingsville you want to visit? We could just ride through town and have everyone whistle at us." Tricia started the engine, listening to it purr in idle before pulling out to the street.

"You know," Tricia said. "I was driving the streets of Kingsville just yesterday. Jesus Morales had tracked down Bruce McDonald. You remember reading about McDonald in the paper? He was the one who was fired from the Public Works Department. He's living in a slum a couple of blocks from here. What do you say we drive by?"

"I did read that article. It said that was the Bruce that Dupree bribed for $50,000, right?"

"Yes. Did you want to visit him?"

"I have a strange feeling that we should drive by."

Tricia drove slowly along the Kingsville streets. In five minutes they turned onto the street of the El Conquistador Apartments.

"He's over there," Tricia said, pointing. "McDonald's in apartment E, the one with the Lincoln parked in front of it."

"That Lincoln certainly looks out of place in that parking lot."

Tricia's mouth dropped open. "That's Barbara Dupree's car! I saw it parked out in front of her place Tuesday! Do you think we should stop?"

"I thought you weren't in the mood to see her."

"That was a few hours ago. I'm dying of curiosity to know why she's visiting Bruce."

Tricia pulled the red sports car into an empty spot near the "A" end of the strip. Together the women crept up to the apartment door. Tricia placed her ear against the door but could hear nothing due to the air conditioner blasting away next to her.

"I'm sure they're up to no good. I'm all for charging right in."

Dovie put out a restraining hand. "Do you want to know what I think they're doing?"

Tricia looked at her with surprise. "Do you mean you have a vision? Does your ESP tell you something?"

Dovie laughed. "No, silly. This is just common sense. A man and a woman who aren't married, meet each other in a cheap apartment out of town. It happens all over the world, I'm sure."

"You haven't seen this place. Cockroaches crawl over piles of filth. I've been to Barbara's house. Cleanliness obsesses her. I can't believe that she would ever have sex in this place. No, I can't see it."

"Maybe she's helping out a friend in need? You know, bringing groceries, or cleaning a little."

"Barbara? Being altruistic? I never trusted Barbara and I'm sure she's up to no good. I've just got to know, Dovie. Let's rush in and surprise them."

Tricia gave the knob a twist. It turned easily. "Close your eyes until we get inside. That way your vision will adjust quickly." Tricia threw open the door and charged into the room.

She opened her eyes to find an astonished Barbara Dupree bending over a portable typewriter sitting on the kitchen table. Barbara stood and squinted. Tricia realized that with the bright light behind her she must appear to Barbara like a black silhouette.

Dovie came in behind her, shut the door, and screamed.

"Look! Look! Look over there on the bed!"

Tricia looked and gasped. Bruce McDonald's dead body lay across the bed, his head a bloody mess. A gun rested loosely in his open right hand. The blast at his right temple had splattered blood and brain tissue all over the sheets. A little blood still flowed, dripping into a morbid puddle on the pillow.

Barbara spoke in a sad, sympathetic voice. "Isn't it an awful tragedy? I just got here and found him like this. Heaven only knows how long he's been dead. I was just reading this suicide note when you came in. I suppose all the drugs, the loss of his wife and career … it all became too much for him. And then the article about him in the paper was the final blow, you know what I mean? Well, at least that's what this suicide note says."

Dovie turned and hid her face against the wall. Tricia felt drawn to look at the dead body close-up. She took his left wrist in her hand, failing to find a pulse. Huge bruises swelled over his eyes. Tricia swallowed hard.

"Have you called 9-1-1?" Dovie asked.

"I looked around. There isn't any phone."

Tricia said, "It won't wash Barbara."

Barbara's voice sounded shrill and harsh. "What do you mean?"

Tricia turned to confront her. She saw fear in Barbara's eyes, the look of a trapped animal.

"You weren't reading that note when we barged in on you. You were writing it. That typewriter wasn't here yesterday. You shot Bruce and tried to set it up to look like a suicide. His body is still warm. As cold as he keeps this room, his body temperature will drop quickly now that he's dead. You must have shot him just minutes before we arrived."

Barbara glanced at Dovie, who had turned to watch her. Barbara let out a long held breath and turned her full attention to Tricia.

"That's crazy!" she said. "Why would I kill Bruce? He was so weak and helpless. Bruce used to be somebody, but now he was all used up."

As she talked she walked over to stand next to Tricia.

"Look at him; sallow, wasted, cadaverous. I didn't kill Bruce. Drugs killed Bruce. The cocaine he snorted poisoned him, eating his soul. You know what I mean? And once his soul was gone the body rotted from the inside out. The man became an empty husk, one who could no longer tolerate his own existence. Can you believe it?

"It's the evil powder, that cocaine. It's like a wild dragon that goes through the woods devouring all the sweet little jungle animals. I've known more than one person who fell victim to its allure, I can tell you that. I suppose you've known some people too. But poor Bruce was one of the worst."

As Barbara rambled on, Tricia looked over at Dovie crumpled on the floor, now facing the corner again. She sat with her head cradled in her arms. Tricia heard her sobbing and saw her shaking. She walked over to Dovie and kneeled behind her to stroke her and comfort her.

Tricia was speaking softly to Dovie when Barbara said, "You don't believe me, do you?"

Without turning Tricia said, "No. I bet you shot him as he slept."

Barbara sighed. "Well, you're right. And what a nuisance you've become. If you hadn't stirred things up in the first place no one would have ever gotten hurt. You know what I mean? I'm just a business woman trying to make a living. Why couldn't you have left me alone? Now I'll have to kill you two as well."

Tricia jumped up as she and Dovie turned in horror. Barbara had taken the gun from Bruce's hand and now pointed it at them. Using both hands, she held a careful steady aim leveled at Tricia's chest.

"I just couldn't have Bruce testify against me, you see. At first I supplied him with a little cocaine to get his favors. Then he demanded that big bribe from me. Well, I had too much money tied up in that project to have him rule against me. So I paid the bribe. But I also recognized that once this guy got the taste of blackmail in his blood, there would be no end of it. You know what I mean? I anonymously let his supervisors know about his cocaine problem. Sometimes it takes just a little pebble to get an avalanche rolling. Once they started looking into Bruce McDonald, his house of cards collapsed.

"And now I'll need to kill you two. I'll type a new note having Bruce explain how the drugs drove him crazy and how sorry he was and all that. With you dead, Miss Patricia Tracy, there won't be anyone investigating my property problems. And, more importantly, no one to finger me for Bruce's death."

Tricia began pacing as she thought. She kept away from Barbara, trying not to force her hand. She wanted to keep her talking.

"Did you send Lupè to kill me last night? How did you know what car I was driving?"

Barbara smirked. "Harry makes a great little private dick. He followed you in your big white Cadillac from your townhouse, to that big house on Ocean Drive, to The Cannery. That was quite the coincidence. I had already arranged to meet Harry there, and it turns out to be the place where you end up."

"Why did you kill Turtle? He didn't do you any harm."

"Turtle? Who's Turtle?"

"Sidney Jones, the black man who bought your car," Tricia explained. Looking over at Dovie she saw her to be white with fear, still sitting in the corner and staring in terror at Barbara. When Tricia looked back to Barbara she found that Barbara was totally ignoring Dovie, keeping the gun fixed on Tricia as the reporter walked the room's perimeter.

"I really have no idea what you're talking about," Barbara said. "I didn't kill Mr. Jones. The paper said he died when his car crashed into a wall. Why would you think I killed him?"

"The police think someone blew up his car."

Barbara shrugged. "It's their job to be suspicious."

Tricia studied Barbara's face. Her blue, bloodshot eyes looked huge behind the black rimmed glasses, staring at her in unblinking concentration. Her hook nose looked like the beak of a predator bird, fixed upon Tricia as prey. As Tricia continued walking, Barbara continued rotating. Eventually Tricia reached the far corner of the room, placing the bed between Barbara and herself. Tricia saw Dovie silently rise to her feet and edge toward Barbara from behind

"Well, it wasn't me! I didn't kill Mr. Jones. I'm just an honest working girl."

"Just an honest working girl? And what did you work as? A drug pusher? You say you supplied Bruce with cocaine. You're responsible for his demise, from beginning to end."

Barbara sneered. "He did that to himself. He used to be somebody. He chose to use the cocaine. I never use that stuff. I'm just a working girl who supplies people with things they want. Selling cocaine makes me money. That's how I got my capital together for my first land development. I have a few connections down at the docks, or meet sailors who've brought in cocaine at local bars. This month I bought several kilograms from a sailor. Got a great price. I brought a little as a going away present to Bruce. Can you believe it? He died happy.

"How about you? Would you like to do a line of snow before you go? It'll ease the pain."

Tricia snorted. "I'm not going anywhere. Just think about it, Barbara. You'll see right off you'd never get away with this. You think the police would believe a double murder/suicide scenario? Never in a million years! You've probably got your fingerprints all over the place—like on the typewriter keys and the door knobs. I'm sure the typewriter belongs to you. I bet the gun is registered in your name, isn't it? And what about the people who have driven by and seen your car in the parking lot? That shiny gold Lincoln sticks out like a black man at a Ku Klux Klan convention. The police will be on your trail before supper."

Barbara's eyebrows furrowed in thought and her gun hand drooped. Dovie reached from behind and grabbed her in a big hug, trapping her forearms. The gun pointed uselessly at the floor.

Tricia raced over and wrenched the gun out of Barbara's grip. The three women fought and kicked and screamed, bites and scratches narrowly avoided. Youth and strength won out, with Barbara's arms tied behind her back, her legs secured to the bed.

Tricia kept watch on Barbara as Dovie left to call the police. She returned the same time that five police cars roared up. Tricia guessed it was the whole Kingsville force.

Tricia and Dovie talked with the police for several hours before they were finally released. Exhausted, they relaxed with beer and tacos at a Mexican dive in Kingsville before driving back to Corpus Christi in the darkening evening. They spoke little, their adrenaline supplies depleted.

They found Scott waiting with the paperwork at the Toyota dealership. On the drive home Tricia couldn't recall what she had signed. Driving in a trance, she aroused only when she pulled her new car into her soot-stained parking spot in front of her townhouse.

Tricia kept her eyes on the bushes while walking toward her door. She couldn't shake the memory of Lupè jumping out at her the other day. She slipped into the townhouse and keyed the door bolt into place. With a large exhale she hadn't realized she had been holding, she released her pent-up anxieties. The only other people with keys were Mel and Mrs. Silverman. She felt safe.

Walking over to the easy chair, she collapsed upon it. In the silent deepening gloom of dusk, Tricia sat quietly, breathing deeply and slowly. She shut her eyes and soon fell asleep.

33

Interview: Morris Cohen
Date: Friday, Sept. 16
Location: Phone Call Seattle, Washington

Note: This call was taped without the knowl-
                edge of the recipient. This transcript is
                for reference only and may not be used as
                evidence.

Cohen: Hello?

Sweeney: Hello. This is Detective Melvin Sweeney of
                the Corpus Christi Police Department. Is
                this Dr. Morris Cohen?

Cohen: Police? This isn't about Nathan again, is
                it?

Sweeney: My apologies, sir. As a matter of fact, I
                am calling about Nathan Cohen.

Cohen: I wish you people would get this straight.
                Every few months I get one of these heart-
                breaking calls. I know I've reported it a
                dozen times.

Sweeney: You've got me at a disadvantage, sir. What
                are you talking about?

Cohen: What do you mean? What am I talking about?
                You called me! You said you're calling
                about Nathan Cohen and I told you I've
                already reported it.

Sweeney: What exactly is it that you've reported?

Cohen: He's dead. He was my son and every year or two you gotta stir up the memories. Can't you get this straight?

Sweeney: My deepest sympathies, sir. When did your son die?

Cohen: The war. That stupid Vietnam war. Nathan was gonna save the world. Went out for ROTC. Listened to the Green Beret theme song in his bedroom at night. Good God. Then they shipped him home in a rotten canvas bag. Now every couple of years you boys have to call me up and stir up the memories. Well let me get this through your thickset skull. Nathan is dead. Benjamin Lewis stole his identity and uses his social security number. Why is it so hard for you to figure that out?

Sweeney: What do you know about Benjamin Lewis?

Cohen: Don't you know nothing? They were all ambushed together in Nam. Lewis lost an eye and almost a leg. Nathan was killed and that damn Lewis stole his identity. He's been using it ever since. Now leave me alone!

The phone call ended.

End of Recording.
MS/sb

34

The ringing of the phone startled Tricia into wakefulness. Listening to the machine answer, she shook off the nightmare hanging just below her consciousness.

"Hello Tricia. This is Mel. Where the heck are you now, I wonder? Call me, okay? I just want to hear you say you're okay. I'm at home." Click.

Tricia smiled. Taking a good deep breath she felt refreshed. She turned on all the lights and the stereo. A Coke from the refrigerator brought her a rush of energy.

She read 11:32 from the clock. Glancing at the answering machine she saw that there were eighteen messages. She listened to them, three days worth. Many of them were friends offering condolences about her mother. The last four were all from Mel, all similar to the one she had heard.

What I could use, she decided, *is a couple of hours out and away from it all. After all, it's not quite midnight on a Friday night. Maybe Mel will want to take me dancing.*

She picked up the phone and pressed the automatic dialer for Mel's apartment.

"Tricia?" he answered hopefully.

"Yes, my love. You must be taking psychic lessons from Dovie."

"Where are you? It's so good to hear your voice! Are you doing okay? Can I do anything for you? I had the strangest feelings that you were in danger."

Tricia smiled. "You are psychic! Barbara Dupree had a gun pointed at me, threatening to kill me. But she's in jail now."

"Good God! Tell me about it!"

"How about at the Western Palms? Put on some jeans and I'll meet you there."

"Baby, I'll always make time for you. It's my new resolution! Western Palms will be great. How about I treat you to a meal first? Say Denny's or Taco Caribe? We can sit and talk. I'm got some important new information."

"What?"

"I now know who killed Maria, Sidney, and Meredith, and I know why. And, I believe you're in great danger!"

"Mel, you're always coming up with great theories, I'll give you that! I'll hop in the shower and meet you at Taco Caribe in an hour. I can hardly wait to hear your newest theories and show you my new car! Bad news about leg room again, I'm afraid. Bring your recorder if you want my official statement about Lupè. Speaking of whom, how did it go with him today?"

"Last I heard this afternoon he was trying to make bail. Judge Parker set it at forty grand, because of the car damage. I'll throw on some slacks and a plaid shirt and see you at Taco Caribe. And Trish …?"

"Yes?"

"I love you! Now don't be late this time. If you're not there by one o'clock I'm going to come after you."

"I love you too, Darling. See you soon." She sent a kiss through the phone before hanging up. She hurried upstairs to start the shower.

Tracy's Tidbits
by Patricia Tracy

Corpus Christi Caller Times
Saturday, September 17, 1994

Death of My Mother

Meredith Randolph Tracy, Corpus Christi matriarch, died yesterday. She died alone, found at the bottom of her stairs when her maid came to clean. The city has lost a leading citizen, and a daughter has lost her mother.

Meredith Randolph Tracy, heir to the Randolph and Tracy fortunes, died yesterday. The Randolphs trace their lineage from the Pilgrims and Daughters of the American Revolution. They boast Civil War Generals, American politicians, industrial achievers, intellectual leaders, and financial geniuses. The Tracys made their money more recently, shrewd investments followed by development of the H.E.B. food chain.

Meredith Randolph Tracy, philanthropist, died yesterday. Meredith shared her fortunes generously. The new museum dedicated a wing in her name, First Baptist Church, a chapel. She chaired the annual United Way Fund drives. She contributed generously to Del Mar College and Corpus Christi State University. Money seemed to flow in endless supply to worthy causes, leaving a legacy of gratitude from many.

Meredith Randolph Tracy, woman of many interests, died yesterday. Her greenhouse cultivated original orchids. World renowned paintings, including a Picasso and a Hopper, decorated her walls. For several years she chaired the annual Regatta, famous for her sailing skills. She walked the streets of world capitals, and saw all the wonders of the modern world.

Meredith Randolph Tracy, my mother, died yesterday. We'd been estranged, rarely speaking these past ten years. She hadn't the time for mother/daughter luncheons or shopping dates with her only child. No phone calls at midnight, just to talk. No spontaneous gifts, "Just because I love you." I never understood the reasons behind our alienation. Nothing I did was good enough, no effort sufficient, no accomplishment noteworthy. Eventually I gave up trying to make amends, believing that I could always do it tomorrow. Now those tender moments that might have been are gone forever.

Meredith Randolph Tracy, recluse, died yesterday. She lived a lonely life in a huge mansion. Before my father's death, our home abounded with people, flowed with guests from around the world, rattled with raucous parties. For the

227

past ten years only Meredith's footsteps echoed in those sad empty halls. She must have preferred that loneliness, some resentment toward mankind forbidding her from loving and refusing to be loved.

Meredith Randolph Tracy died yesterday; died all alone. Though she wasn't much of a mother, she was the only one I'll ever have. I'll miss her dearly.

35

Tricia luxuriated in the feel of the hot water beating on her back. She had finished soaping, shampooing, and rinsing. Now she stood enjoying those last few minutes of hedonism, the joy of the hot water massage for its own sake. She knew she needed to get out and dress to meet Mel at the Taco Caribe, but she granted herself another five minutes of pleasure. The water massager beat a steady rhythm down her upper spine as she stood, her head bowed slightly, eyes closed, breathing quietly.

With a crash the shower rod and curtain flew off the wall. Tricia jumped back against the shower stall, staring in terror at Lupè Garcia. Holding the dripping shower curtain in his left hand, his switchblade shining in his casted right, he leered at her. His gaze traveled slowly downward from her face, pausing to take in her erect nipples on the reddened breasts, then fixing at her crotch.

Tricia trembled with fear and abhorrence. Cowering against the back wall, she tried to cover her breasts and pubic area with her hands. Lupè's putrid breath reeked of alcohol, his grime stained clothes stank of pungent body odors and filth. Sweat beaded across his forehead. The steam released from the shower coated his face and clothes with a layer of mist.

"I'm gonna enjoy this, you stuck up *puta*," Lupè said with slurred words. He swayed on his feet, still holding the shower curtain across his front as a pool of water collected on the bathroom floor.

"I bet your box is as tight as a taquito," he said, staring at her hand covered crotch. His leer stretched ear to ear, displaying an uneven graveyard of yellow tipped tombstones.

The hot water beating down on Tricia provided inspiration. She grabbed her shower massager from its harness, aimed for Lupè's face, and turned the temperature to full hot.

Lupè screamed as the blast of water scalded him. He raised the curtain to protect himself, deflecting Tricia's assault.

He cursed in anger and pain, advancing on Tricia from behind the protection of the shower curtain. It acted as an effective shield, the shower curtain rod banging against the toilet with a hollow metallic clang.

As the curtain came at her like a crushing wall, Tricia looked around desperately. She grabbed the open shampoo bottle and poured its contents onto the floor in front of Lupè's feet. With his next step his foot went sliding out to the side and he crashed to the floor. His head struck the tub edge with a resounding thunk. He crouched dazed. His back arched from bent knees to the tub rim. His left hand grabbed the rim. The right one, in the cast, hung beside him. He rested his head on the porcelain edge, twisted to the right. A steady stream of blood poured into the tub at Tricia's feet.

Tricia turned off the water and stepped up on top of Lupè's shoulders. She jumped up in the air and came down on his shoulders as hard as she could. The weight was too much for even Lupè's thick neck to stand. With a booming crack his head snapped back as his trunk collapsed to the ground. As he fell, Tricia almost lost her balance, grabbing onto the sink to stop from tumbling off.

Once steady, she looked down on her perch, gasping with horror. Lupè's head was twisted one hundred and eighty degrees, his eyes open and unseeing, his mouth gaping open. A large depression in his right temple poured blood from split skin, adding a red color to the inch deep pool of water on her bathroom floor.

Tricia stood transfixed, unable to believe that she had just killed a man. She panted, fright and action having brought her heart racing to its limit. Struggling to control her breathing, she listened intently, hearing only the hum of the air conditioner. With a shiver she realized that she was wet, naked, and cold.

Climbing carefully off of Lupè's body, she stepped gingerly through the water. Her terrycloth robe had avoided most of the shower assault. Determined not to look back at the body, she grabbed fresh towels, one for her hair and a couple for the bathroom door opening.

She walked into her bedroom and picked up the phone to call 911.

The phone had no dial tone. She pressed the disconnect button several times, but the phone refused to give a dial tone. After hanging up the receiver she stared at it, her lips pushed out in a pout. With a worried shrug she headed to the stairs to see if she would have more luck with the downstairs phone.

On reaching the platform at the turn of the stairs she looked in astonishment at the man standing below looking up at her. Thursday night, hardly more than twenty-four hours ago, she had written him off as a rejecting scoundrel. This morning, she had rejected him again in favor of Mel. But now, seeing him standing there with a boyish grin on his handsome face, the magical spell she had felt the first time she had laid eyes on him came rushing back.

"Bill!" she shouted, running down to jump into his arms.

He wore black leather gloves, adding to a firm grip that hugged her with warmth and security. She luxuriated in that hug, bending her knees to nestle her head into his strong chest. Bill bent his head down and kissed her scalp.

She smelled his delightful aroma, the sea air and the human life. They kissed deeply and lovingly. Finally, feeling weak with the emotions, she climbed down.

"What are you doing here? They told me you had gone away! How did you get in?" She threw out her questions in rapid fire.

Bill stared into her eyes, his one beautiful auburn right eye piercing into her heart.

"I had to come back to tell you I love you."

As she looked into his face, tears flowed down her own. The joy of having him here, proving Mel wrong about him, on top of the emotional trauma she had just been through overwhelmed her. She felt weak and giddy. As she started to collapse, Bill reached out to catch her.

"What's wrong, Tricia? You look like you're going to faint."

She allowed him to pull her to him again, feeding on his strength and kindness.

"Oh, Bill, it was awful! Lupè Garcia just attacked me in the shower! I think … I think I just killed him!"

Tricia noted Bill's look of astonishment. "Oh, how terrible for you. Where is he? Would you like me to go check on him?"

Tricia nodded weakly. "Upstairs on the floor at the shower."

Tricia waited at the bottom of the steps. He returned quickly.

"That's an incredibly wet mess. And you're right, he's dead. I would never have thought that you could do that. Do you practice karate?"

Tricia had to laugh. This was the second time someone had asked her that in regards to Lupè in just a few days.

"No. I'm lucky and persistent — and desperate as well. How do you suppose he got in here? I remember bolting the door."

Bill hesitated before answering. "Actually, I let him in."

Tricia's jaw dropped in astonishment. "What?"

Bill reached into his pocket and held up some keys. "That day you left your purse on my boat I had some duplicate keys made. I've been setting Lupè up for two weeks. I suppose I got him a little too drunk this time. Oh well, I can still make it work out, I guess."

"You mean …" Tricia stumbled over the enormity of the concept. "You mean you intend to kill me? You sent Lupè to my shower to rape and kill me? But … why? I thought you loved me?"

Bill nodded slowly. "That's the unfortunate part. I actually do like you tremendously. Maybe I even love you. Yet I can't let that interfere with my plans."

Tricia ran and picked up the kitchen phone. No dial tone.

"I'm afraid I cut the lines," Bill said.

She collapsed into a dining room chair and shook her head sadly. "So Mel was right all along. You are a killer after the inheritance."

Bill stepped back, a bitter, wary expression on his face. "What? How did you know?" He spat out the words, like blood spurting from a wound.

"Oh yes, Bill. My boyfriend, Detective Mel Sweeney, knows all about you. He knows that you're working for my cousin. He suspects you of murdering my mother, Maria Garcia, and Sidney Jones too! He knows all about your past and your motivations. You might as well give it up, Bill."

Bill looked confused. "Your cousin? Who's your cousin?"

"Bob Randolph. Surely you're not going to deny it? You just admitted it!"

"Bob Randolph, the fat editor? Ah, so the police think he's behind all this? I see, they think I killed Mereidth for his sake so he can get the money. Why, that works out perfectly for me. They'll still pin this one on Lupè. Even if they tried to find Bill Tucker they'd never find him. Bill Tucker doesn't exist!"

Tricia felt overwhelmed with sadness. She still couldn't believe that Bill would really harm her.

"So, Mel was right? Bob hired you to kill Maria because she was blackmailing him, and then hired you to kill Meredith and now me to get the fortunes?"

Bill laughed, settling into a chair across the table from Tricia.

"Not even close. Your cousin Bob Randolph has absolutely nothing to do with this. I killed Maria and Sidney Jones to protect myself. They both recognized me from my past and my whole plan depends on my anonymity.

"Maria Garcia figured out who I was in a tavern one evening. Apparently she had letters that my mother had written to her mother about my war wounds, and even an old photograph. She thought I was going home with her to have sex. I drugged Lupè at the tavern. After screwing her, I killed her and hid her body in that well. Their damn dog barked so much I thought I was going to have to kill him too. At first I was just going to set him up to take the fall for her murder, but he turned out to be such a great patsy that I figured to use him as your murderer.

"Sidney Jones was another bit of bad luck. He and I served together with the Green Berets in Nam. When he recognized me at the park that day, I followed him home and sliced his throat, staging the car accident and explosion."

Tricia struggled to get her dry mouth to work. "Bill. I'm totally lost. If you're not doing this for Bob Randolph, what possible reason could you have for killing these people?"

Bill smiled widely and jumped his eyebrows. "You have no idea at all, do you? Well, My Beauty. You were right about my doing it for the inheritance, but it's not for Bob's purpose, but my own. You see, I'm your cousin."

"My cousin? What are you talking about? I don't have any cousins."

"The secret's been well kept, hasn't it? All the better for me. You told me a couple of days ago that you didn't even know until this week that your father had a sister. My mother was your father's sister. She became pregnant at age fifteen, and ran off to Norfolk. Not until last year, just before she died, did she tell me about her past and the Tracy fortune. She let me know something else, too. I have some closet skeletons to share with you about your father that explain some of your problems."

"My problems?" Tricia asked incredulously. "I don't have any problems. You're the one going around killing people."

Bill laughed. "Your point is certainly valid. I grew up rough. My mother immersed herself in drugs and alcohol, supporting us with prostitution until she was too old to do anything but live off welfare and, though she kept it secret, a monthly stipend from the trust. I joined the marines when I was young, turning into a very successful killer in Viet Nam. Sidney Jones and I and another kid, Nathan Cohen, were a special squad that worked behind enemy lines. We got ambushed one day, where I lost this eye and almost my leg. Nathan got killed and Sidney snapped. Once I recovered, and out of the army, I took over Nathan's identity and made my living from being a bodyguard, or sometimes as a contract killer. Until I realized the easy money is in drug smuggling."

"How will killing me get you any money?" Tricia asked. She looked at him sadly. She kept expecting her adrenaline to pump, her body to react to this threat on her life. Somehow, though, she couldn't rouse herself to fight another battle. Maybe her energies had been exhausted in the fights with Barbara and Lupè. Maybe she couldn't believe that someone who loved her and who she loved could really kill her.

"It's a bit complicated," Bill said. "Since I arrived in Corpus Christi a month ago my whole attention has been devoted to obtaining the Tracy fortune. I already had Matthews' name from the checks he sent my mother. Posing as your lawyer, I sent him requests for the documents I needed. Meredith's will states that when she died, practically all the Randolph/Tracy fortune went to you. Technically, though, it goes to the Tracy trust until you reach age twenty-five. If you die after you reach twenty-five, then there will be a mess, an estate battle. But should you die before you reach twenty-five, all of the Tracy trust goes to the nearest surviving Tracy relative. That, my dear, is me. That's why you must die tonight.

"I sought out Alma Trevino as a means of reaching you. She was very helpful on setting up my alibi, making it look convincing that I had left the country before Meredith and you each met your untimely deaths. I plan to never return here, allowing my lawyers to obtain my money. I've even used my other identity, Nathan Cohen, for everyone in town but you and Alma. There never would have been a connection between William Tucker and Benjamin Lewis.

"I tried to get close to you by suggesting you hire me as a bodyguard, but even with Lupè in the picture, you wouldn't bite at that. I blew up your car both to scare you and to slow you down.

"A little alcohol and camaraderie made Lupè putty in my hands. He made a great fall guy for Maria's murderer, and will be for yours as well. I needed to keep him out of jail, so I hired an excellent lawyer to represent him, and yesterday provided bail money from my cocaine sales, though there's not much left of that now. That night at the Mayor's reception I couldn't let him kill you because I hadn't taken care of your mother yet. He almost ruined everything that Tuesday night when I was tied up with Jones and he attacked you here. Of course, after he killed you tonight I would have had to kill him too."

Tricia reached across the table to try to hold Bill's hands, but he withdrew his.

"But, Bill, why kill me? It doesn't make sense. We love each other. We could marry. Then you'd have all your money. I'm sure we'd be happy together. We both love adventure and excitement. Imagine what we could do with our money. We could travel the world! You wouldn't have to run drugs or kill people. Think of it! We'd gamble in Monte Carlo! We'd ski in the Alps! Oh, the life we could lead."

Bill raised an eyebrow in thought. "You do entice me, My Beauty. Ah, if only such a beatific ending could come to my life's saga. Not that I deserve it."

He smiled and winked at her. "I'm afraid it could never work out. Though you could be fun, and I imagine I could reform, neither you nor the police could really ever forgive me for my past. You already know me as a murderer and a drug smuggler. I fear I have other nasty deeds speckling my history that you would find rather unsavory."

Tricia sat forward in her chair, staring across the table into Bill's eye. "I could forgive you, Darling. I'm sure we could make it work!"

Bill smiled, but shook his head. "I'm afraid not, My Beauty. Even if it weren't for my past, I'm afraid there's another serious objection to our matrimony. Suppose you wanted to have children?"

Tricia felt confused. "Well, I do sort of want to have children some day. Why? Are you … sterile?"

This time Bill's smile was accompanied by a laugh. "Hardly. What I'm trying to get at is that we're too closely related to each other to marry."

Tricia shook her head. "We're first cousins. First cousins can marry."

Bill looked back at her, a strange bemused expression on his face. Tricia could see that he was considering how to explain himself.

"Do you remember on the boat talking about your inability to enjoy sex? Yet when you were asleep you could have quite an experience. Oh, don't worry. I used a condom. I wouldn't want to leave physical evidence on you."

"You <u>raped</u> me in my sleep? You Bastard! I hate you!" Tricia pushed away from the table, grabbed the salt shaker and threw it at him.

Bill laughed. "Our first lover's spat, hmm? Back to my point, though. Have you ever sought counseling to understand where all your sexual hang-ups come from?"

Tricia shook her head. She felt mortified at having been abused in her sleep. Yet that feeling became eclipsed by a sudden nervousness. "I don't want to hear about this, Bill."

"I'm sure you don't. But you must. Haven't you ever wondered why you were so attracted to me? Is it just my suave manner? Or perhaps the excitement of adventures?"

"Sure."

"No!" Bill practically shouted. "Look at me, Tricia. Look at me closely. Who do I remind you of?"

Tricia examined Bill's features carefully. She shook her head.

"Oh, come on, girl. Look again." He slowly turned his face back and forth so that she could get a full view of his profile as well as the front. Tricia felt her mouth grow dry as her pulse quickened. She turned her back to him and walked to stand in the corner, facing the wall.

"I have no idea what you're talking about," she insisted, her muffled voice drifting back to him.

"Turn around and look at me, Tricia. Even your boyfriend noticed the resemblance the first time he laid eyes on me at the dock, though he couldn't place it. Denying the truth is not going to make it go away. Yes, that's better. Now, are you willing to admit it?"

Tricia stared at Bill's handsome face, auburn eye, strong nose, and high cheekbones. She knew who he meant. "No! I don't know who you're talking about!"

"Your mouth says 'no-no', your eyes say 'yes-yes'. I look just like your father, don't I? Admit it, Tricia. I've seen pictures."

"Well, you are his nephew. It's not <u>that</u> surprising that you should have some resemblance."

"Some resemblance? I'm practically the reincarnation. And you want to know why? It's because I have more than just a nephew's share of genes. My mother was fifteen when I was conceived. That was 1950. How old was your dad then?"

Tricia calculated for a moment. "Eighteen."

"My Mom told me she was the victim of abuse by her brother. We're more than just cousins, Tricia. I'm your half brother."

"You tell me so many lies, Bill. You're saying my Dad raped his younger sister? Why should I believe you?"

Bill laughed again, a deep throat rolling laugh. "Cut to the quick, don't you, My Beauty? Until my Mom told me this last year I had always wondered who my father was. Well, this is one lifelong quest that I intend to prove. I've got your blood sample and one from my mother. With DNA testing I'll be able to establish how much genetic material we share. If we share over fifty per cent that will prove we have the same father. If the test results come back at twenty five per cent or so, then I guess my mother was lying and it was just a stranger that fathered me. I'll know in about two months."

"You have no moral scruples about killing your own sister?"

"For the millions of dollars I'll inherit, no, not a one. From penniless scoundrel to multi-millionaire patron of the arts, it's my dream come true. There's another reason to hurry this up. I'm forty-three years old. How old was your Dad when he died?"

Just as it did every time, the thought of her father's death brought tears to Tricia's eyes. "Fifty-two," she answered.

"I've already had two heart attacks, including one angioplasty. I don't have the years to wait, Tricia. If I'm ever going to enjoy the Tracy fortune it's got to be now!"

"All of this was completely unnecessary, Bill. All you had to do was come to me and identify yourself. We have plenty of money. I'm sure our lawyers could have worked out something."

Bill snickered. "Can you honestly see your mother giving a black sheep like me a million dollars just for old time's sake? Ha!"

Tricia had to agree with that. "Still, I could have given you money. I still can. I promise. Look, let's just sleep on it tonight. Tomorrow we can go visit my lawyer and make the arrangements."

"I don't think so, My Beauty. Tomorrow, rather today, is Saturday, not a lawyer friendly day. If I stick around this berg your police boyfriend will have me in the slammer by nightfall. I don't relish the idea of spending the last few years of my life rotting in jail. But your invitation to sleep on it tonight is tempting. Your young beautiful body would bring out sexual longings in even the most celibate of men, a qualification for which I don't qualify."

Tricia pulled the robe tighter around her body, feeling naked and exposed.

"Even though you're probably my sister, I certainly enjoyed our one experience," Bill continued. "Maybe I take after my father? However, that brings us back to the problems I alluded to earlier. Again I ask, why do you suppose you're so attracted to me?"

"I suppose you're right. You do remind me of my father. And there's no doubt about it, I loved my father. So, what's your point?"

"Look, My Beauty, let me put one and one together for you. You loved your father to an almost unnatural degree, right?"

"Right."

"Your mother resented you for no apparent reason, right?"

"Right."

"You have sexual hang ups that are rather extreme, right?"

"Well. Maybe."

"Your father is a known child molester, documented by my mother's testimony, right?"

Tricia stared at him. "You … you mean…. Are you saying that my father used to sleep with me and that's why I…. And that's why my mother …"

Bill looked at her quietly. Ever so slightly he nodded.

Tricia's hands felt icy. She struggled to breathe, gasping and choking. From deep subconscious vaults, long locked and hidden, dark images of her father coming into her room at night came erupting into her memory. The feel of his mustache on her face made her lips twitch. The hardness of his penis entering her too young vagina made her crotch muscles squeeze anew in protest. Smells, sounds, and touches of helpless memory crashed upon her. Agony and worthlessness took hold of her soul, choking her sense of self, destroying her desire to live.

"Oh. Oh. Oh my God. I want to die. I deserve to die. How can I go on living with this?" Falling to a heap in the corner, she crossed her arms, hugging herself tightly and rocking. Her body shivered in anguish.

Bill stood up from his chair. Leaving his cane next to his chair, he limped the few feet required to stand over her.

"Well, fortunately, I can help out on that request. I hate to do this. But now I believe we've said all there is to say."

Tricia looked up at him. She didn't want to die, she knew that. Yet she didn't have the strength to resist. She felt as helpless as a child, or perhaps a small wounded bird. Her face stretched in pitiful agony, silently begging for mercy.

Bill bent down and grasped her two hands at the wrist where they crossed. He placed his other gloved hand over her mouth, squeezing her nose between his thumb and index finger. By pushing back with that hand, he trapped her head in the corner, making it impossible for Tricia to shake him off.

She immediately felt air hunger, unable to move her breath in or out. She realized how much she wanted to live, to fight, and to survive. She struggled, desperately trying to kick out at him, to free a hand, or to bite his. She heard him saying something about putting her in the bathtub, making it look like she had drowned in the struggle against Lupè. In only a matter of seconds she felt herself grow weak. Her head and chest felt as if they would explode. Blackness came across her eyes like a lowering curtain.

A loud explosion came to her ears. For just a moment she thought it must be her throat exploding in its effort to breathe. Suddenly her mouth was clear. She gasped, breathing in and out desperately. Bill fell on top of her, a heavy dead weight. Blood poured out from his mouth, spouting out a red fountain from what was left of his head. She pushed him off, watching him roll limply before her.

Looking up she saw Mel standing at the open door. He still held his pistol in both hands, pointing to a spot just above her head. From its barrel a wisp of smoke waved at her.

His mouth was set in a determined clench, but his eyes looked glazed and unbelieving. Slowly he lowered his gun, still staring at her in silent disbelief at how close he had come to not being in time. Neither of them could say anything. They both stared in wonder.

"You ... you okay Tricia?" Mel finally asked.

She stood up and ran to him, totally uncaring of how awful she must look with Bill's blood all over her, the robe flapping open. He apparently didn't care either, for he grabbed her in both arms, hugged her tightly, then kissed her over and over and over again.

"Oh my God, Mel! I love you! I love you! I love you!" She returned his kisses and hugs, holding him tightly and crying. She eventually asked, "How did you ever know to come to my rescue?"

"I told you I was worried about you. When you didn't show up on time at the Taco Caribe I called here. There was no answer and no machine, so I rushed over. I owe Mother Mary a nine day novena. It's a debt I'll gladly pay!"

"Don't look at me, Mel, I'm too much of a mess." Tricia said this without any desire for her command to be followed.

"Tricia, you are the most beautiful woman in the whole world, no matter what mess you're in. Come on. I'll help you up to the shower."

She looked up at him in horror. "Oh, Mel! Lupè's dead on my bathroom floor! I killed him!"

Mel looked at her in astonishment. "How did that happen?"

Tricia's words came through her sobs. "He attacked me in the shower. When he slipped on the floor I jumped on him and broke his neck."

"He attacked you in the shower? Clearly it was self defense. Let me go check on him." Mel took the stairs three at a time, checked the shower, and descended slowly.

"He's quite dead. I can't believe I left you in such danger. Thank God you're finally safe. With Lupè and Ben Lewis both dead, these dangers have passed. But, knowing you, you'll soon be up to your neck in some other sort of scheme. The only way I know of keeping you safe is to marry you. Please, Tricia. I love you. I could never stand to lose you again. Please tell me you'll marry me."

Tricia looked at him in surprise. For a moment she hesitated. Then she reached up to kiss him long and passionately. When done she confirmed, "Yes! Yes! A thousand times YES! And we have to do it soon!"

"Soon?" Mel asked with a raised eyebrow. "The sooner the better as far as I'm concerned. But is there any reason it has to be done soon?"

Tricia nodded. "Oh, definitely. We have to marry before I turn twenty-five so I know you're not marrying me for my money." She reached up and kissed him again, a long kind kiss signaling commitment forever.

THE END

978-0-595-49883-3
0-595-49883-3

Printed in the United States
113968LV00001B/130-195/P